ERIC AND THE DIVORCEE

by

PETER CHILD

To Vivienne

With best wishes

Peter

Benbow Publications

Published in 2011 by Benbow Publications

British Library
Cataloguing in Publication Data.

ISBN: 978-0-9558063-5-3

Printed by Lightning Source UK Ltd
Chapter House
Pitfield
Kiln Farm
Milton Keynes
MK11 3LW

First Edition

OTHER TITLES BY THE AUTHOR

ERIC THE ROMANTIC

THE MICHEL RONAY SERIES:

MARSEILLE TAXI
AUGUST IN GRAMBOIS
CHRISTMAS IN MARSEILLE
CATASTROPHE IN LE TOUQUET
RETURN TO MARSEILLE

THE INSPECTOR HADLEY SERIES:

THE TAVISTOCK SQUARE MURDERS
THE TOWER OF LONDON MURDERS
THE GOLD BULLION MURDERS
THE AMERICAN MURDERS
THE DIAMOND MURDERS
THE ROYAL RUSSIAN MURDERS
THE SATAN MURDERS
THE MEDICAL MURDERS
THE WESTMINSTER MURDERS
THE GIGOLO MURDERS

NON-FICTION

NOTES FOR GOOD DRIVERS
NOTES FOR COMPANY DRIVERS
VEHICLE PAINTER'S NOTES
VEHICLE FINE FINISHING
VEHICLE FABRICATIONS IN GRP

ACKNOWLEDGEMENTS

Once again, I wish to gratefully acknowledge the help and assistance given to me by Sue Gresham, who edited and formatted the book and Wendy Tobitt, for the excellent cover presentation. Without these talented and patient ladies this book would not have been possible.

Peter Child

INTRODUCTION

Do you believe in Angels?

Divorce is a difficult situation for any woman to cope with, so when relatives offer their advice on what to do next and how to begin a new life, it is not always helpful. However, when a tall handsome stranger arrives unexpectedly on the scene offering guidance and comfort, any woman would be foolish to turn down the opportunity to place her future happiness in his strong hands.

Unfortunately Eric Blood Axe, a Viking guardian angel, is only on his second solo mission and is still learning how to carry out his allotted tasks without causing mayhem...

CHAPTER 1

CLARE MEETS TONY

The trouble with Tony was that he was such a charmer and looked so bloody gorgeous naked. From his broad shoulders down to his neat waist and little bum with dimples, not to mention his other physical attribute, he was just simply gorgeous! However, I've already said that.

I met him at a party. I had been invited by my best friend Jane, whose cousin Melanie organised the catastrophe at her place to celebrate getting a new job, well, any excuse would do! I was not looking forward to it much as I'd had a bad time after being dumped by the latest clown who called himself my 'everlasting' lover and prospective husband.

At the party I had been deserted by Jane and boxed into a corner of the room by a slightly cross-eyed, red nosed Neanderthal, who kept telling me that he only lived to play rugby. At last he wandered off to get another pint of lager and I sighed with relief before sipping my glass of red wine. I glanced up just as Tony came into the crowded room... our eyes met for a brief moment and I thought 'wow!'

I looked down at my glass as he made his way across the room in my direction and I wondered if he was actually going to speak to me. I hoped and hoped again that he would... then suddenly he was in front of me, so I looked up into his handsome face and said 'hi.'

He paused for a moment then said, 'I'd like to talk to you but I'm afraid I can't.'

'Why's that?' I asked.

'Because you're so beautiful that I couldn't think of what to say, so I'll just stand here looking at you while you tell me all about yourself... then I promise to leave you alone and never trouble you again.'

I thought 'oh trouble me, do trouble me again' before I smiled and said 'really?'

'Yes and when I get to work on Monday I'll tell everybody that

I met the most beautiful woman I've ever seen… and she'll be in my thoughts forever' he said.

I thought 'wow' again, then 'what an opener', my knees went weak before I asked, 'so where's work?' as I tried to compose myself.

'Euro Concordia Aviation' he replied.

'And what do you do there?'

'I'm a test pilot on the development team of our new fast jet interceptor for NATO' he replied.

I thought 'oh… my… God!'

'But it's not as glamorous as it sounds' he added with a smile.

I thought 'you could have fooled me' before I said 'really?' again, in what I hoped was a sophisticated tone.

'No, we also have a number of corporate executive jets, which the company hires out, so occasionally when I'm not test flying I have to fly farty old businessmen to various places in the world.'

'Really' I said again before I thought 'well if you'd like to take me, you could bang me up against a bulkhead anytime you like whilst the bloody thing is flying on auto pilot.'

'Yes, it's a touch boring sometimes' he said with a smile.

'I suppose you've got a uniform with gold wings and things?' I said picturing him in dark blue jacket with wings over his top left pocket and stripes on his sleeve… oh, how I do love a man in uniform.

'Yes, but I only wear it so the old businessmen think that I know what I'm doing with all the levers, bells and whistles in the cockpit' he replied with a grin.

'And what does your wife say about you flying off into the sunset?' I asked, thinking that would slow him down, but he laughed and replied 'I'm not married… I mean, what woman in her right mind would marry me?'

I thought 'only the world's entire population of single women and half the married ones,' as my knees turned to custard and an itch started down below, but I replied innocently 'I've no idea.'

'Precisely.'

'So what do they call you at Euro Concordia Aviation?' I asked as I tried to recover.

'They call me Tony but my friends call me Captain Franklin' he replied with a mischievous grin.

'So what category do I come in?' I asked.

'Oh, you're most certainly a new friend.'

'That's good to know.'

'Yes it is, because I don't normally allow any new friends into my circle until one of the old one's die' he said.

'Well I hope no one's gone on the critical list because of me' I replied with a smile and he laughed.

'No, I promise you they're all safe... so tell me your name.'

'I'm Clare, Captain Franklin' I replied and he laughed again.

'Now, Clare, in just a few minutes you've managed to find out all there is to know about me, so I guess you must be a femme fatale interrogator in Military Intelligence or something' he said.

I thought 'I wish' before replying lamely 'I work for a car dealership.'

'They must sell Bentley's or Aston Martin's with you there.'

'Neither, it's BMW's' I replied.

'Ah, the Germans' he said with a smile.

'Yes.'

'And what do you do for them?'

'Produce endless accounts for rich people who don't pay' I replied.

'The free market economy, the back bone of civilised society' he said with a grin.

I decided to change the subject and asked, 'so, what do you do when you're not flying or attending naff parties?'

'Oh, I just try and relax' he replied his blue eyes twinkling.

'Give me a for instance' I said with a smile, eager to know what he would say.

'Well as my job is a bit dangerous sometimes, I need time alone to think about the meaning of life - and other things' he said.

'Go on.'

'So, I often soak in a bath surrounded by candles, then cook a nice meal, I'm particularly fond of Thai food, sit quietly sipping a good wine, whilst reading a romantic book with a happy ending. and possibly listen to some Mozart' he said as he looked into my very soul with his gorgeous blue eyes. My ankles turned into jelly, matching my custard knees.

I thought 'so there is a God after all and I quickly prayed... please help me to catch this heavenly creature'.

I had just finished praying when Jane arrived and said, 'Clare, come and see Simon, he's Melanie's brother and he's dying to meet you.'

I thought 'bugger Simon... let him die' but said 'in a minute, Jane I'm busy at the moment.'

'Don't let me keep you, Clare' said Tony and I could have killed Jane with my bare hands! I looked at her but she just smiled and said 'come on, don't be shy.'

'I'm not' I replied then looking up into the heavenly creatures eyes I said, 'I won't be long, I promise you.'

'There's no hurry, I'll be here for a while yet' he replied with a smile.

Passing my lager clutching Neanderthal, I followed Jane across the room to Simon, to whom Jane introduced me.

'I've heard a lot about you, Clare' he gurgled with a silly grin.

'Well I'll try and live it down' I replied. He giggled as I glanced back across the room to Tony who was now talking to a long legged blonde, with dubious hair colour, wearing a short red dress which was ridiculously low cut and far too tight for her. You know her bulging type, frustrated and once round the block with emotional baggage. My heart raced as she laughed at something he said. God, I could have killed Jane again for this and I made up my mind to get back to the heavenly one before 'blondie' could get her claws too deeply into him. Tony said something else, then 'blondie' threw back her head with laughter once again and touched his arm, as silly women do who want to impress a man. I didn't like the laughter or the arm touching but suddenly I was aware of Simon speaking to me.

'So what do you do?' he asked... as if it mattered.

'I work for a BMW dealership' I replied lamely.

'Wow... how cool is that!' he exclaimed with a silly grin.

'I've no idea' I replied.

'BMW's are one of my favourite cars, especially the 5 series, I mean they are just the best value top performance car that's available anywhere, absolutely no one can beat them' he said enthusiastically.

'You sound like one of our salesmen' I said in a disinterested tone.

'You're very lucky to get a job there' he said.

4

'Am I?'

'Yes, BMW are very fussy about who they employ these days' he said and I thought 'thanks a bunch!' as I glanced back across the room and saw to my horror that a petite dark haired girl had joined the dubious blonde and was trying to attract Tony's attention. My blood pressure couldn't stand much more of this torment, so I hatched a plan to make my escape and get back to Tony.

'I must go to the little girl's room' I said. Simon nodded and I made my way across to where Jane was talking to an earnest looking bearded type with a scarf tied round his neck.

'Excuse me, Jane where's the loo?' I asked in a whisper.

'Oh Clare... you must say hello to Rupert, he's a...' began Jane

'Hello Rupert' I interrupted then repeated through clenched teeth 'where's the bloody loo?'

'Oh, down near the kitchen, or if that's busy you'll have to use the one at the top of the stairs' she replied.

'Thanks' I said, handed her my glass of wine then hurried off towards the kitchen. That was busy and two silly giggling girls with smudged makeup were waiting outside with their legs crossed, so I made a dash for the stairs. I had just reached the naughty step when suddenly Tony appeared from the noisy room and smiled at me.

'Hello you' he said disarmingly.

'Hello.'

'I hope you're not running away just yet' he said

'No, just trying to find the loo' I replied.

'Thank heavens for that, I thought you'd deserted me' he said with a smile and I thought 'never in this lifetime, baby blue eyes' but replied with a smile 'no, I wouldn't do that.'

'Well when you've found it, come and find me' he said with a twinkle in his eyes.

'I will' I replied and made my way up the stairs. The bathroom was free and I hurriedly tinkled, tidied my hair, touched up my lip-gloss and breathed deeply before returning to the noisy party in search of the chosen one. He was now chatting to an old guy and to my relief 'blondie' had disappeared but the dark petite one was still hovering like an anxious bird of prey. I crossed the room and said 'well here I am at last.'

Tony smiled down at me and said 'good, now let me get you something to drink whilst you chat to Phil here and tell him all about yourself.'

'Thanks, I'll have a red wine' I said with a smile, feeling really wanted. Tony disappeared into the crowd and Phil said 'Tony's been telling me all about you.'

I thought 'oh goody, goody' but said in a surprised tone 'has he?'

'Yes, it seems you've made quite an impression on him and I must tell you that Tony's girl friends all come in one size… leggy and beautiful, and you fit the bill nicely.' I could have kissed him for that but replied 'that's good to hear.'

'I'm sure, so how come you know Melanie?'

'I don't really, but my friend Jane is Melanie's cousin so she invited me' I replied.

'Well in that case thank heavens for family friends' he said.

'Too true, are you a relation?'

'No, I'm just Melanie's old boss' he replied sadly.

'Oh.'

'I'm glad she's got such a bright future in front of her now but I am very sorry to lose her' he said as Tony arrived back with my wine and a glass of orange for himself. He handed me my drink and said with a smile 'cheers' and I whispered 'cheers' before sipping the wine.

'So what do you do in your spare time after you've finished chasing BMW customers and attending unbelievably awful parties?' asked Tony.

'Not a lot really' I replied.

'What about your boyfriends?' he asked.

'I haven't got one' I replied but thinking 'you're the next successful candidate and no matter what you say or do, your resistance will be futile.'

'I can't believe that' he said with a smile.

'Neither can I' added Phil.

'It's true, I promise you' I said with a silly giggle before taking another sip of wine to steady myself.

'I bet they're really queuing up outside your door' said Phil.

'I wish' I replied.

'Well, what a hopeless lot they all are round here' said Tony.

'No wonder our population is shrinking' said Phil.

'Too true' said Tony with a smile. I could have kissed him there and then. I wondered how I should play the situation without scaring him away. Then Jane appeared once again and said 'Clare, Simon is waiting for you.'

'Don't let us keep you' said Tony. I just grinned and nodded as my blood pressure increased to a serious level, which would soon require my admittance to a hospital's intensive care unit.

'I'll catch you later' I said with a smile and he nodded. As I followed Jane across the crowded room, I wondered why Tony had not tried to persuade me to stay with him, perhaps he had something planned for later, so my heart was full of hope once again. I wondered if I would end up in a bath with him, surrounded by candles. Oh God, make it happen sooner rather than later! Also, I do like Thai food and Mozart... well... just a little I think.

My eyes glazed over when I looked up into Simon's face as he asked 'do you live local?' There followed about ten minutes of dreadful and banal conversation with me fencing away silly remarks like some desperate and demented Scaramouch. It seemed like hours before I was suddenly aware of Tony standing beside me and I glanced up at him with relief.

'Sorry to interrupt, but could I just have a quick word with you Clare?' he asked and Simon nodded, mumbling 'sure' before drifting away into the crowd of guffawing Neanderthals.

'I'm flying to Paris tomorrow afternoon and...' he started and I interrupted with the thought 'would you like to take me with you?'... 'so, I've got to go now and get an early night.'

I thought 'what a bloody shame' but said 'oh, really?'

'Yes... but if you're ready to leave this shambles, I'd be happy to drive you home, if you think you can trust me' he said. I thought 'it's not you who's got to be trusted it's me!' but replied 'oh, yes please... I'll just get my coat.'

Within moments I had said 'goodnight' to those who mattered and my heart raced with expectations as Tony guided me down the path to the road, where his gorgeous red Jaguar coupé stood gleaming in the street lamplight. He clicked his key, the lights flashed and the door locks opened. He brushed gently passed me, opened the door and the smell of the leather seats wafted up as I slid into the sleek sports car. The interior lights stayed on until he was seated behind the wheel, he turned to me as he started the purring engine and said 'I couldn't possibly leave you there with that mob of dreadful creatures.'

'Thank God you rescued me, my knight in shining armour' I replied with a giggle but thinking 'am I really in for an early bath with candles?'

'My pleasure' he said before the Jaguar swept effortlessly away down the road with me feeling... well, sort of seduced already by the events of the evening. As my dear Mother says, 'you never know what's round the corner'.

'So where do you live?' he asked as we reached the bottom of the road.

'In Romford' I replied, but added hastily 'with my Mother.'

'Ah, that's not too far, we'll be there quite soon' he said as the Jaguar purred along at speed.

'You needn't hurry, it's still quite early and I'm not expected in just yet' I said.

'I'm sure, but I've got to get home to rest and be ready for my flight tomorrow' he said.

'So where do you live?'

'At Cranfield' he replied.

'Where's that?'

'It's a small village near Bedford.'

'How nice.'

'Yes it is... and it's very close to the airfield where I'm based' he said.

'How convenient' I said, wondering if this gorgeous man was too wrapped up with flying to be interested in settling down.

'So it's all bed and flying for you then?' I asked.

'No, not at all... I do try to fit in a social life when I can' he replied and I thought of his leggy girlfriends for a moment, but dismissed them because I was on a mission which I intended to win - knocking out the competition by any foul means.

'And when do you find time for that?' I asked.

'Well quite often... for instance, I'm flying several business men over to Paris tomorrow afternoon, then flying onto Rome,

8

staying overnight, then bringing two VIP's back to Luton... after that I'm free for a day before I start test flying again... so would you like to have dinner with me on Monday evening?'

I remained speechless for a few seconds whilst my head calmed down from the first excited rush of lust and replied demurely 'yes... that would be lovely, Tony, thank you.'

'That's good... because I thought you might say 'no'' he said quietly.

I thought 'never!' but asked 'whatever made you think that?'

'I just wondered if...'

'If what?' I asked as he faltered.

'Well... there was someone else' he replied.

'No, there's no one at the moment' I replied firmly, but seconds later thought 'I shouldn't have been so definite... I don't want him to think he has no future competition.'

'Oh, I thought Simon might be...' he began but I interrupted him and said 'oh, no, not Simon.'

'Well I'm glad about that.'

'He's not my type' I said.

'So what is your type?' he asked and my brain went into overdrive trying to think of a clever answer.

'I'm not sure really... but I'll know as soon as I've found him' I replied.

'Well, let me know when you do' he said with a laugh.

'You'll be the very first to know' I said, adding 'please could you turn the heat down a little?' which gave me time to think and compose myself.

'Oh I'm sorry, Clare... are you too hot?'

I thought 'oh brother, if you only knew!' but said 'yes, just a little, I think it's the cheap plonk that I've been drinking' I replied as he adjusted the air conditioning.

'There... but do tell me if you're still too hot' he said.

'I will, but that feels better already' I said with a smile as cool air gently wafted at me from the vents.

'Good... I don't want you to feel uncomfortable.'

'Thank you.'

'It's the duty of all pilots to ensure that their passengers are safe and comfortable at all times' he said.

'I'm sure.'

'It's drummed into us from the very start of our flight training' he said seriously.

'How considerate... now tell me about cooking Thai food' I said as I wondered if he'd invite me to his place for dinner on Monday, followed by a little Mozart music and a relaxing, candlelit bath.

'Well, it's very easy really, everything is light and needs only a short time in the wok so the meal is quick and tasty' he said.

'Sounds delicious' I said whilst thinking 'I hope its dinner at his place' but he dashed my expectations by saying 'but I know this little Italian place that's serves fantastic lasagne... do you like Italian food?'

'Oh I do... I love it' I replied trying hard not to show my disappointment.

'Good' he said, as I glanced out of the windscreen and saw the sign for Romford... it was only ten miles away. I thought 'God... I hope my Mother's not still up watching some silly late night film on the television... but I bet she is.'

My Mother and I have not been on the best of terms lately... well, ever since I moved back home from the flat I had shared with Jane. That arrangement didn't suit me really, because perhaps we are too much alike so I'm stuck with Mother until I can afford a place of my own.

My Mother thinks that all daughters should be married and having babies when they are young... so, having just passed my twenty-seventh birthday with no reasonable man in sight, I have been given up for dead by her. When I look in the mirror some mornings I think I'm turning into my Mother, which is awful. We seem to row a lot and she keeps telling me I'll end up like her... all alone and pruning roses. My Father, bless him, had an affair with his secretary and when Mother found out she divorced him without a second thought... now she regrets it. Father married his secretary, Nicole, and they seem quite happy, which annoys my Mother intensely. There's no pleasing some people.

'A penny for your thoughts' said Tony, which brought me back to reality.

'Oh... er, I don't think I can invite you in tonight for coffee... it's my Mother you know, she's not sleeping too well...'

'Don't worry, Clare, I had no intention of staying because I need to get home' he interrupted and I breathed a sigh of relief. If my Mother caught sight of this gorgeous man too soon she'd be putting her big fat foot in it at every turn and wrecking any chance I had of catching him. I would need time to prepare him for the inevitable confrontation when she'd ask daft questions like 'I think all women should be married by their early twenties, don't you?' or 'don't you agree that if a woman isn't married by the time she's thirty she should take the first man that comes along?' I cringed at the very thought of it all and decided to keep Tony out of harm's way for as long as possible.

'We're nearly there' he said as another signpost for Romford flashed by.

'There's no hurry' I said as calmly as I could but we were soon in the town and I guided Tony to my home in Brentwood Gardens. He switched off the engine and we sat in silence for a moment before he said in a whisper 'I've had a wonderful evening, Clare and I'm so glad that I've met you,' then he leaned over and kissed me gently on the lips.

'Oh, Tony' I whispered back.

'I have to go now... but I'll collect you on Monday evening, about seven... is that alright?'

'Oh, yes.'

'Then goodnight' he said before he gently kissed me again.

'Goodnight, Tony.'

I stepped out of the Jaguar, closed the door and watched as it sped away down to the main road, turned left and disappeared. My heart was singing as I made my way up to the house and let myself in. I could hear the television on full blast and went into the lounge where Mother, glasses perched on the end of her nose, was busy foraging around in a box of Milk Tray chocolates.

'You're back early' she said, still looking at the screen. 'Had a good time?'

'Well it was alright... I suppose' I replied as I slumped down in the armchair.

'Meet any body nice?' she asked as she popped another chocolate into her mouth.

'No... not really' I lied.

'But did you meet anyone at all?' she asked firmly.

'Yes…'

'Who?' she interrupted.

'His name's Tony…'

'He sounds nice.'

'Yes, I think he may be.'

'Good… are you going to see him again?'

'Probably.'

'Well has he asked you out?'

'Yes.'

'When?'

'Monday, but I'm still thinking about it' I replied and thought 'I wish she'd shut up, watch the bloody box and scoff her chocolates.'

'What's there to think about?' she asked before she scooped up another chocolate.

'I don't know…'

'Is he gay?' she interrupted.

'No.'

'Married?'

'No.'

'Then it sounds to me like you're getting too fussy in your old age' she said with a touch of malice, then added 'you'll regret it.'

'I think I'll go to bed… I've got one of your headaches coming on!' I said and got up.

'Ah… I've touched a raw nerve at last' she said before popping another chocolate.

Sunday dragged by and I constantly thought of Tony. I wondered if he had left for Paris yet, I kept looking at the clock and wishing I was with him. Mother got on my nerves because she kept wittering on about my brother David, his wife Angela and their baby Naomi. In the end, I really couldn't be bothered with it all and went to bed early, leaving her glued to the television.

I felt fine on Monday morning because the gorgeous one, who I decided was sinfully handsome, was taking me out for dinner! As I drove to work, I thought that nothing could spoil my day and possibly I wouldn't go to work on Tuesday if Tony made a night of it! Oh, what luxury to be laying in bed with him… my Pagan love God, who must be completely satisfied at all costs… whilst my boss Roger Wilkes, manager of the accounts department, worried about the customers unpaid bills.

When I strode into the office, Tina looked up from her screen and said 'hi, you look pleased with yourself this morning.'

'Oh, I am' I replied, as I sat down at my desk.

'And why is that may I ask?'

'I'm going out to dinner this evening' I replied.

'Ohhh, on a Monday… that's a bit strange isn't it?'

'I don't think so' I replied.

'So tell me… who with?' she asked with a smirk.

'A nice man.'

'Oh…ha… ha… I didn't think it was a woman… so where did you find him?'

'At a party on Saturday' I replied.

'What's his name?'

'Tony.'

'Why is he going out with you for heaven's sake?'

'He thinks I'm lovely…'

'Is he blind?' she interrupted with a giggle.

'No… he's a pilot…'

'Has he run out of stewardesses then?' she asked as Roger Wilkes came into the office.

'You're late again this morning Clare, I've told you about your timekeeping before' said Wilkes as he adjusted his glasses.

'Yes, Mr Wilkes, I'm sorry… it's my Mother, she's not too well at the moment' I replied.

'Then get her to see a Doctor. This is a list of overdue accounts that must be followed up today, so please see to it' he said as he placed the paper on my desk and hurried away to his own office.

The rest of the day dragged on with the occasional interruption from Tina asking inane questions about Tony and where was he taking me to dinner. I tried to remain patient but in the end I had to tell her to shut up and get on with her work. There is only the two of us in the office and I think I'm slightly in charge, but I'm not sure as it's never been made official and Tina resents it… not knowing that is.

I got home just after six, told Mother I was going out, and knew that the intended one would be outside in less than an hour. I showered, dried my hair as I plastered on my 'slap' and chose my 'killer' low cut black dress for this evening. I wore my comfortable black high heels, took what I needed from my handbag, and put it into a little black clutch bag. I was ready and thought I looked good in the mirror. I'm a brunette, quite tall with firm boobs, long legs and quite a pleasing face with brown eyes... Tony says I'm beautiful... and I have to agree! I put some of my favourite Givenchy perfume, 'L'amour', behind my ears, a touch in my cleavage and a drop on my hanky. So... all done now and ready to be whisked away for dinner and whatever comes after... I hope... I hope!

I went downstairs, presented myself to Mother, who was busy in the kitchen, and asked 'how do I look?'

She glanced at me up and down then said 'alright, I suppose, but what's that smell?'

'It's my perfume... its Givenchy 'L'amour'' I replied in an exasperated tone.

'Well, whatever it is, you've got far too much on' she said.

'Well it's too late now, I can't take it off' I said firmly before going into the lounge. I glanced at the clock and it was just after seven, I looked out of the window just as Tony's Jaguar pulled up outside. My heart pounded and I called out 'I'm off now... don't wait up!'

'No I won't' called Mother as I put on my coat and hurried out of the front door.

Tony was all smiles as he opened the car door for me.

'Hello you' he said as he gave me a little kiss on my cheek and I smiled, whispered 'hello' then slid into the warm, comfy, leather interior of the Jaguar. The car sped away down Brentwood Gardens and Tony drove out to the Southend Arterial road.

'So where you taking me?'

'To a little Italian restaurant called 'Il Farenzia'... the food is fantastic and it's on the sea front at Westcliffe' he replied.

'Sounds lovely... and we can go for a swim afterwards' I said and he laughed.

'I don't think so... but we could have a walk along the front in the moonlight.'

'That would be nice.'

The 'Il Farenzia' is owned by two brothers, Luigi and Pietro, they welcomed Tony with smiles and little bows before Luigi showed us to a reserved table for two in an alcove at the back of the warm, candlelit restaurant. I was feeling relaxed, sexy and dreamy all at the same time... it was lovely. Luigi handed menus to both of us and said in his thick Italian accent 'I canna recommenda the lasagne tonight... it is particularly gooda!'

'Then we'll both have it, Luigi' said Tony and I thought 'I do love a man who takes control.' Tony glanced at me and asked 'is that alright, Clare?' spoiling my illusion for a moment but I nodded and whispered 'yes, that's fine.'

'Now... whata you like to starta witha?' asked Luigi and after glancing down the list we both chose avocado pears with prawns.

'Ah, bene... bene... now whata woulda you like to drinka?' asked Luigi. Tony glanced at the wine list and ordered a bottle of Chianti. The smiling Italian hurried away and Tony looked at me and said 'you look absolutely fabulous tonight.' The candle in the huge red goblet in the centre of the table flickered and I thought 'this evening is going to be spiritual' then said 'thank you... I do try my best.'

The food was simply delicious and we hardly spoke until we had finished our desserts of soft ice creams topped with chocolate sauce. After coffee, Tony paid the bill and we said 'goodnight' to the smiling brothers. We walked along the promenade in the cool night air, I held Tony's arm and glanced up at him and said 'thank you, the meal was fantastic.'

'I told you it would be good' he said, before bending down to kiss me. I was in heaven and said 'we should do this more often.' He laughed and replied 'I was just thinking that, so how about dinner at my place on Saturday?' I was speechless for a moment as Thai food, Mozart and a candlelit bath flashed before my eyes again, I replied 'oh, that would be nice... are you going to cook some Thai food?'

'Yes... if you like.'

'That'll be great... then we can listen to some Mozart' I said with a smile.

'Why not?' he said and I thought 'then you can bathe me and take me to bed.'

We drove slowly back to Romford and talked all the way about our jobs and hopes for the future. I learned a lot about his flying and thought how brave he was to test a new jet fighter with his two colleagues, Matt and Paul. They were like the three Musketeers, all for one and one for all. By the time we turned into Brentwood Gardens I was hopelessly in love with this amusing, intelligent, sinfully handsome man. I wanted to spend the rest of my life with him, without a shadow of a doubt. I only hoped he felt the same about me. After he stopped the car and switched off the engine we kissed passionately for some while before I said 'I must go in now… work tomorrow.'

'Me too… I'm test flying until Thursday then taking some more VIP's to Brussels on Friday' he said.

'Well I hope you're back in time to cook dinner on Saturday' I said firmly.

He laughed and replied 'yes, I will be… and I'll pick you up at about seven again… is that okay?'

'Oh, yes… I'll be ready' I replied and he kissed me passionately.

The rest of the week dragged slowly by like a limping man pulling a lame donkey. My frustration was only punctuated by rows with Mother about nothing in particular, silly remarks from Tina and more prodding from Mr Wilkes about my inattention to the importance of the job in hand.

Saturday dawned at last and I spent the morning sorting out my flimsy black lace underwear with the red roses, matching suspender belt and fish net stockings. I didn't want Tony to think I was a tart when he undressed me, but on the other hand, I was determined to keep his interest up as he uncovered his prize. I chose my backless red dress and slipped it on just to make sure that it still fitted OK because I hadn't worn it since Greg dumped me. What an absolute tosser he was! All over me like a rash at first then cold as ice when he realised I was serious! Commitment was never in his vocabulary but never mind, that's all in the past now and with a bit of luck, I have the man of my dreams. My dress looked alright and I breathed a sigh of relief.

Over lunch of soup and cheese sandwiches, Mother was asking too many questions about Tony and I tried to placate her with non-committal answers as I didn't want her to meet him yet.

'You don't seem very certain… are you sure about him?'

'Yes, quite sure' I replied.

'Well in that case I only hope you know what you're doing this time, I mean that Greg was a...'

'I do know!' I interrupted, not wishing to be reminded of that hopeless moron.

'We'll wait and see, but I won't hold my breath…'

'No, please don't' I interrupted and she remained silent for a few moments then said 'I think there's something you're not telling me, Clare.'

'There's nothing, honestly… Tony's a nice person and, when I'm ready, I'll ask him to come home so you can meet him' I said and she looked at me then just said 'mmm' in a disbelieving way.

'So what does 'mmm' mean?' I asked.

'Nothing… but I hope you remember that lying to me is futile, I always find everything out in the end' she said before she bit into a sandwich.

'Oh… don't I know it!'

I was all dressed up and ready to go by six thirty and just dabbed my Givenchy perfume in all the right places before I went down to the lounge to wait.

Mother looked at me, pushed her glasses up her nose and said 'I must say that you look a bit better than you did the last time you went out with this chap.'

'Why thank you, Mother dear' I said with a touch of sarcasm, she shook her head and tutted.

We stayed silent as she watched the television and I waited impatiently for my 'soon to be' lover to arrive. I kept glancing at the clock and just before seven I saw the Jaguar pull up outside. My heart leapt and I said 'here he is… I'm off now.'

'Bye' she replied still watching the box.

The drive round the M25 and up the M1 to his neat house on the outskirts of Cranfield village was effortless and I was in a relaxed heavenly mood when we arrived.

'I hope you'll approve of my cooking tonight' he said as he opened the front door and guided me into his warm home.

'I'm sure it will be fine' I replied and thought 'the way I'm feeling at the moment you could serve me up beans on toast and I'd be satisfied!'

The house was tidy, nicely furnished and comfortably open plan. Tony put on some light background music and I asked 'I suppose the Mozart comes later then?' He laughed and replied 'only if you want.'

I thought 'I know what I want later and only hope that you want the same thing, my baby blue eyes!'

'Now what can I get you to drink?' he asked as I sank down into his soft, cream leather settee.

'Have you a gin and tonic?'

'I have' he replied and went to a kitchen cupboard and took out a bottle. He poured the drinks then joined me and with ice tinkling in our glasses, we sat together before he said 'cheers... here's to us... and our future.' I liked that so smiled and said 'cheers' before we touched glasses.

Whilst he cooked the food, I sat at the candlelit table and watched. He was like a master chef in action and I was suitably impressed. When the meal of diced chicken breasts was served on a bed of soft, steaming rice, the aroma of the spices was only surpassed by the flavours. We drank a large bottle of light white wine and by the end of the main course I was already quite 'squiffy'.

'I hope you're not going to take advantage of me tonight' I said in a slightly slurred tone.

'Wouldn't dream of it' he replied with a captivating smile.

'Good' I replied but thought 'pity.'

'Are you ready for a sweet yet?' he asked.

I thought 'I'm ready for anything' but replied 'yes, I think so.'

'There's a choice... you can have either cherries in brandy or fruit salad' he said.

'What's in the fruit salad?' I stupidly asked.

'Fruit.'

'I thought so... it's always the same wherever you go... I'll have the cherries then' I slurred and he smiled.

'I think you are little unsteady' he said.

'Have you only just noticed?'

'Probably.'

'Well it's all your fault... you're the cause' I said, trying to point a very unsteady finger at him.

'Me?' he grinned.

'And you know it... you only brought me here to feed me delicious food, get me drunk then have your wicked way with me' I said.

'Well I must admit... it did cross my mind...'

'See! See!' I interrupted loudly.

'But I think that you're so gorgeous Clare that I really can't resist you' he said in a whisper.

'Oh, I know I am' I said, then added 'are you going to put the Mozart on before we have a bath?'

'If you like... but do you need a bath?'

'Yes... I'm feeling disgustingly dirty!' I replied with a giggle and he laughed.

We ate the cherries and drank more white wine then we sat and kissed on the settee before he whispered 'I'll go and run the bath now and light the candles.'

'If you would... I'm feeling dirtier by the minute' I said. He smiled and left me to gather my heavenly thoughts.

In the bedroom he undressed me slowly and gave me gentle kisses as each layer was removed, kissing my naked body all over when it was finally exposed. He led me into the warm, candlelit bathroom and helped me into the bath before undressing in front of me. He was gorgeous naked and my heart fluttered with excitement as he climbed into the foaming water.

'This is so nice' I said with a smile.

'Indeed it is.'

He washed me all over and we soaked for a while before getting out and drying off. It is so relaxing to have a handsome naked man dry you with warm towels... I can really recommend it!

He led me into the bedroom where he made love to me, gently at first then as I became more and more excited he thrust up into me with such wonderful force that I had a shattering orgasm and he came at the same time. It was absolutely fabulous and I wanted to cry with emotion but just kissed him so passionately that he struggled to breath.

God... it was all so wonderful... but I thought it was too good to last... and it was!

CHAPTER 2

CLARE MEETS ERIC

The next few weeks flew by at breakneck speed and Tony spent all his available free time with me. We had dinner at 'Il Farenzia' several times as well as the 'Steak House' in Bedford, which is a lovely restaurant in an old watermill by the river. We made love at his house as often as we could. Then I arranged for him to meet Mother!

I warned him about her and made sure she understood that I really wanted Tony and I would happily murder her if she put a foot wrong when they met. She smiled and told me that she only wanted me to be happy… get married... and move away from home!

Although I was nervous, everything went well over the Sunday lunch of roast beef with all the trimmings and I must admit that Mother was on her very best behaviour. Not only had she cooked a delicious meal, smiled at all the right times, laughed at Tony's jokes, but also said nothing about Greg and the other losers who had dumped me!

I was feeling relieved as we drove back to Cranfield and that evening Tony proposed to me. When he asked, 'will you marry me, Clare?' I just whispered 'oh, yes, my darling, yes…'

It was just a month from when I had met him at the party. I couldn't believe my good fortune and I was so happy. I thought 'you never know who, or what, is around the next corner… it could be the love of your life… or a big win on the lottery!' That's positive as well as so true!

The next morning I phoned work to tell them I wouldn't be in and we went into Bedford to buy a ring. After visiting several jewellers I found just what I wanted… three pure white diamonds, mounted in a gold cross over. The assistant was all smiles, Tony paid her with his plastic and I kissed him as he slipped it on my finger.

When I told Mother that evening and showed her the ring, she was overjoyed and went immediately into 'arrangement mode'. Invitations, guest lists, catering, church… the whole nine yards…

she was in her element and I couldn't slow her down, that is, until I told her that Dad would be invited … and Nicole. She pulled a face, sighed and said 'I suppose they'll have to come… but your aunts will be unhappy about it.'

'Well it's my day and they'll just have to put up with it won't they?'

'They might not come when they know your Father will be there with… her' said Mother, emphasising the 'her'.

'Then they'll have to stay away and we'll save on the catering bill' I replied.

'You're as uncaring as your Father' she said with another sigh.

'Well it's not the way I see it' I replied before I went up to my room.

When I told Jane she was very happy for me but said that Simon would be disappointed. I thought 'Simon will have to learn that in life you can't have everything you want!'

At work on the Tuesday, Tina looked a little 'po' faced when I showed her my ring, she kept saying 'but you've only known him for a couple of weeks!'

'A month' I corrected her.

'Don't you think it's a bit too soon?'

'No… when you meet the right man you always know immediately' I replied smugly.

'Well I hope you know what you're doing' she said dismissively before she gazed back at her computer screen and started tapping away at her keyboard.

I met Tony's widowed Mother, Linda, a very sweet lady and we instantly bonded. I only wished that my Mother was as understanding and gentle as this lovely, relaxed woman. Soon afterwards I met Tony's sister, Samantha, her husband Bob and their two little girls Lucy and Amelia, who wanted to be bridesmaids. Of course, I agreed and everyone was very happy with that arrangement. I asked Jane to be my matron of honour and she smirked a little but said 'yes'. I was pleased because she is a pretty brunette, tall as me and has a sense of humour.

When I first told Dad on the phone, he was delighted with the news and invited us over for dinner. He and Tony hit it off straight away, whilst Nicole stayed a bit aloof, but that's how she always is... so none of us took any notice. I guess she was dreading the wedding and the inevitable confrontation with Mother and my two aunts.

Everything was set, including the honeymoon, which Tony had organised in Paris. We were going to stay at the Georges Cinque Hotel for a wonderful week and would be waited on hand and foot. What could be a better place for a honeymoon than Paris in the spring?

Tony had looked at the forward flight schedules and noticed that Matt was flying out to Charles de Gaulle airport on the Sunday after our wedding. He was going to collect some Scottish business people and fly them back to Edinburgh. The flight operations manager agreed that Tony and I could fly over to Paris in the empty HS 125 jet.

We were married in St Edmund's church at three o'clock. on Saturday April the 23rd, St George's day. Dad gave me away as Mother dabbed her eyes, Nicole stayed aloof under her enormous hat, whilst everyone else, including the bridesmaids, remained fairly calm.

After the ceremony, when my shiny new husband and I walked slowly down the aisle, nodding and smiling at all the family, I noticed a good looking man sitting alone in the very last pew. I had not seen him when I arrived on Dad's arm so I guessed he must have slipped into the church after the ceremony had begun. He smiled at me and I tried hard to think if I knew him... but I didn't... and it worried me for a moment. Was he a friend of Greg's who had come to spy on me and spoil my golden day? I glanced at him again and thought 'whoever you are, you're a very handsome guy... so where were you when I needed a tall, good looking bloke with a tan, blue eyes and a mop of blonde hair?'

Suddenly we were out in the sunshine and the photographer was trying to get us organised. We almost did as we were told and after a lot of temperamental fuss, accompanied by silly giggling, he was eventually satisfied with the results of his artistic camera work. After that excitement was over, Tony and I made our way to the waiting limousine, followed by excited guests throwing confetti. I climbed into the limousine with confetti showering out of every fold in my dress, whilst Tony smiled and chatted briefly to Paul, who had been the best man. I glanced up as Paul closed the car door and saw the handsome stranger standing behind the guests, towering above them all. He smiled at me and I was quite un-nerved by his presence, so quickly looked away.

'You look pale, darling... are you alright?' asked Tony as the limousine drove off.

'Yes... I'm fine, Tony... my new husband' I replied and we kissed.

The reception went off wonderfully well and exactly as planned. Paul's speech was very amusing and only matched by my Dad's... even Mother had to smile. The food was excellent, the Champagne perfect and the music played by the jazz quartet was fitting for the occasion. Tony and I had the first dance and all the guests cheered! Everyone was well behaved and, other than Lucy spilling her orange juice all over her bridesmaids dress and Auntie Joyce, there were no unfortunate incidents. By the time we left the party I had drunk too much Champagne, kissed everybody twice and was glad that it was all over. We spent the first night in the nearby Excelsior Hotel where we fell into a deep sleep immediately we climbed into bed.

After dragging ourselves out of bed the next morning we had a light breakfast of toast and black coffee to sober up before we set off to our house in Cranfield. The flight departure time was three thirty from the airfield, which gave us time to pack our final things, have a sandwich for lunch, more coffee and drive round to the offices of Euro Concordia Aviation.

Tony introduced me to the Operations Manager, Giles Hutton, as Mrs Franklin, and I felt so pleased with my new title. Then I met Matt, as we shook hands I thought 'he looks like Brad Pitt... why are pilot's so handsome?'

'Hello, Clare... I'm so pleased to meet you at last... Tony has not stopped talking about you... and I can see why' Matt said with a captivating smile. I thought 'how can I reply to that?' and said 'why thank you... it's a shame that you couldn't come to the wedding yesterday.'

'I know… I'm sorry I missed it, but I was still in France at NATO headquarters and only got back late last night' he replied.

'Then you're forgiven' I said and he laughed.

'That's good because I'd hate to have an unforgiving passenger on board!'

I was led out to the very smart, small executive jet parked by the control tower. The co-pilot, Peter, was already at the controls carrying out the start up checks. Tony and I sat in the comfortable leather seats either side of the narrow aisle at the front of the plush cabin whilst Matt went up to the cockpit and sat in the Captain's seat.

Tony smiled at me as the engines were started up and we fastened our seat belts before we taxied away slowly towards the runway.

'It'll only take about 45 minutes or so to get to Paris.'

'That's quick.'

'Yes it is… then I've got you all to myself!' he said with a grin and I smiled.

When the jet was standing at the runway threshold waiting for permission to take off, I glanced out of my window and to my surprise I saw a tall man standing alone by the perimeter fence. I was certain that it was the stranger at the church and the hairs stood up on the back of my neck. I was quite un-nerved and quickly looked away as the engine noise increased and the aircraft moved onto the runway. Within moments the noise from the engines grew even louder and suddenly we were hurtling down the runway… and airborne.

Matt climbed the aircraft rapidly to its operating height and when it levelled off Tony undid his seat belt and told me to do the same. I smiled and sat quietly for a few minutes watching the clouds as they drifted slowly by but could not get the handsome stranger out of my mind. Eventually I looked at Tony and asked 'at the wedding, did you notice a tall guy sitting at the back of the church?'

'No, darling, I can't say I did… was he a relative of yours?'

'No, I'd never seen him before' I replied.

'Well it was probably just one of the local's who popped in to see us' he said with a grin. Nevertheless, it worried me that Tony hadn't noticed this guy... I mean he was tall, good looking and you couldn't help noticing him... I began to wonder if I had imagined him.

We landed at Charles de Gaulle airport just under an hour later and taxied to the dispersal for private jets. Matt and Peter shut everything down and we all climbed out of the baby jet. Peter helped Tony with our luggage and we followed Matt into the VIP Reception. Our passports were checked by the customs officers and we were free to go. We said 'goodbye' to the boys and Matt gave me a kiss on the cheek and said 'Tony's a very lucky man.'

'That's what I keep telling him' I replied and they all laughed.

The Georges Cinque Hotel was absolutely splendid and Tony had managed to book us into the honeymoon suite for the week. I couldn't believe it! The bedroom was heaven and from the first night onwards I didn't want to leave it. The bathroom was made for lovers and had every conceivable perfume, along with a selection of gels that only the French could dream up. We made love every which way that you could imagine and ended up totally exhausted every night!

We strolled along by the Seine holding hands in the spring sunshine, went up the Eiffel Tower and marvelled at the view and had dinner three nights running at 'Le Bistro Romaine' in the Champs-Élysées, because the food there was so good. My favourite meal was on the first night when we had homard á l'americaine, which is lobster cooked in brandy; followed by boeuf en daube, tender beef cooked in red wine with herbs... it was delicious! We drank a bottle of Burgundy and had Crepes Suzette followed by coffee and brandy... I was in heaven and fast putting on weight.

However, there was one incident that worried me a little. It happened when we were wandering around Montmartre looking in the bijou shops. I thought I saw the stranger from the church watching me at a distance, but he suddenly vanished in the crowd so I dismissed it as being my silly imagination again... because why would this guy want to follow me to Paris? I decided not to tell Tony.

Unfortunately, everything so good has to come to an end and we left the most romantic city on earth and caught the Euro express from Gare de Nord on the following Saturday.

It seemed that from the moment we arrived back at Cranfield Tony virtually disappeared! I knew he'd be busy flying farty old businessmen about and testing the new jet fighter but I did expect him to be at home with me sometimes. It came as a bit of a shock to be alone so much after all the love and attention that I had experienced on honeymoon.

The reality of it all kicked in, I was not happy to be back at work, and it was an added pain driving to Hamilton Motors in Romford every day. I decided to look for a new job locally and in the meantime, stay at Mother's when Tony was away. She was unhappy about that but when I convinced her that it was only until I found a new job she reluctantly agreed.

'I suppose I can put up with you in small doses' she said.

'It's mutual' I replied.

'But why is Tony away so much?' she asked.

'He's just very busy at the moment.'

'I'm sure he is, but he should come home more often than he does' she said as she put the kettle on.

'I know' I said with a sigh.

'Is everything alright?' she asked, which touched a raw nerve.

'Yes… it's fine, it's just that…'

'Just what?' she interrupted, fixing me with one of her 'looks'.

'I just wish he wasn't so busy… that's all' I replied.

'Mmm.'

'And what does 'mmm' mean?'

'Oh nothing' she replied before she made the tea but I knew what she was thinking and it didn't please me. I felt that perhaps I had married him much too quickly before thinking through what life would be like with a man who was so wrapped up in his flying career. It was like a drug to him and he couldn't get enough. I was only just beginning to realise that… and what made it worse was that Mother also knew. I couldn't bear it if she ever said 'I told you so.'

When Tony was at home we started to argue about his time away and I just couldn't make him understand how unhappy I was.

'But you knew all about my flying when you married me' he said.

'I know… but I didn't think you'd be away all the bloody time!'

'Well then you're more stupid than I thought!'

'Thanks for that! All I want is to be with my husband occasionally and have some life with him… going out to dinner with friends would be nice once in a while!' I shouted before he walked out and slammed the bedroom door. I sat on the bed and cried more often than not.

I went for several job interviews at fairly uninteresting companies in Bedford, Milton Keynes and Northampton. I wasn't successful and in a way I was glad, but it left me stuck at Hamilton Motors and with Mother. I felt trapped by circumstances and what made it worse was that I realised it was all of my own making. After Greg dumped me I should have tried to get promoted at work and find a flat of my own. Why, oh why, did I have to meet and fall in love with Tony then marry him so quickly? I couldn't live without him and was finding it impossible to live with him!

It was in the July when I first suspected that he was seeing someone. In the four months after we were first married the arguments had become bitter and he did nothing to make me happy. It was a terrible disappointment to me and I didn't know whether to tell Mother or not… so, I decided to tell Jane instead. We went to 'The Red Lion', our busy local pub in Romford to drown my sorrows.

'Oh Clare… I'm so sorry' Jane said when I had finished my tale of woe.

'Well… I suppose it's all my own fault' I said with a sigh as I gazed into my gin and tonic.

'No it's not!'

'I certainly know how to pick 'em' I said.

'That's true… Greg was a….'

'Don't mention him!' I interrupted loudly, which startled the drinkers at the next table in the noisy pub.

'What are you going to do now?' she asked.

'I don't know, do I?' I replied impatiently.

'Well I think it's time for firm action' she said.

'Like what?' I asked defiantly.

'Tell him that if he prefers his precious 'flying' to a wife who adores him, then he should bugger off and find someone else he can tread all over… he has the choice' she said angrily.

'I think he's already found her' I said lamely with a lump in my throat and I thought 'God, why is this happening to me?'

'Well, if you think that, the sooner you tell him to 'piss off' the better, in my opinion!'

'It's easy for you to say that… but I still love him' I said in a whisper as the tears started.

'Oh don't cry, Clare… no man is worth it… we all know they're such bloody liars' she said in a soothing tone. I nodded and searched for a tissue in my bag.

'Let's have another drink' she said with a smile, I nodded and dabbed my eyes.

We left the pub and sauntered back to my house, with me feeling no better emotionally and slightly the worse for wear. Mother was glued to the television whilst munching through a large bar of Galaxy and only nodded when I asked her if she wanted a coffee. Jane followed me into the kitchen and I struggled to make three cups of the dark reviver whilst she told me all about her 'on-off' romance with Rupert, the bearded guy at the party. Apparently, he was an author, but unfortunately hadn't had anything published yet and had so many rejection slips he used them to wallpaper his loo. Jane said she was attracted to him but he lived permanently in his own fantasy world where he said there was no room for a woman. Men… I ask you!

The following weekend Tony arrived home and was all smiles. He looked like the cat that had been at the cream. I fancied I caught a whiff of perfume on him when he undressed but decided not to say anything for the moment. That Saturday night he said he was too tired to see to my needs and I turned over with an exasperated sigh. I thought 'I can't put up with this much longer… he's always away and when he does come home he doesn't want to know me… I'm beginning to think the handsome stranger from church would have been a better bet!' I eventually went to sleep feeling frustrated and bloody angry once again. Tony flew away on the Sunday morning to France and we parted with hardly a word said between us. I drove back to Mother's in the afternoon traffic feeling lonely and a bit tearful.

I returned home to Cranfield the next Wednesday evening to get some things, pick up the post and make sure that the house was alright. I was just opening the latest outrageous gas bill when the phone rang. I picked it up and said 'hello' as I wondered if it was Tony calling from France. There followed a moments silence from the caller before a female voice asked 'is Tony there please?'

'No he's not… who's calling?'

'Oh, er, it doesn't matter… I call him at work some other time' she replied.

'He's in France at the moment' I volunteered, hoping I could find out who this female was… as if I couldn't guess!

'Oh, is he… well it's not important.'

'Is there any message?'

'No, no thank you.'

'Are you sure, Miss?' I persisted and could feel her discomfort.

'Quite sure, thank you.'

'Right… so may I have your name and phone number please?' I asked.

'Er, what for?' she asked anxiously.

'It's for security reasons, my husband is involved in top secret work testing aircraft so every call made to this ex-directory number has to be recorded' I lied convincingly. She hung up, so I dialled 1471 but the caller withheld the number… how very convenient!

I drove back to Mother's that night because feeling the way I did, I just couldn't face the rush hour traffic the next morning. On the journey I decided to tell her what was troubling me but knew that any sympathy for me would be minimal. I hoped that she might be able to give some advice… I mean, that's what parents are for… isn't it?

When I arrived home she was watching the television and only nodded when I walked in and sat down.

'I didn't expect to see you back here tonight' she said.

'No' I replied then focused on the screen and asked lamely 'is it good?'

'So, so... it's about a woman, who murders her husband and makes it look like an accident' she replied.

'Why?'

'Why what?'

'Did she murder him?'

'Because he's having affairs left right and centre.'

'Typical.'

'They're all the same' she said, I nodded and thought 'but why?'

I waited until the film had finished and the guilty wife was imprisoned for life before asking 'can we talk?'

'What about?' she asked as she clicked off the television and stared at me.

'Me.'

'Ah... I was right... I knew there was something wrong, its Tony isn't it?'

'Yes.'

'Well go on then.'

I hesitated before blurting out 'I think he's seeing someone else.'

'I'm not surprised' she said in a flat, unemotional tone.

'Why do you say that?'

'For a start he's a man and therefore can't help it... a good looking one at that, with loads of charm that women can't resist, I'm sure they've been chucking themselves at him since his schooldays she replied.

'But he's a married...'

'I know, but that doesn't make any difference, no man can resist a woman on a plate and I expect there's a whole dinner service of them just waiting' she interrupted firmly.

'I suppose so' I replied lamely... then I thought of the blonde at the party. My God... was it her? I suddenly imagined her lying naked on a huge plate! It was a hideous sight! All that pale, saggy and uncontrolled wobbly flesh!

'You should never have got married, I thought you were making a mistake from the moment I saw him!' said Mother interrupting my thoughts.

'Well why didn't you say something?' I asked angrily

'Would you have listened? The answer to that is 'no'!'

'Oh dear God… what a mess.'

'You made it' she said and I felt angry.

'Bloody hell! Why can't you have some sympathy for me for a change?'

'I do but…'

'If it was David in this state you'd be all over him!' I shouted.

'But he's not and you are!' she replied angrily.

'It's no bloody use talking to you… I'm going to bed!'

'Just wait a minute will you?'

'Why?'

'You're too impatient and that's been the problem all along, so sit still whilst we talk' she said calmly. I pulled a face and remained in my chair.

'Now what makes you think he's seeing someone?' she asked. I told her about the perfume, the phone call, and elaborated on the fact that I wasn't having my needs met anymore.

'Men are all the same, Clare, on honeymoon they could eat you alive and soon afterwards they wished they had' she said and I had to laugh.

'Surely not all men are like that?' I queried.

'Take it from me… that's my experience with your Father and both your aunts have told me the same… once they've had their fill of your tasty bits they lose interest rapidly.'

'Oh dear God' I murmured.

'It's part of being married, so get used to it.'

'Do I have to?'

'Yes… you either put up or shut up and if you can't, then as a last resort, get a divorce' she replied.

'Well I'll have to think about it' I said slowly and felt the tears welling up. I thought 'why on earth did he have to do this to me?'

'Yes… and take your time, my advice is to do nothing hasty, you might regret it' she said and I thought how she regretted divorcing Dad.

'I won't' I mumbled.

'That's good to hear… now I think you should talk to him and try and find out what's been going on.'

'Yes, I will…'

'But do it calmly' she interrupted.

'Okay.'

'Calmly' she repeated slowly.

'Alright, alright' I said testily, as one does when being lectured by a parent.

I returned to Cranfield after work on Friday hoping that Tony would arrive home from France that night. He did, and I was pleased to see him all smiles when he came into the house.

'And how's my little wife tonight?' he asked before he kissed me.

'All the better for seeing you, whoever you are, handsome stranger' I replied.

'Ah… there's nothing like unbridled sex with a stranger' he grinned.

'Well, I live in the hope that I'll find out soon' I said and he laughed.

'Tonight could be the night' he said before he kissed me again. I thought 'this is a bit better than usual so perhaps I'm wrong about my husband.'

I rustled up cheese omelettes with chips and peas whilst Tony poured the drinks. He seemed to be his light-hearted self once again and I relaxed completely…I was now confused… perhaps I had been wrong about him. After dinner we sat and kissed on the settee for a while until the bloody phone rang and my heart stopped. He got up to answer it but I could tell he didn't want to… I'm funny like that... feline with a sixth sense, you know what I mean.

'Hello' he said quietly.

I thought I heard the voice of a woman speaking and he turned slightly away from me.

'Who is it?' I asked calmly and he faced me, waved his finger then turned away again.

'No, no… I'm afraid I can't do that until tomorrow evening' he said.

Do what? I wondered… give 'Miss Mysterious' a good seeing too?'

'Right… right, I'll be there, yes… yes, I'll organise the flight, leave it with me... I'll take care of everything, goodbye' he said and hung up.

'More work?' I queried.

'I'm afraid so, darling.'

'Who was it?'

'It was a secretary who works for one of our regular customers... she wants a flight to Brussels for him tomorrow... would you believe it?'

'No, I wouldn't' I replied and Tony looked a little flushed at my reply.

'Why, darling?' he asked as he sat beside me.

'Because she would have phoned the office in working hours to book a flight, not phone the pilot at home on a Friday night' I said and he went a little pale.

'Well, I can promise you that these businessmen make instant decisions and...'

'She phoned on Wednesday' I interrupted.

'How do you know that?'

'I recognised her voice' I lied and he looked quite shocked.

'Well, er, I expect...'

'She wanted to make arrangements for a night out with you... ending up with a good screw no doubt!' I shouted and he went red in the face.

'Clare!'

'That's me... your poor suffering wife, who's not going to put up with it any longer!' I shouted.

'But Clare...'

'I bet it's that overweight blonde tart in the red dress you met at the party!'

'Clare, I promise you...'

'Oh... fuck off Tony!' I screamed, then stormed out of the room and went upstairs to bed with tears streaming down my cheeks.

When he eventually came to bed, I was fast asleep and didn't wake until the morning.

We hardly spoke over our breakfast of toast and coffee. Tony left just after ten o'clock saying 'I'll be back tomorrow afternoon about five.'

'You can please yourself' I mumbled, he shook his head in

despair before walking out and slamming the front door.

Things went downhill pretty rapidly from then on. I was convinced he was seeing other women and he never denied it. He always just shook his head and wandered off every time I asked him where he'd been and who with. It couldn't go on any more and when we had a blazing row, before I walked out for the last time, he said it was for the best. I asked why and he replied that he had enough of my nagging, which was distracting him, and he was certain to have a crash and kill himself if it went on any longer! Well, I ask you…

Mother was not pleased when I moved back permanently with her and had to bite her lip several times to stop herself from blurting out 'I told you so.' David recommended his solicitor in Romford to get the divorce proceedings under way but I found it difficult to talk to the small, balding man with thick glasses about my private life. Mr Clarke was sympathetic and did his best to re-assure me, telling me that it would be over quite soon, but every time I went to his office it reminded me of visits to the dentist when I was a child. It gave me the shudders…

After many evenings at 'The Red Lion' with Jane, talking endlessly about the fickle cruelty of men, I decided to really bury myself in work and try to get promoted so that I could afford a place of my own. If I didn't, I was sure that I would end up smothering Mother or putting something nasty in her bedtime drink! I knew it would be best for me to move out as soon as possible and Jane agreed because my Mother was becoming insufferable. For example, after a little retail therapy with Jane, I bought a smart handbag and a pair of red high-heeled shoes with black bows. When I showed them to Mother she said 'I don't know why you always have to buy shoes that make you look like a transvestite!' Well I ask you…

It was now the beginning of September and I could hardly believe that it was only six months ago that I had been swept me off my feet and married Tony. My mind was still in a muddle with everything so I decided to go for long walks on Sunday mornings in our nearby park. It would give me some peace to think about my life and try to get it into some perspective whilst admiring the golden autumn leaves. I thought that I should try to relax more and be 'in tune' with nature... it might help.

On my last walk, I was sauntering along the path, glancing at the trees and across to the small lake, where some ducks were splashing about amongst the reeds, when suddenly I noticed a man sitting alone on a bench. I thought I recognised him and my mind went into a whirl... was it the handsome stranger from the church? It certainly looked like him, but I could be wrong so I walked a little quicker towards him and he turned to face me then smiled. Good God... it was him and I thought 'what do I do now?' My instinct told me to hurry on by and pretend I didn't see him. As I got close to him he said 'hello, Clare.' I froze inside and stopped immediately.

'Do I know you?' I asked as firmly as I could whilst gazing stony faced into his twinkling blue eyes and I thought 'whoever you are, you're a handsome stranger.'

'No, but I know you' he replied and I thought 'just my luck... all I need now is a mad stalker in my life to make it a complete disaster!'

'How do you know me?' I asked anxiously as I glanced around for someone to help but the park was empty with not even a sweaty jogger in sight.

'Please sit with me for a moment and I'll tell you' he replied with a gorgeous smile.

'I'm not sure that's a good idea' I said.

'Please' he half whispered... and boy did he have a persuasive whisper! I felt that I couldn't resist him and sat down slowly at the other end of the park bench and just stared at him. Without a doubt he was sinfully handsome with his tanned face, fair hair and blue eyes.

'My name is Eric and I've come to help you...' he began and I thought 'into bed' before he continued 'with guidance for your future happiness.' I thought 'oh yeah' and nodded... he was obviously some nut so I thought it best to humour him and then run for it when I got the chance!

'How very kind of you' I said in my achingly polite voice.

'It is my duty' he said and I was suddenly aware of his peculiar clipped accent.

'Duty?'

'Yes, Clare.'

'You're not from round here are you?' I asked, hurriedly changing the subject and not wanting to know too much about his 'duty' in case he was from the Salvation Army or something.

'No, I'm originally from Norway' he replied with a smile, and I wondered what a tall Norwegian was doing in Essex.

'You were at my wedding' I said firmly.

'Yes, I was there, and you looked very beautiful that day' he replied and I began to think that this Norwegian was not at all bad... I've always had a soft spot for the Continentals, I mean to say, they're usually so complimentary to women... such a contrast to the local Neanderthals.

'Thank you' I replied with a smile then said 'and you were in Paris.' I thought that would shake him but it didn't seem to.

'Yes, I was there' he replied calmly.

'Spying on me?'

'No, just making sure you were safe' he replied and I thought 'I'm puzzled by this nut, what does he want?... Other than the usual that all men want, that is' but said 'really.'

'I know you've had some upsets with your husband...'

'How do you know about that?' I interrupted angrily.

'I have to know everything to be able to help you' he replied calmly but I was suddenly very anxious. I mean who was this guy? Was he working for Mr Clarke? He didn't look like someone who would be stuck in an office all day surrounded by paperwork. With his tan he looked more like an outdoor man to me and he was dressed in a kind of leather waistcoat trimmed with fur and tight leather trousers but I supposed that's how Norwegians kept warm.

'Go on' I said in a suspicious tone.

'And now you must part forever' he said.

'Yes, we're getting a divorce' I said.

'I know.'

'So do you work for Mr Clarke?' I asked, feeling sure I was right about that.

'No, I don't know this man' he replied, which mystified me.

'Well I think you'd better tell me what you do know and how you think that you can help me' I said taking firm control of the situation.

'All in good time' he said with a smile and suddenly I felt a little more relaxed. He was having quite an effect on me but I was still confused by everything he said and my emotions were on a roller coaster ride.

'Does my husband know about you?' I asked.

'No… I only have to look after you, his angel will look after him' he replied.

'Angel? Do you think you're an angel or something?' I asked wide eyed as my emotional roller coaster suddenly went speeding downhill.

'Yes, I'm here to guide you and…'

'You're nothing but a bloody nut case… so leave me alone!' I shouted before I jumped up and hurried back towards home. I glanced over my shoulder several times at him and was relieved to see that he stayed where he was on the bench.

When I arrived at the house I was still shaking so I made a strong coffee to calm myself. It was just my luck to meet a madman when all I wanted was some time alone to think. I tried to put him out of my mind but couldn't do it. I started reading the Sunday paper and although I was distracted for the moment by the latest political scandal involving money, my thoughts went back to Eric. I thought 'what if it was true and he was my guardian angel?' I felt guilty and remembered that my dear Mother always complains that I am too hasty. I should have given Eric more time to explain himself and tell me what he was going to do for me… I needed some help for sure. After awhile I felt much better and thought that if Eric was my angel, although I don't believe in them for one minute, he would re-appear again sometime and I would give him a chance to explain himself. The rest of the day passed quite smoothly, other than a few sharp exchanges with Mother about nothing in particular.

The next morning I arrived in the office before Tina and started on the customer's overdue list. I had just finished when Mr Wilkes came into the office and said 'you're early this morning, Clare.'

'Yes… it's the new me' I replied with a smile.

'Ah, it's good to see that you're casting off old habits and making a positive start to your work' he said with a false smile. He was a workaholic and I never liked him.

'I am' I said with a smug grin.

'Now when Tina eventually arrives I want you both to come into my office as I have something important to tell you' he said.

'Yes, Mr Wilkes' I nodded as he glanced at his watch, looked at Tina's empty chair and 'tut tutted' before he hurried away. I was still wondering what it was all about when Tina breezed in a few minutes later.

'You're early' she said as she unloaded her large bag to the floor with a thump.

'I am and you're late.'

'I know… the bloody traffic this morning…'

'Wilkes has been in already and said he wants to see us in his office' I interrupted.

'I wonder why?' she said as she tidied a place on her desk before plonking her lunch box in the space.

'When you're ready we'll find out' I replied.

Mr Wilkes looked concerned when we entered his office and he waved us to sit in front of his glass topped desk covered with little neat piles of paper. He leaned back in his black executive chair, gazed at the ceiling for a moment then, glancing at us in turn, said 'there have been some important changes in the organisation where senior management have promoted dedicated staff…' and I thought 'that's good news for me'.

'And I'm pleased to tell you that Mr Schenker has been recalled to Head Office in Germany to take up an important position within the management structure' continued Wilkes. He was a really pompous company man and if he was sliced across the middle I'm sure he would have BMW printed right though his body.

'And that means that we will have a new area manager who will oversee both warranty claims and customer accounts.' Tina and I waited for the grand announcement… was it our Mr Wilkes who would be leaving us? Dear God, please make it so.

'The new manager is Mr Hammond and he will be visiting us in the next few days so I want to make sure that everything is how it should be, we don't want him to find any errors in our system, do we?'

'No, Mr Wilkes' we chorused.

'Good... now I'll be checking everything carefully after lunch so I suggest that you use this morning to list all the outstanding accounts ready for my inspection later' he said, we nodded and after being dismissed like school children, returned to our office.

'So we've another new picky twerp to contend with' said Tina as she slumped down in her chair.

'Well, he sounds English for a change' I said.

'I bet he'll be just like old Schenker... ve nefer don't do this like this in Germany' Tina said in an accent as she pulled a face.

'We'll know in a couple of days' I said with a grin.

When I arrived home on the Wednesday there was a letter from Mr Clarke asking me to make another appointment to see him... no wonder these legal worms are so rich! I was still feeling depressed when I went to work the next morning and it was made worse when Wilkes came into the office all of a bother and told us that Mr Hammond would be arriving today. I was not emotionally ready for another pain in my life but it seemed as if I was going to get one... I was not disappointed!

CHAPTER 3

JEFF MEETS CLARE

The moment I saw Clare I fell in love with her. I know that sounds stupid but it's true. How many people have said they knew instantly when they met the love of their life and wanted to spend the rest of eternity with them? The answer is thousands... possibly millions!

True love is a difficult thing to explain in words but somehow you just know deep inside when it happens to you.

I arrived at Hamilton Motors in Romford about three in the afternoon and was immediately shown up to the Managing Director's office where Victor Black stood up to welcome me.

'I'm very pleased to meet you Mr Hammond and congratulations on your new appointment' said Black as we shook hands.

'Oh, thank you and please call me Jeff' I said with a smile.

'Ah, I see you're a man who likes informality' said Black as he waved me to a seat.

'Yes, I find it takes down barriers and allows us to get good results from the staff' I replied.

'I'm glad to hear it, we always had good audit reports from Mr Schenker and I hope we'll continue getting the same from you' said Black. I knew that this was not absolutely true as Otto Schenker had written several confidential reports critical of the way the accounts were handled at Hamilton Motors. I smiled and said 'time will tell' which seemed to disturb Black a little, so I guessed he knew the truth.

'Of course, now would you like to see Roger Wilkes in accounts or George Thomas in warranty first?' asked Black.

'I'll start with Roger Wilkes if I may' I replied.

'Right... I'll call him now' said Black as he picked up his desk phone and tapped in the number.

Wilkes appeared almost immediately as if he was waiting outside the door like an eager buyer at the January sales. After introductions and some small talk we went to his office where he pontificated on high for some time about his systems. However, I was not impressed with his 'fluffy' and overlong explanations because before joining BMW as a manager, I had spent ten years in the Army as a tank captain with the Seventh Armoured Brigade. In my military career I was used to quick, direct and decisive action, not endless words, but I had adjusted to civilian life, so I remained patient. When he eventually finished he said 'I have two very good accounts clerks who do all the donkey work, would you like to meet them now?'

'Yes, what are their names?'

'Mrs Franklin is the senior and Miss Woods is her junior' replied Wilkes as he stood up from his desk. I followed him down the corridor to their office and was introduced to them. When Clare smiled at me I was absolutely smitten! I thought that she was stunningly beautiful with such gorgeous brown eyes and a firm figure. When she stood up to shake hands she was almost as tall as me and I could have kissed her there and then!

Miss Tina Woods was a petite, busty blonde with too much green eye shadow that did nothing for her appearance and I immediately thought that she looked like the proverbial Essex girl.

Wilkes asked Clare to bring up the latest account details on her screen for me and I noticed that she had no rings on her hand and wondered why. Was she divorced or did she just prefer not to wear them for some reason? As I glanced at the figures on her screen I caught the gentle whiff of her perfume, which sent my senses reeling. I thought 'I've been single for too long after my marriage disaster and I need to have someone like Clare... correction... I need Clare in my life.'

I looked at the total of outstanding debts whilst Wilkes droned on relentlessly but I could only think about this delightful woman close to me. I made all the right comments about the accounts then said to Wilkes that I wished to see him in his office. He looked a little anxious but nodded, I thanked Clare and Tina before following him out into the corridor.

When we reached his office Wilkes said 'I hope that you found everything satisfactory, I mean the system that...' but I interrupted him saying 'it all looks fine to me, Roger.'

'Oh, oh, thank you, Jeff' he replied with a look of relief.

'But I'd like to spend a little more time with your department looking at the system which I think could be adopted and used by the other Dealerships in our network' I said knowing that would please him and allow me to spend some time getting to know Clare.

'Of course, Jeff, you're most welcome' he beamed.

'Good... when I've seen George Thomas in warranty I'll come back and go through your system again with Clare' I said.

'That's absolutely fine' he said with a smile.

The warranty claims were mostly for minor things and there were very few of them. I was pleased to find that George Thomas had everything under tight control so I left his office quite satisfied and returned to see Wilkes.

'I've prepared a spread sheet for you, Jeff, so you can pinpoint the main thrust of our recovery rate where it peaks' said Wilkes.

'Thanks, Roger, I'll take that with me and study it before I call again sometime next week' I said.

'Right... now I'll get Clare to show you our system again and run through it once more.'

'Yes, if you would please.'

I followed him along to her office, 'Jeff would like to see the system again so would you please run through it and answer any questions he may have?'

'Yes, Mr Wilkes' she replied but the look on her face told me that she was not happy... and neither was Tina, who scowled before gazing back at her screen. I sat next to the heavenly creature and tried to concentrate on what she was saying but all I could think about was how I would get her to come out with me. When she had finished explaining the system she looked at me with her lovely soft eyes and asked 'is there anything else you'd like to know?' I thought 'yes, are you free for dinner tonight?' but said 'no, not at the moment Clare, you've explained everything, thank you.' She smiled and said 'good.'

'But I will be coming back next week, after I've thought about it to see if we can make any improvements' I said and her face fell again. I suppose that she had hoped she had seen the last of me for the time being.

I was feeling on top of the world as I drove back to my

comfortable flat in Brentwood. After I poured a drink, I sank down on the settee and wondered how I was going to get Clare alone to ask her for a date. I knew that senior management did not approve of emotional involvement with junior staff, but I really didn't care. My future happiness was my top priority after several years of lonely existence after my wayward wife, Evelyn, went off with her boss, Ashford, following several so called 'business trips' abroad. She now lived as his mistress whilst he remained married to his long suffering wife Jean. Why do women put up with it? And why is it that some women leave their brains in neutral when a sweet talking bastard comes along and persuades them to leave their husbands? I'll probably never know. I pondered for awhile before a plan started to emerge whereby I could have Clare to myself... then suddenly I had it! I sang as I cooked up spaghetti Bolognese for one and poured another glass of red wine in celebration.

The next morning I phoned David Lovegrove, the accounts manager at Thames Motors in Southend and told him about the refined system that Wilkes had developed at Hamilton Motors. He sounded less than keen on a new system at first but as I was the area manager he quickly acquiesced to my request to bring Clare to demonstrate to him and his staff. It was agreed that I would bring Clare over on the following Wednesday morning. I then phoned Hugh James at Blackwell's in Chelmsford and repeated the exercise. He agreed to see us on the Wednesday afternoon, which meant I would have Clare to myself all day. I planned to take her to lunch at 'The Windmill', a lovely pub in Pilgrims Hatch, that served wonderful food and I would invite her out to dinner as we enjoyed a relaxed drink. It was perfect... providing that Wilkes did not throw a spanner in the works for some reason. I phoned Wilkes and told him that I would call in on Monday with some ideas to discuss and he seemed pleased. I wished him a good weekend and he reciprocated.

On the Saturday morning I played a round of golf with my older brother Richard and on the fourth green I told him all about Clare.

'Well you seem to be in a pretty hopeless state over this woman' said Richard as he lined up his putter and swung it gently to and fro.

'I am.'

'And what if she says 'no'?' he asked as he struck the ball firmly and it trickled towards the hole.

'I'm sure I can persuade her to come out on a date' I replied as the ball disappeared.

'You couldn't persuade Evelyn to stay with you' he said looking at me squarely and resting on his putter. That hurt... but I knew it was true because I had tried everything to keep my lovely wife with me and out of Ashford's hands, but failed miserably. This old, smarmy, adulterous wretch of a man had seduced all his secretaries before Evelyn became his PA. I met him several times at his firms 'do's' and saw immediately what sort of old lecher he was. He undressed every woman with a leer, whilst Jean just stood passively by and tried to ignore his crude and offensive behaviour. I told Evelyn repeatedly that she would be next on his list for horizontal line dancing but she always laughed and replied 'I'm not interested in that old fart!'

However, after he started taking her away on the business trips to Turkey he obviously worked hard at it and managed to seduce her and our marriage broke up. I did not want a divorce and forgave her indiscretions then begged her to leave her job and never see the old rat again but she insisted on a divorce saying that he was the only man who would ever really make her happy. When I tried to remind her of all our happy days before she met Ashford, she said that she had never been happy with me in fact she had been quite miserable ever since we first met. I was stunned, bewildered and profoundly saddened by that and reluctantly agreed to her wish for a 'quickie' divorce. She moved out and straight into a flat that Ashford had bought for her close to where he lived with Jean in Harpenden, where I presume she remains to this day. Evelyn has never been in contact with me or any of my family, who were as shocked as I was when she started her affair with Ashford, a married man with a sickening history of adultery - and old enough to be her father.

I spent Sunday morning reading the papers and consuming too much coffee before putting on the washing machine, which was now full of shirts, pants and odd socks. When that was done and I tidied myself up and drove over to my parents for lunch. They lived comfortably in a bungalow on the outskirts of Epping. Dad kept the garden neat and tidy, after he retired from teaching, whilst Mum maintained a spotless home. They were very happy in their own little world and were very upset at the break-up of my marriage. It was such a contrast to their own life together as well as Richard's happy marriage to Susan with their two children, Tom and Hazel.

After opening the front door Mum kissed me and said 'we've got roast lamb today, dear.'

'Sounds wonderful' I replied as Dad came in from the back garden.

'Make sure you wipe your feet' she called out to him as I followed her to the kitchen.

'I always do' he replied as he stood at the back door.

'That'll be the day' she said, as he grinned.

'Hello son.'

'Hello Dad.'

'Time for a drink before lunch I think… so what are we all having?' said Dad.

'I'll just have a little sherry' said Mum as she bent down to look at the joint of lamb in the oven.

'Right… sherry alright for you?' asked Dad.

'Yes, thanks' I replied.

After lunch I told them all about Clare and they looked very pleased with my news but then Mum asked 'now is she single or has she got a husband tucked away somewhere?'

'I really don't know… I think she may be divorced' I replied.

'Well dear, you'd better find out before you get too involved' said Mum firmly.

'I will, her boss called her Mrs Franklin but she doesn't wear any rings' I said.

'If she is married just you make sure you don't cause any problems and break it up' said Mum firmly.

'No I certainly won't… I know how bloody awful that is' I replied and they both nodded.

I returned home that evening feeling very happy and looked

forward to Monday morning when I would drive to Hamilton Motors and see Clare again. I felt confident that everything was going nicely to plan, then at about nine o'clock the phone rang and it was Dad.

'Now, your Mother and I have been talking about this girl Clare, and we're a bit worried' he said.

'Why Dad?'

'Well, we're anxious that you don't get too involved too quickly... I mean you seem to be infatuated with her and if she's married or perhaps doesn't feel the same about you... you could be badly hurt again' he replied.

'Oh don't worry Dad' I said.

'We do, son, because when Evelyn left you, you were in such a state for a long while... we really didn't know what you were going to do' he said hesitantly.

'Like commit suicide?' I asked with a grin.

'It did cross our minds occasionally' he replied.

'Tell Mum not to worry and don't you worry either, I'm just fine and if Clare is married or not interested in me, then no harm done and I will carry on as usual' I said.

'I'm glad to hear it son... I'm sure you'll find someone nice one day.'

'I may have already found her, Dad.'

'Well I hope for your sake that you have' he said.

'So do I... and thanks for the call, Dad.'

'Okay... goodbye, son.'

After I put the phone down, I thought 'it's nice to have parents who really care about you and I'm really lucky to have mine.'

I poured myself a glass of wine and went over Wilkes' accounts system again and studied his spread sheet before going to bed relaxed and sleeping soundly until the next morning.

It was just after ten o'clock when I arrived at Hamilton Motors and I could hardly wait to see Clare. I went up to Roger Wilkes' office, knocked and entered. He smiled when he saw me and waved me to a seat.

'So Jeff, did you have any ideas over the weekend on improving my system?' he asked.

'No, not really, Roger, as far as I can see you've done a pretty good job' I replied.

'That's good to hear!'

'In fact, I've decided to take your system for trial at two other Dealerships' I said and his face lit up.

'Really?'

'Yes, I've arranged to see David Lovegrove at Thames Motors and Hugh James at Blackwell's on Wednesday' I replied.

'Well that's fantastic!'

'Of course I'll need Clare for the day so she can demonstrate your system and answer any questions' I said with a smile.

'Oh dear.'

'What's wrong?' I asked anxiously.

'Well she's not in today... she phoned up first thing and said her mother was ill again' he replied.

'Do you think she'll be back by Wednesday?' I asked.

'I hope so, Jeff, but I can't be sure' he replied and my heart sank at the news.

'Well, never mind, we'll just have to wait and see' I said bravely.

'If Clare's not back by then why don't you take Tina with you?... she can demonstrate most of it' he said and my mind froze at the very thought of being trapped with Tina for the day.

'I'm sure that Tina is very competent but I think that as Clare is the senior person she should accompany me on such an important issue... I mean we wouldn't want anything to go wrong and jeopardise the demonstration' I replied diplomatically.

'No, no... I'm sure you're right' he said and I relaxed.

'Is there any chance that you can contact her before Wednesday and find out if she'll be in?' I asked gently.

'Yes, if she's not at work tomorrow, I'll phone her at home and find out for you' he replied.

'Thanks Roger, otherwise I'll have to cancel the appointments until another time' I said.

'Give me a call at about ten tomorrow, Jeff... I should have some news by then' said Wilkes.

'Thanks, I will.'

I left Hamilton Motors feeling down and spent the rest of the day going through my work load on automatic. I kept wondering if

Clare lived with her Mother because she was divorced or separated from her husband and hoped that was the case. I couldn't get her out of my mind and was failing to concentrate on anything, so when I returned home that evening I just threw a pizza into the oven for a quick meal before I remembered the washing machine was still full of clothes.

The next morning I called Wilkes at exactly ten o'clock and asked if he had any news.

'Yes, Clare is back at work today, Jeff and I've already told her about your appointments for tomorrow and she says she'll be ready when you are.' My heart leapt!

'That's good, I'll pick her up at about this time in the morning' I said.

'Okay, Jeff, I'll see you tomorrow.'

Time drags so slowly when you're waiting for something good to arrive even if you know for certain that it is coming, the wait is still unbearable.

On the Wednesday morning I got up extra early, showered, shaved and had a good breakfast before choosing my best shirt, matching tie and smartest blue suit to wear. I thought I looked positively the bee's knees and strode out of the flat full of confidence, absolutely sure that Clare would agree to a date with me. My imagination soared as I drove the company BMW towards Romford and I could see us in the future being happy and contented, with possibly two or more kids. Life was at last worth living after my dark lonely days without Evelyn. Those sad days were all behind me now. I know that you can never change the past, so it is futile to waste any precious time in the present worrying about what has gone forever. My future was with Clare and I just knew instinctively deep down that we would be very happy together.

I arrived at ten and went straight up to Wilkes' office.

'Morning, Jeff, I think she's all ready for you' he said with a smile.

'That's good.'

'What time do you think you'll be back?' he asked.

'Oh, depending on how it goes… possibly about five or so' I replied.

'That's okay then… I want Clare to finish some work before she goes home tonight' he said.

'Right, I promise to have her back before five then.'

'Thanks… I'll just go and get her' he said as he stood up from his desk and disappeared out of the office. He arrived back within minutes with Clare, who looked absolutely fabulous. She was wearing a neat, dark grey, pin striped suit over a pink blouse with a bow at the neck. Her hair was gathered up in a French roll and her makeup was subtle, which enhanced her lovely face and her soft brown eyes. She smiled and said 'good morning.'

'Good morning, Clare, I'm glad that you could make it today' I said.

'Yes, so am I, when Mr Wilkes told me about your plans I was very pleased to help' she said.

'That's excellent… so shall we go?'

We chatted about work nearly all the way to Thames Motors at Southend but as we reached the outskirts of the town there was lull in the conversation so I said 'Roger Wilkes told me that your Mother was ill, I hope she's better now.'

'Yes… she's much better, thank you.'

'Hasn't she got anybody else to look after her except you?' I asked.

'I'm afraid not' Clare replied.

'So do you live near her?'

'I live with my Mother' she replied sharply and my heart leapt.

'Oh.'

'I'm back at home because I'm going through a painful divorce at the moment' she said in a firm tone as if to say 'mind your own business.'

'Oh, I'm sorry' I said, hoping that I didn't sound too happy with the news.

'Don't be sorry… it seems to happen to most people these days' she said glancing out of the side window.

'I'm afraid it does… it happened to me a few years ago, so I know what you're going through' I said.

'Good… then you'll understand that I don't want to talk about it' she said firmly as she looked stony faced at me.

'Of course… I'm sorry' I said meekly.

We remained silent until we pulled into the forecourt of Thames Motors.

'David Lovegrove is the accounts manager here and I'm sure you'll get along with him and his team, they're a nice bunch' I said as I parked near the showroom.

'I hope so' she said before she got out of the car but her body language told me that she was not happy. I cursed myself for being too inquisitive as I had obviously touched a raw nerve and it was clear that she was right in the middle of her divorce. It gave me some hope that she might find a dinner date a welcome distraction.

David and his people were welcoming and after coffee in his office Clare demonstrated Wilkes' accounts system. They did not seem duly impressed and asked lots of questions, which Clare answered without hesitation. She obviously was on top of her job and they realised that, but nevertheless they found objections to the proposed system. It was ever thus… people instinctively hate change of any sort to their work routines. Afterwards in David's office he said that he would think about Wilkes' system and would let me know his thoughts after he had discussed it with his Managing Director. I took that as a 'no' but smiled and agreed that he should see if it fitted his customer profile before making a decision.

It was just after twelve when we left Thames Motors and as we drove out of Southend I said 'I know a nice place where we can stop for lunch.'

'Is it on our way?' she asked in a suspicious tone.

'Yes… its 'The Windmill' pub at Pilgrims Hatch' I replied with a smile.

'That's alright then…' she said and after a pause, asked 'I don't think they were very impressed this morning, do you?'

'Possibly not, but I know David will think about it seriously before he makes any decision' I replied.

'Mmm' she said unconvincingly before glancing out of the side window.

I tried to amuse her with silly stories about my hopeless attempts at playing golf but I could not get her to smile and all she said was 'really' in a disinterested tone. I found the conversation hard work and was relieved when we pulled into the car park at 'The Windmill'. This was not going to plan and there was a further set back when she caught sight of a tall man sitting alone at a table in the beer garden in front of the pub. He looked like a farm labourer, he was a big bloke, bare armed and wearing a sort of leather waistcoat. Clare stared at him for some moments and went quite pale before I hurried her into the cosy pub.

'Do you know that chap outside?' I asked anxiously.

She hesitated then replied 'er, no, no, I don't know him…'

'Are you sure?'

'Yes' she replied, but I could sense the anxiety in her voice.

'That's okay then… what'll you have to drink?' I asked as we moved towards the busy bar.

'A gin and tonic please.'

'Right… the food's good here, so decide what you'd like to eat… it's all chalked up over there' I said pointing to the blackboard over the stone fireplace. She moved away towards it as I caught the bartender's attention and ordered two gin and tonics. After I paid and collected the drinks I turned to see Clare staring out of the window. When I reached her I looked outside but saw nothing in the beer garden. It seemed the mystery man had disappeared.

'You look as if you've seen a ghost' I said as she turned to face me quickly and I could see she was now very pale.

'No… no, it's just…'

'Just what?' I interrupted.

'Oh, nothing' she replied with a shake of her head as I handed her an ice tinkling glass of gin.

'I think there is…'

'Just leave it will you?' she interrupted angrily.

'I'm sorry I'm sure… I didn't mean to pry, but you do look a bit shaken up and I'm concerned about you, so if I can do anything to help I will' I said calmly and we remained silent for a few moments.

'Sorry for going off like that' she said quietly.

'You needn't apologise… I'm sure that you're under a lot of

strain at the moment and perhaps it wasn't a good idea to ask you to come out today' I said.

'No, no, it's fine, really... I'm enjoying it... gives me a break away from the office' she said with a smile as the colour returned to her cheeks and I thought she looked very beautiful.

'Cheers... here's to systems' I said and she smiled as she touched my glass and murmured 'systems.'

We sipped our gins before I asked 'so what are you having for lunch?'

'I haven't looked yet' she replied, glancing at the black board.

'The cottage pie is always good' I said helpfully.

'No... I don't think so, er, I think I'll have the chicken with chips in a basket' she said.

'Right... I'll join you.'

After I had ordered our lunches we found a small table in the corner of the bar and sat quietly sipping our drinks. She looked a little better and I didn't know whether to ask about the mysterious stranger or keep quiet about him. I decided it would be better to talk about work... so I did.

'So tell me, Clare, what are your future career plans?' I asked with a smile.

'Well, I'd like to find out if there's any chance of promotion at Hamilton's because I do intend to stay there' she replied.

'I'm pleased to hear it, what have you in mind?'

'I really don't know, but if there's nowhere for me to go in Hamilton's then perhaps area accounts' she replied.

'Or corporate sales accounts... have you considered that?' I asked as a bar maid brought our lunches over.

'No, I hadn't... do you know if there are any vacancies that would suit me?'

'Not off the top of my head but I could find out for you' I replied and she smiled then said 'thanks... now this looks good' as she picked up her cutlery.

We enjoyed the chicken and said little until we had finished. Then I persuaded her to have homemade apple pie with custard and ice cream for dessert, followed by coffee.

Clare seemed to mellow and relax after we had finished the

meal so I decided this was the moment to ask her out, thinking 'it's now or never'.

'This place is a favourite of mine and I often bring business people here' I said.

'I can see why' she replied with a smile.

'Yes... the food's always good and it's such a picturesque pub... the German's love it when they come over from head office' I said.

'I'm sure.'

'But I know another little place where the food is even better' I said.

'Really?'

'Yes... so would you like to have dinner there with me?' I asked as my heart began to thump faster than usual. She looked at me for a moment and slowly shook her head.

'Thanks for asking... but I really don't think we should get involved' she replied.

'I'm only asking you to come out for dinner... not run away with me' I said plaintively.

'I expect that comes later' she said and I had to smile before saying 'possibly.'

'Probably' she said with a grin.

'Oh Clare, don't say 'no' like all the other women' I said pleadingly.

'You know that the company is not happy about managers dating junior staff...'

'Yes I'm aware of that' I interrupted.

'Well then... as I'm looking for promotion it would count against me if we were...'

'Nobody need know' I interrupted.

'Somebody always knows... besides, I'm really not in the mood to start anything with a man... even dinner with a perfectly harmless person like you is a step too far for me at the moment' she said.

'I understand' I said gazing down at my empty coffee cup in disappointment.

'Men in general and one in particular are not my flavour of the month, so you'll have to ask someone else to have dinner with you' she said firmly.

'It's not because of that chap you saw outside is it?' I asked and she looked stunned.

'No it isn't!'

'But you do know him?' I persisted foolishly and she hesitated for a moment before replying 'I have seen him before but I don't know who he is.'

'Is he stalking you?'

'No… not really.'

'What does 'not really' mean?'

'He was at my wedding and recently I saw him in the park' she said.

'So he's a friend then?'

'No… I don't know what he is' she replied angrily and I knew I had gone too far.

'Sorry Clare, I was only trying to help…'

'Well you're not!'

'Right… I'll just shut up then…'

'Please do!' she interrupted.

'But if I can be of any help, you only have to say the word' I said calmly.

'I'll remember that… now shall we go?' she asked firmly and I nodded.

When we walked outside I saw the labourer was back and sitting at the table in the beer garden. He looked at Clare and smiled. She glanced at him for a split second then made her way quickly towards the car park. I hesitated for a moment then strode over to him and as I got closer I could see he was a big bloke, but it didn't deter me.

'Hi' I said bravely as he looked up and replied 'hello.'

'Who are you?'

'My name's is Eric' he replied in a clipped tone.

'Are you being a bit of nuisance to that young lady' I said pointing towards Clare.

'No I don't think so' he replied with a smile.

'Then why are you following her?'

'To make sure that she is always safe' he replied.

'Well let me tell you Eric, she's more than capable of looking after herself and she's also got me as her back up!'

'That's good to know.'

'So I suggest that you stay well away from her in future or I'll…'

'Do what?' he interrupted with a disarming smile.

'I'll, I'll bloody well…' I blustered but he just smiled again then stood up and I was stunned by his height.

'Take Clare to work and I'll explain everything soon, I promise' he said before striding out of the garden and away down the road. I was left struggling to think what to say or do. I stood for a moment then walked to the car park where Clare was waiting by the BMW.

'I wish you hadn't spoken to him' she said firmly before she got into the car.

'I'm only trying to protect you' I said calmly.

'Well you're making a bloody mess of it so just stay out of my affairs and let me deal with them on my own!' she exclaimed as she slammed the door shut.

'Right… sorry for trying to help I'm sure!' I said angrily before starting the car and driving off.

We did not speak on the journey to Blackwell's and I was relieved when we pulled into their spacious forecourt and parked. This whole episode over lunch had been a complete disaster and I could not imagine how I was ever going to recover the situation. I felt certain that I had lost any chance of dating Clare forever and was fed up to the back teeth. Oh dear God… what a mess!

We went into the showroom and up to Hugh James' office where I introduced a sullen faced Clare to him. After some polite small talk we went along to the office where she demonstrated the new system to the ladies who dealt with the accounts. Hugh and his staff were not overly impressed and I left my proposal with him to discuss with his Managing Director in due course. I was just glad to get out of the place and decided on the trip back to Romford to have one last go at persuading Clare to have dinner with me.

I put on some background music to soothe her savage breast and said 'I know we haven't got off to a very good start but…'

'Please don't start all that again… I've had enough today… I really have!' she interrupted. I paused for a moment then said in a resigned tone 'okay, I understand.'

We did not speak again until we reached Hamilton's and frankly I was glad. All my hopes had been dashed today so I intended to leave Clare as soon as possible, go home and pour myself a large scotch and forget all about her. Obviously she was not the right one for me, although I had believed she was when I first saw her, but now I would happily leave her to the tender mercies of Eric... whoever the hell he was! I thought that perhaps she liked big labouring types! I didn't know or care now... it was all over, not that it ever got started.

We went up to Wilkes' office where I thanked her for her help and smiled at him when he asked if it had been a successful day. I assured him the accounts managers had seen the system and were discussing it now with their respective principle's to see if it fitted their customer profiles. He seemed pleased and I told him that I would be in touch as soon as I had something further to discuss. I said one last goodbye to Clare who struggled to give me a half smile and as I left Hamilton's a weight seemed to lift from my shoulders.

I drove slowly home in the rush hour traffic listening to the radio whilst mulling over the day's events. I came to the conclusion that I was hopeless with women and shouldn't even bother trying any more. I decided that from now on I would be a golf playing bachelor, becoming mellow as I aged. This would enable me to observe the misfortunes of those who had foolishly married the wrong one whilst I remained content and aloof from the battle of the sexes! I felt comfortably smug as I pulled into my parking space.

It was just before midnight when I climbed into bed and put the light out. I lay in the lonely darkness of my room for a while wondering what I had done to deserve all this unhappiness. After the euphoria of my earlier stupid decision I suddenly felt dismayed once again at not having a woman in my life. Who was I kidding? I needed someone to love, cherish and spend the rest of my days with, is that too much to ask? The loss of Evelyn to the adulterous old rat still haunted my thoughts and all I could see in front of me now was the damp, unremitting fog of inner loneliness.

So bugger Clare! And who was this bloke Eric anyway?

CHAPTER 4

CLARE TAKES A BREAK

When Wilkes introduced Jeff Hammond to us I thought he looked quite reasonable and hoped that he would be different to our Herr Schenker, but I was wrong. He just kept staring at me when we were first introduced so I didn't know what to think, although it crossed my mind that if he didn't blink soon he'd go blind! He only glanced at Tina and when I showed him the system on my screen he leaned over my shoulder and came a bit too close for comfort. Wilkes was prattling away as usual whilst I tried to demonstrate how we kept the delayed payments to a minimum. Hammond said all the right things but I wasn't convinced that he was very interested in Wilkes' system. He seemed to be in a world of his own... perhaps that's how all accounts managers are these days and they only see cash flow and bottom line profits, not real people.

When he and Wilkes left our office Tina said 'he's a bit of a funny one isn't he?'

'D'you think so?'

'Yeah I do... he got ever so close to you and I swear he was sniffing your hair' she replied and I shivered slightly.

'Oh God' I whispered.

'I bet he's not married' said Tina.

'How do you know?'

'He's got that look about him' she replied.

'D'you think he's gay then?'

'No, he's just a loner, I've seen them down the club on Saturdays... they just hang about half pissed leering at all the girls but never have the balls to chat anybody up' she replied.

'And you're an expert?'

'I am at spotting the likes of him... he's a real 'knicker sniffer' if ever I saw one' she replied and I had to laugh.

'Knicker sniffer?'

'Yeah, I bet he'll have a few pairs of lace scanties amongst his porno mags and DVD's' she said.

'Well it takes all sorts' I said as I began tapping away at my key board.

'I bet he lives alone in a pokey flat somewhere…'

'With drawers full of knickers!' I interrupted with a laugh.

'And a cat!' she added with a grin.

'If only the Germans knew about their new area manager' I said pompously and Tina laughed, adding 'old Schenker would have a fit… ve haf ways of stopping you sniffink!' We still were in fits of laughter when Wilkes came in and told us that Hammond would be back for another run through the system after he had been to the warranty department. When we were alone Tina said 'I think he fancies you, that's why he's coming back.'

'Well, I don't fancy him.'

'I don't blame you.'

'I hope he's not going to be a pain' I said firmly.

'I bet he will be… all lonely old knicker sniffers are!'

I was still grinning when Wilkes came back with Hammond. I tried to keep a straight face as I went through the system again but had to look away from Tina when she winked at me and sniffed.

When my ordeal our new area manager was over he thanked me and went back to Wilkes' office.

'See, he'll be back again and again, just you wait and see' said Tina.

'Oh God, I hope not.'

The next few days passed quite quickly. I phoned my solicitor, Mr Clarke, and made an appointment for the next Monday. I took the day off and phoned in to tell Wilkes that Mother was ill, well she had been a bit of a pain most of the weekend, so I used her as my excuse. She had the nerve to tell me over Sunday lunch that I should start evening classes in something or other to take my mind off the divorce. I told her that evening classes were full of middle aged men in cardigans with comb over's looking for sex! That was the very last place on Earth I wanted to be at the moment… it would be worse than amateur dramatics! She did not take my refusal kindly and said 'as you're hurtling towards thirty now, you should make the most of any chance you get to find a decent man!' I was not amused and she made me angry when she finally said in her martyr voice 'I'm only trying to help, dear.' We hardly spoke for the rest of the day and I went to bed early leaving her to watch some idiotic talent programme on the television. Nowadays we have to watch endless football, cooking or gardening programmes or so called 'searching for a star' or something equally stupid... 'dumbing down' is fast becoming an art form in its own right!

My interview with Mr Clarke was drab and upsetting. He prattled on about the house at Cranfield and Tony's objection that I should have half the value as a settlement because we had been married for such a short time and anyway it was his house. Quite honestly I didn't give a damn about it all... I just wanted to be completely free of the unhappiness and sadness at losing my lovely handsome husband to his womanising way of life. I knew deep down that he would never change.

Mr Clarke peered through his thick glasses and assured me he would do his best to settle matters as soon as possible. I told him that I could ask for nothing more and I left his office feeling as if I just been to the dentist and had a major extraction... decidedly groggy and just wanting to go home to bed.

I returned to work on the Tuesday feeling just about ordinary and was settling down to the customary chore of updating the list of late paying customers, when Wilkes came in and asked how Mother was. I told him she was better but I knew he didn't believe that she had been ill. As Tina and I were having our mid-morning break Wilkes appeared again and told me that Hammond had organised a day out to demonstrate our system to two other Dealerships. I was surprised and sceptical about spending the day with Hammond but obviously I had to go, so I decided to make the best of it.

'Mind how you go with him' said Tina after Wilkes left the office.

'I will.'

'He's got you to himself for the whole day and that could be tricky' she said with a grin before she sniffed loudly and I started to giggle.

'Oh do stop it' I said.

'And if he wants to take you home to show you his pussy, just say 'no'!'

'Or see his knicker drawers' I added and we both laughed.

I wore my pin striped grey suit with a pink blouse for the day out with Hammond and tidied myself up nicely before leaving home. I hoped to make a good impression on the managers at the other Dealerships just in case they were looking for someone to head up their accounts departments. Mother only caught a glimpse of me as I rushed out the front door and called out 'is something special on at work today then?'

'Possibly' I called back before slamming the door shut. I couldn't be bothered to stop and go into long discussions with her at the moment.

It was just after ten when Wilkes came into the office and asked me if I was ready to leave with Hammond. I said I was, nodded to Tina, who smirked as I followed Wilkes to his office. Hammond stared at me strangely before we left. I felt awkward in the car with him at first but as we drove towards Southend and he chatted about work I began to relax a little. He asked me about Mother and I knew he was fishing for something about me, so I told him that I was in the middle of a divorce and didn't want to talk about it. He said he was divorced, so I guess Tina was right about him living alone and I wondered if she was also right about the knickers and the cat! After our short, sharp conversation about me, he shut up... thank God.

I demonstrated our system to the manager and his girls at Thames Motors but I could see that they were not that impressed. After some polite conversation with Mr Lovegrove, we left and started on the journey to Blackwell's at Chelmsford.

We were just leaving Southend when Hammond said he knew a nice place for lunch and I was a bit suspicious but he assured me it was on our way. When we arrived at 'The Windmill' I was quite captivated by it. The pub was set back from the road and had a thatched roof with white walls and open green shutters either side of tiny picturesque windows. There was a beer garden neatly laid out in front of the pub with wooden tables and sitting alone at a table was a smiling Eric! My insides turned to ice and I felt sick as

I glanced at him as I hurried passed, asking myself 'why was he here?' Once we were inside the pub I realised that Hammond knew something was up and then he asked about the stranger outside, I tried to deny that I knew Eric. My nerves were on edge but a gin and tonic relaxed me a little then after lunch Hammond asked me out on a date! Could you believe it? I said 'no' and meant it... he was not my type and never would be. He was not happy but I didn't care... men were not my favourite people at that particular moment. As we left the pub he had the bloody nerve to go and speak to Eric who smiled, said something before he strode off up the road. What an absolute pratt this bloke Hammond was! He was even more unhappy when I told him to mind his own business! My day out was not going at all well.

I repeated the demonstration at Blackwell's but it was obvious to me that they had no intentions of changing their system. We left after all the usual banal chat and on the way back to Romford, Hammond started on me again! I said 'no' once more and he shut up. I was glad when we arrived back at Hamilton's and was relieved when he left after speaking senseless platitudes to Wilkes. God... these men, who do they think they are?

I arrived home that night feeling like a mad woman's underclothes... all over the bloody place! Mother didn't help.

'So anything exciting happen at work today?' she asked as she put the kettle on.

'If you must know it was a complete disaster' I replied as I slumped down on a chair at the kitchen table.

'Well... I expect it was all because you were too hasty as usual' she said in a flat tone and I just sighed then put my head in my hands.

'Oh God' I murmured.

'You'll feel better when you've had something to eat... we've got chicken and chips for dinner' she said and I just moaned.

I was feeling really depressed when Jane came to my rescue a few days later in 'The Red Lion'.

'Let's go on holiday' she said brightly after we had finished our first drink and discussed the foibles of men... one man in particular.

'I'd like to but I can't afford it… this bloody divorce is going to cost me a fortune' I replied.

'Listen… my Uncle Frank, he's Melanie's dad, has a small holiday house in a village somewhere in Provence, he said I could go there anytime I wanted, provided it didn't clash with his holiday with Aunt Grace. So, as it's almost the middle of September now, we could go for a short break and soak up the last of the sun' she said with a smile.

'It sounds wonderful, but I…'

'Oh just let's go for a week… it'll do us both good and it won't cost a lot. Uncle Frank is a sweetie and he won't charge us any rent, so we only have to find the air fare and some spending money, surely you can afford that' she interrupted enthusiastically. I thought for a moment and said 'yes, why not? I've got some holiday owing, so yes, let's go and leave it all behind… and bugger the expense!'

A week later we flew on Easy Jet from Luton to Marseille. Jane had arranged for a hire car at Marignane Airport so we climbed into the front seats of the little white Fiat after packing our over full suitcases onto the back seat. Jane had not driven a left hand drive car before and we had a few near misses with frantic French taxi drivers hooting madly at us as we pulled slowly out of the car park and headed towards the autoroute. Luckily it was still daylight and as we had quite a long journey to Grambois we were relieved, because we didn't fancy our chances of finding the place in the dark.

Uncle Frank had drawn a map from the airport right to the door of his house and that was where it all went wrong. I mean, I'm usually quite good with maps but this one seemed to leave out so many details that it was obvious that we would get lost at some point on the journey. As we approached Marseille on the autoroute Jane kept asking 'which way now?'

'I'm not sure… it's not clear…' I replied each time.

'Oh for God's sake, Clare… do try and help me!' she said in desperation.

'Just keep going for the moment… I'm looking for a sign that says 'Aix''

'You keep saying that but there are so many signs over the motorway with lanes going off in all directions... it's confusing me and these bloody drivers don't help... I swear they're all mad!'

We ended up following the signs to 'Centre Ville –Toutes Directions', which was a mistake and eventually arrived at the harbour in Marseille which was full of sailing boats bobbing gently at their moorings. Jane pulled over and stopped the car outside a restaurant.

'So what do we bloody well do now?' she asked angrily.

'Let's take a break, have a walk and find somewhere to have a drink' I replied because I could see she was flustered.

'Clare, we haven't got time for all that!' she replied.

'I thought we were on holiday...'

'But we're lost!' she interrupted.

'No we're not, we're by the harbour in Marseille... and I don't think we'll starve to death looking at all the restaurants around the place' I replied as someone tapped at my window. I turned away from Jane and saw a handsome smiling face. I wound the window down and he said something in French and I looked blank then replied 'je suis Anglais' which is all I know.

'Ah... are you on holiday?' he asked in perfect English with a broken biscuit accent, which turns some women on but was wasted on me at the time.

'Yes, we are' I replied with a smile.

'And are you alright?' he asked.

'We're lost' Jane piped up with a smile.

'Ah, well... you're in Marseille, by the harbour, mademoiselle' he replied and Jane sighed... I think it was the 'mademoiselle' coupled with his smile that did it for her.

'We guessed' I said and he nodded.

'So, where do you want to go to?' he asked.

'A place called Grambois' I replied.

'I've never heard of it... is it far away?'

'It's a village in Provence' I replied.

'Do you know where it is near?' he asked.

'Well, our map says the nearest place is Pertuis' I replied.

'I don't know where that is... so let me have a look at your map' he said with a smile. I handed him Frank's sketch and he shook his head.

'Mon Dieu… no wonder you're lost…'

'Can you help us please?' asked Jane with a smile.

'But of course, mademoiselle' he replied.

'Thank you so much… monsieur… monsieur?' she asked… fishing for his name.

'My name is Pierre, Pierre Dalmas' he replied and Jane sighed again whilst I thought 'if this goes on much longer we'll be spending the whole week in Marseille with these two gazing into each other's eyes!'

'And I'm Jane and this is my friend Clare.'

'Enchanté, mademoiselles… now when you left the airport you should have taken the autoroute to Aix…'

'I was looking for the sign to Aix' I interrupted.

'Bien sûr, it is a bit confusing because there are so many exits.'

'You can say that again' I said.

'Now when you get to Aix, you take the road to Pertuis… then it says here, the D956 to Grambois, so there you are.'

'Thank you… now how do we get to Aix from here?' I asked.

'You're by the Old Port and if you carry on this side of the harbour, the road leads to the start of the autoroute, which runs along the coast to Monaco, soon there is a turn off which will take you up to Aix' he said as he handed the map back to me.

'Thank you' I said.

'But I should wait until the rush hour is over…'

'You mean it gets busier?' interrupted Jane as she glanced quickly at the stream of traffic hurtling by, bumper to bumper.

'Oui, Jane, the road to the autoroute will soon be jammed packed and it stays that way for about two hours' he replied.

'Oh God' whispered Jane.

'But if you would like to have something to drink with me whilst you wait…' he began and I thought 'oh oh, here we go!'

'Yes, that would be very nice, thank you, Pierre' said Jane and I winced.

'Bon, you can leave your car here…'

'Where are we going?' I interrupted, thinking we were about to be trafficked as sex slaves to somewhere hot and dusty.

'In here' he said pointing to the restaurant behind him then he added 'my Aunt Monique owns it with my cousins.'

'Oh how lovely' said Jane and she was out of the car before I could undo my seat belt.

La Galleot was cool inside and beautifully laid out with pristine white tablecloths and gleaming cutlery. There were a few early evening customers being served by a pretty waitress as Pierre introduced us to his Aunt and her two sons. None of them spoke English so Pierre had to translate and we were soon made very welcome. We sat at a table in the window so we could keep an eye on our car whilst we drank refreshing lime cordials in tall glasses filled with tinkling ice. How fortunate to have stopped where we did. Pierre explained he was just leaving the restaurant and saw us when we pulled up and told us that we looked hopelessly lost.

'Well Pierre, I'm glad you came to our rescue' said Jane.

'I am too' he said in a half whisper, gazing into her eyes as she fluttered her eyelashes before glancing down at her cordial. I thought 'God... this might end up being very painful and I wasn't emotionally ready for another 'love at first sight' saga!' Then I glanced out of the window at the car and bugger me... I saw Eric walk by!

I had a moment of panic then tried to think clearly before I decided to confront him... I mean... what on earth was he doing here?

'Excuse me, I need something from the car' I said to the others but I needn't have bothered because they were in a pink fluffy world of their own and didn't hear me. I hurried out of the restaurant and looked in the direction that Eric had taken. I couldn't see where he had gone for a moment then looking around I saw him across the road sitting on a long bench overlooking the harbour. I eventually crossed safely in between speeding drivers who were obviously rushing home to their wives or somebody else's... well you know what the French are like... and joined Eric on the bench.

'Hello, Eric.'

He turned to face me and smiled saying 'hello, Clare.'

He looked handsome, dressed in tight leather trousers and a white, sleeveless, open necked shirt that contrasted with his tan. His skin seemed to glisten and his teeth were so white... I suppose that's because of all the oily fish the Norwegians eat.

'So what brings you here?' I asked in my curious tone.

'You of course.'

'Why me?' I asked now feeling more relaxed in his company. I mean, if he wanted to do something awful to me he would have surely done it by now.

'Because your well being and happiness is my only concern' he replied. I was beginning to like this good looking Norwegian more and more. I thought 'it's funny how your mood can change quickly when someone says something nice to you.'

'Well I really don't know whether to give you a kiss or run away and hide' I said with a grin.

'Oh you must never kiss me…'

'Why not?' I interrupted.

'Because you must not get emotionally involved with me…'

'Why's that?' I demanded.

'It is my duty to help and guide you and not anything else' he replied.

'Well it might help me if you showed me some affection… I mean, I am having a bad time at the moment' I said firmly as my mood changed back again.

'I realise that, but I am not available to you' he said solemnly. Now there is nothing so attractive to a red blooded woman on holiday than a handsome man who is temporarily unavailable… I stress 'temporarily'.

'So I guess you're married then?' I asked.

'No, I'm not' he replied with a smile as I had another mood swing and thought 'oh goody, goody… Weetabix for breakfast… here we go!'

'Have you a special woman in your life?' I asked coyly.

'No, not really, although I have had several under me on the furs by the fire in the long house' he said with a big grin.

'How nice' I replied with a smile whilst thinking 'some girls have all the luck.'

'Yes it was.'

'Now tell me, who are you really and why are you following me?' I asked firmly, determined to sort out the truth about this man. He looked away from me and gathered his thoughts for a moment then said 'my name is Eric Blood Axe…'

'Oh God!' I interrupted then thought 'I knew it… he's a mad axe man!'

'And I am a Viking…'

'They're all dead!' I said firmly.

'That is true… but some of us did not live out our full lives and have been instructed to act as guides to people who need help.'

'Why didn't you live out your full life… as if I believe you're dead' I said.

'I was killed fighting Saxons' he replied in such a matter of fact tone that I, almost, half believed him.

'So are you alive or dead at the moment?' I asked… I mean to say… this conversation was getting silly.

'That is too complicated to answer, but for you… I am alive' he replied.

'I'm very pleased to hear it as I wouldn't like to be sitting on a bench in Marseille talking to a corpse!' I said and he laughed.

'Neither would I' he replied and I smiled.

'So tell me, how do you propose to guide me and why do you want to do it?' I asked.

'It is obvious that you are a very head strong woman and difficult…'

'What?' I shrieked… strong I may be, but difficult… certainly not!

'You can't see yourself…'

'This is not going well Eric' I interrupted.

'It's as I feared' he said.

'Well say something nice about me otherwise I'll run away and hide!'

He looked into my eyes and said 'I really believe that you would try.'

'There's no doubt about it' I said and he paused for a moment, nodded his head slightly then said 'I think that I should leave you for awhile and we can talk later at Grambois…'

'How do you know about Grambois?' I interrupted in surprise but he ignored my question and said 'when you are settled there and less anxious you will be easier to talk to, so I will see you in a few days.'

I just stared in amazement as he stood up and strode away towards the heart of the bustling city. I was completely bewildered by what had just happened so I sat for a few minutes and tried to pull myself together before returning to La Galleot.

'Who was that tall bloke you were talking to?' asked Jane immediately I sat down at the table. I really didn't know what to say to her and mumbled 'he was at my wedding and I recognised him.'

'So what's he doing here?' she asked.

'I think he's on holiday.'

'Bit of a coincidence isn't it?'

'Possibly.'

'You're not keeping something secret are you Clare?' she asked in a sly inquisitive tone.

'No… not really.'

'What does 'not really' mean?'

'I'm sure Pierre doesn't want to hear about it, so I'll tell you later… could I have another drink, please… that one was delicious' I said, hoping my request would be a quick diversion from Jane's questioning, Pierre nodded and called to the waitress. I breathed an inward sigh of relief and hoped Jane would shut up about Eric. Friends… sometimes they're worse than family!

We talked about England and discovered that Pierre came regularly to London to visit his sister who had married a teacher and lived in Ilford. Jane was delighted by that news and suggested that we should all meet up for dinner the next time that Pierre came over to stay. Pierre readily agreed and I could see love blossoming before my very eyes… it was touching and reminded me of when I first met Tony. I hoped for Jane's sake that anything between them would last longer than my disaster. After they had exchanged telephone numbers Pierre insisted that he treat us to dinner before we set off to Grambois, we readily agreed. As we were in Marseille where fresh fish is a 'must' on all menu's he suggested that we had the soup of the day, which was Bisque, followed by Sole Meunière, cooked in butter and parsley. It was delicious and melted in our mouths. Without a doubt Aunt Monique certainly knew how to cook fish. We finished the meal with cheese but we only had one glass of white wine as we needed to stay alert for our journey to Grambois.

It was almost seven o'clock when we said our 'goodbyes' and gave kisses to Pierre, his Aunt Monique and her two sons before we set off towards the autoroute. The traffic was quite light compared with what we had seen earlier and we made good progress on the road for several miles when we both saw the overhead sign to Aix. I breathed a sigh of relief as Jane drove down the slip road and on to the road that would hopefully take us straight to Aix. As we settled down on the journey I knew Jane would start asking questions and she did.

'So tell me, Clare, who was that bloke?'

'His name is Eric, but I really don't know much about him' I replied.

'So what do you know?'

'Well, I first noticed him at the wedding... didn't you see him there?'

'No, was he at the reception?'

'No, only at the church.'

'I wonder how I missed him because he's tall and good looking' she said.

'Yes he is.'

'Did he say why he's here?' she asked and wondered for a few moments whether I should tell her everything... it all sounded so ridiculous but I thought if Jane knew she might see something that perhaps I was missing.

'He said he's here to see that I'm alright...'

'How nice... but a bit spooky unless you've got something going with him that you're not telling me about' she interrupted.

'I'm confused by what he says...'

'You're not the first woman who's been confused by a man!' she said firmly.

'Look, if you want to know about Eric then just shut up and listen will you?'

'Promise.'

'Right... now he says he's an angel...'

'What?' she shrieked in surprise and the car swerved as she wobbled the steering wheel.

'He says he's been sent to guide me...'

'Well, that's the best 'legs opening' line yet!'

'Will you just shut up and concentrate on the driving otherwise we'll be in heaven ourselves in a minute and if he really is an angel you'll be able talk to him yourself!'

'Surely you don't believe that crap, do you?'

'I don't know what to think' I replied.

'Oh Clare... I think you're heading for another disaster' she said sadly.

I spent the rest of the journey to Aix telling her everything I knew about Eric, including Hammond's silly confrontation with him outside the pub. I was pleased that she agreed with me that Hammond was a complete pratt.

As we approached Aix I concentrated on the map and looked out for signs that would direct us to Pertuis but I couldn't see any, so we ended up following the signs for 'Centre Ville – Toutes Directions' once again. It was now becoming quite dark and I began to get worried when Jane saw a sign that said 'Pertuis' and we were on our way out of Aix. We hardly spoke, other than to complain about the silly French road signs and wondered how anybody visiting the place actually found their way anywhere.

By the time we reached Pertuis it was completely dark and I hoped that we would be able to find the D956 to Grambois. I mean to say... was this village out in the sticks or what? When we reached the town square suddenly there it was in the headlights... the sign that read D956 to Grambois! We cheered and both felt very relieved as Jane accelerated the little Fiat down the road and out of Pertuis.

We saw the lights of Grambois some distance away because it is perched on the top of a hill. We were surprised at how steep the road was up to the medieval village, where, according to Uncle Frank's map, we had to park the car in the square then make our way to his house on foot. Several people were wandering about in the gloom as we parked the Fiat by a wall and the only bright light came from a bar in the corner of the square.

'I don't like the look of this' said Jane as she glanced around at several curious onlookers.

'Neither do I.'

'Well here goes' she said as we climbed out and unloaded our suitcases.

The map showed that we had to go through an arch at the top of the square and along a narrow street called Rue Jardine, until we reached number 10 where Christine Deville lived. She had the key to Frank's house, which was next door. We were both anxious about going down the dark cobbled street but had to summon up our courage, I wished that Eric was with us. All the terraced houses were very small and I wondered what we had let ourselves in for. We eventually found number 10 and Jane knocked hard on the wooden door. We waited for a few moments then a light came on behind the small window in the door and it was opened by a very attractive young woman.

'Ah... bonsoir ma petites, you're here at last!' she said, we both nodded and said 'yes... at last.'

'Come in, come in' she said and stood back for us to enter.

'Leave your cases and come in here' she said as she led the way into a lovely room that was warm, bright and comfortably furnished.

'I'm Jane and this is my friend Clare.'

'Enchanté... and I am Christine, now have you eaten, mon amis?' she asked as she waved us to sit on a large red velvet sofa.

'Yes, we had dinner in Marseille' Jane replied.

'Très bien... then something to drink now?' she said with a smile.

'Yes please' I said.

'What would you like?'

'Have you a brandy please?' I asked... feeling the need for one after the day's adventures.

'Bien sûr... and for you?' she asked Jane.

'The same please.'

'Bon' she said with a smile before going to a huge sideboard with a large number of bottles on a tray. Jane and I glanced at one another and smiled as I thought 'Uncle Frank's got himself an attractive neighbour to look after his keys and I wonder what else she does for him?' By the expression on Jane's face I think she was having the same thought.

'Now tell me, have you had a good journey?' Christine asked as she handed us goblets half full of brandy.

'It seems as if we've been travelling forever' I replied as Christine joined us with a large brandy.

'I know how you feel, it is awful these days and everywhere is so crowded... that's why I stay here as much as possible and only go to Monaco when I have a new painting to show' she said.

'So, are you're an artist then?' asked Jane.

'Oui, I am. Cheers ma petites, welcome to Grambois and bonne vacance' she said as she raised her glass. We said 'cheers' and sipped the brandy, which hit the spot and I thought 'this could be a very interesting holiday after all.'

'So what do you paint?' I asked.

'Some country scenes, petite villages, Provence is very beautiful and of course the light down here is fantastic for artists... but my nude studies are the most popular with the gallery' she replied.

'How exciting' said Jane.

'May we see some of your work?' I asked.

'Bien sûr' she replied with a smile.

'Uncle Frank never told me he had a famous artist living next door' said Jane.

'Oh, I am not famous ma petite, just someone who likes painting and manages to make a living at it' she replied.

'And your English is very good' I said.

'Oui, I studied art in London for awhile, but after an affair which ended unhappily I had to come back to Grambois... he was married you see' she replied.

'I know how you feel' I said gloomily before taking another large sip of brandy.

'Are you married?' she asked.

'I was... but not long enough to do any permanent damage' I replied.

'Ah... love is a complicated business and someone always gets hurt' she said with a sigh and we all sat for a few moments in silence. Then Jane said brightly 'will you show us some of your paintings.'

'Not tonight... you need to see them in daylight, besides you must be tired now, so have a good night's rest and I will show them to you in the morning' she replied.

'It makes sense' I said.

'Bon, now when Frank phoned me saying that you were coming today I bought you some food, it's all in the fridge next door' she said with a smile.

'Oh thank you, how much do we owe you?' said Jane.

'I left the bill on the kitchen table so you can pay when you come tomorrow... I'll just get the keys now' she said before she hurried into the next room returning with the keys.

Christine showed us to the door, kissed us and wished us 'bon nuit'.

Uncle Frank and Aunt Grace's holiday home was a revelation inside. It was well furnished with old style furniture but very comfortable. The kitchen was a mixture of old and modern, with a large black cooking range in a recessed fireplace and fitted cupboards that toned in well with the décor. We found tea, coffee and sugar in the cupboards as well as lots of tinned food that they had brought from England... mostly from Sainsbury's. There was a good stock of wine in a large rack by the door and an enormous fridge, when Jane opened it we were amazed at the amount of food in there. Christine had obviously 'mega' shopped and bought enough to feed us for a week! Besides the butter, milk, cheeses, apricots, olives, strawberries, cream and ham there were croissants, brioche and chocolates.

'God, how the French stuff themselves' I said.

'It's a wonder that they are not all over weight' said Jane.

'I wonder what the bill is for this little lot' I said as Jane picked up the receipt from the table.

'It says twenty five Euros and thirty cents' she said.

'That's cheap.'

'It certainly is... now how about a cup of tea before we turn in?'

We sat in the lounge drinking a refreshing cup of Earl Grey and relaxing.

'Well, Clare, I never thought we'd ever get here.'

'Neither did I.'

'But we made it at last... so we can laze around for a week, please ourselves and not worry about a thing' said Jane.

'Oh what heaven' I said, then after a few moments my curious nature got the better of me and I asked 'do you think Uncle Frank is giving her one next door?'

'I wouldn't be surprised knowing him, she's very attractive' she replied.

'And she's probably looking for a little bit of tender appreciation without commitment after being dumped by another married rat!'

Jane sighed, nodded and said 'they're all the same... I bet Pierre has got a wife or some other female hidden away somewhere.'

'You don't know that.'

'No, I don't... let's go to bed, Clare, I'm really knackered!'

I slept like a log and woke the next morning when I heard Jane wandering about in the kitchen. I pulled on my jeans, slipped on a T shirt and went to find her. As I went into the lounge, on my way through to the kitchen, I stopped because I was completely stunned by the magnificent view out of the picture window. The village was so high up you could see for miles. There were gently rolling hills peppered with small white houses with orange terra cotta roofs nestling amongst tall trees. The clear sky was an azure blue and I understood what Christine said about the light... it was wonderful.

'Now how about that view?' asked Jane as she came into the room.

'It's fantastic.'

'I thought that when I opened the curtains' she said.

'Your Uncle Frank and Aunt Grace have good taste' I said.

'They have, now come and have some coffee with croissants with honey.'

An hour later we were ready to call in and see Christine, pay her for the food and have a quick glance at her paintings before exploring the village.

'Bonjour ma petites, did you sleep well?' she asked with a smile when we entered her house.

'We did, thank you' Jane replied.

'Bon, now would you like some coffee?'

'No thanks, we've just had breakfast... I've brought the money for the food' said Jane as she handed the Euros to Christine.

'Merci, did I get enough for you?'

'Oh yes, plenty, thanks' I said.

'We'll be fat little pigs by the time we leave here' said Jane.

'Oh, non! You both have lovely figures... and I've been thinking that I should paint you before you leave' she said as she looked us up and down then I thought 'oh, oh, here we go... I think she might be a bit of a lesbian.'

'In the nude?' asked Jane.

'But of course' Christine replied.

'I don't think…'I began.

'Come up to my studio and see what I have just finished' she interrupted with a smile. She led us up the narrow stairs to a room that she used as her studio. It had a huge picture window that let in so much light it was almost like being outside. There were paintings all over the place and the one on her easel was of her. She was naked and reclining on the red sofa in her lounge. The painting was truly beautiful and her figure was so tanned and proportional it was perfect. We stood for a moment looking at it before she said 'I have painted my body as I would like it to be… what woman can do that?'

'Not many' I replied.

'I don't know whether to keep it to remind me when I am old and wrinkly or sell it to the gallery' she said with a giggle.

'I'm sure they'd pay a lot for it… you look really beautiful' said Jane.

'Merci… when I paint you I will make you both look even more beautiful than you are' she said with a smile.

'If we agree, I hope you won't show Uncle Frank the painting when you've finished it' said Jane.

'Why not?'

'Because he might get ideas about us and Aunt Grace wouldn't like it' replied Jane.

'Oh, she will take no notice… it's art ma petite, and nobody can be upset by true art, besides, Frank likes coming in here to see my work when Grace goes off shopping' said Christine and I thought 'I bet he does!'

I looked around and saw several paintings that were propped up against a bureau in the corner and noticed that the same girl appeared in each.

'Does this girl live in the village?' I asked casually.

'Oui, that is Evette, she lives over the bar and poses a lot for me… I sell her paintings to the gallery and then I pay her a percentage… she is very happy with our arrangement' replied Christine.

'She's lovely' I said.

'Oui, and I am very fond of her.'

Then I noticed an open sketch pad perched at the back of the untidy bureau that was littered with tubes of oil paint and saw a face I recognised. I went cold inside before I pointed and asked 'who is this?'

'Ah, he's a Norwegian tourist called Eric... I saw him sitting in the square a few days ago and asked if I could draw him... I think he has such an interesting and handsome face, don't you?' replied Christine. Suddenly Jane was by my side staring down at the pencil drawing.

'Oh... my... God' she whispered slowly.

'Precisely' I whispered back.

CHAPTER 5

CLARE MEETS MICHEL

We left Christine without telling her that I knew Eric and made our way in silence to the bar, hoping a reviving coffee would help us recover from the shock. We sat at a little table outside in the sun and waited for someone to serve us. Jane kept looking at me strangely until I asked 'what?'

'It's so spooky that it must be true' she said.

'What is?'

'That he's an angel' she replied as a boy holding a tray arrived and said something. We glanced at him, smiled and Jane said slowly 'deux café, monsieur.' The boy nodded and murmured something back before hurrying away.

'Jane... I think I'm going mad with all this!' I said angrily.

'With all what?' she asked.

'How can you say that when you know exactly 'what'... I've got some nut who says he's an angel stalking me and popping up unexpectedly... a lousy husband... a Mother who's driving me to distraction... and a knicker sniffer who wants to take me out!' I replied loudly.

'A what?' asked Jane with a puzzled look on her face.

'Oh... it's what Tina calls that pratt Hammond' I replied.

'Why does she call him that?'

'She thinks he's a loner who lives with a cat, has a collection of porno mags and sniffs knickers' I replied then had to laugh at the silliness of what I had said.

'Blimey... you do seem to attract them don't you?' she said with a grin.

'I do.'

'I think that what you need is a steady bloke like Simon...'

'Oh no... not Simon' I interrupted.

'Why not?'

'He'd bore me to death in five minutes' I replied.

'Well if you ask me he's a much better bet than...'

'I know... I know... you're only trying to help' I interrupted hastily as the boy arrived with our coffee.

We sat in silence and drank the coffee whilst gazing out at the wonderful view beyond the open square. I tried to get everything into some perspective but my mind was just hazy and I couldn't think clearly about anything.

'Do you think Eric will pop up here again?' asked Jane.

'He said he would, but I really don't know... so it wouldn't surprise me' I replied.

'Christine thought he was interesting.'

'She did...'

'And she wants to paint us... what do you think about that?'

'It would be a bit of a laugh and take my mind of things' I replied with a grin.

'Then let's do it!' Jane said.

'It would certainly add something to the holiday!'

We wandered around the pretty village until lunchtime and then made our way back to the house. It was now hot and we were glad to get inside in the cool. We decided to be very Provençal and eat our way through the selection of cheeses, drink a bottle or two of Frank's wine then finish off lunch with strawberries and cream. And if we were not too drunk or sick after all that, we would go and tell Christine that we were ready to pose for her whenever she wanted.

'If Christine showed our paintings to Frank he'd have a fit!' I exclaimed with a giggle.

'Or Grace... she'd never let us stay here again!' said Jane.

'I'm not surprised' I said as I unsteadily poured another glass of red wine for each of us.

'But I'm sure Christine would only show Frank when Grace was out shopping' said Jane and we both laughed.

'I bet she'll sell our paintings to the gallery for a huge sum...'

'Hey... why don't we ask her for a percentage of the price?' said Jane.

'What a good idea, it could pay for the holiday!'

'We'll ask for the same rate as Evette.'

'That seems reasonable to me... so why not?'

We sat and giggled as we finished off the rest of the wine and were feeling quite squiffy when we summoned up enough courage to go and knock at Christine's door.

'Ah, ma petites, come in' she said with a smile and I somehow guessed she knew that we were going to offer ourselves for her artistic interpretation. I'm funny like that.

We went through to her lounge and sat on the red sofa.

'Would you like something to drink or have you had enough already?' she asked with a mischievous grin.

'Is it that obvious?' I asked in a slurred tone and she laughed.

'Oui, it is.'

'Then I think we'll have to say no thank you' said Jane.

'Très bien... now have you something you want to say?' she asked.

'Yes, we've been thinking about your offer to paint us...' I began.

'Ah, bon, you are just in time' she interrupted.

'In time for what?' I asked.

'I have prepared a canvas for Evette and I would have started painting her this afternoon, but now you're here you can both take her place' replied Christine.

'I'm not sure that we...' I began.

'There's no time like the present... besides you are only here for a week so we must start now' Christine interrupted.

'Are you going to sell our paintings?' asked Jane.

'There will be only one painting with you together...'

'Together?' I interrupted.

'Oui.'

'So do you plan to sell it to the gallery?' asked Jane.

'Perhaps, but I will keep it for awhile and think about it' she replied.

'Well, if you do, we'd like a percentage of the money' Jane said firmly.

'Bien sûr... we can talk about that later, so ma petites let's go up to the studio and begin!' she said enthusiastically.

We followed her up to the sunlit studio where she told us to get undressed. Jane and I had seen each other's boobs on many occasions when we'd been trying on bra's that didn't fit comfortably... they never do... but we had never been naked together. Jane was shy but I felt quite relaxed and was soon standing completely naked in front of my friend and the artist.

'C'est magnifique' whispered Christine as she gazed at me and her eyes widened when Jane stood next to me.

'Ma petites... this is going to be so good... it will be my masterpiece!'

'So how do want to paint us?' I asked.

'I want to capture your beauty and show it to the world... I have been thinking how I want you to pose ever since I first met you' said Christine.

'Really?' I said.

'Oui, now I want you, Jane, to sit on this' she said as she placed a bar stool in the light from the window. Jane did as she was asked, then Christine moved a small table next to her, on her right.

'Now put your hand on the table and lean slightly back... I want you to hold this mirror in your other hand' and she picked up a small silver handled mirror from the cluttered bureau and gave it to Jane.

'Turn your head to your left and look up at yourself... raise your arm slightly... a little higher' she said and Jane did as she was told.

'Perfect... now Clare, you stand behind Jane and put both hands on her shoulders, move slightly to your left and look straight ahead at me' said Christine. I did as she asked and felt a little tingle of excitement when I put my hands on Jane's bare flesh. I don't know whether it was the wine, or the sun shining in on us but I felt so relaxed and spiritual. I suddenly thought of Eric and wondered what he would do if he saw me naked like this. My mind began to wander. Would he remain 'unavailable' or kiss me and then gently touch my boobs? Perhaps he would kiss them before rubbing his fingers gently over my nipples... then kneel down and carry on kissing me all the way to... well, never mind... I tried to forget Eric and concentrate on what Christine was saying.

'Now, imagine if you will, that you had just kissed each other and you were about to kiss again, when Jane decides to look at herself in the mirror. So Clare, just look down at Jane and let your emotions show in your eyes' said Christine as she stepped back behind her easel and began sketching rapidly on the large canvas. This was heaven and I felt as if I was in a trance.

It seemed an age that we posed motionless and I was relieved when Christine said 'this is going well, so let's stop for a rest and have something to drink.'

'Oh yes' said Jane.

We sat on a sofa in the corner of the studio out of the direct sunlight and looked at each other as Christine went downstairs to get some refreshment.

'Well what do you think?' asked Jane with a coy smile.

'It's so good and I feel completely relaxed for once' I replied.

'It does seem so natural to be like this and have no inhibitions... I think I might pose for another painting... just on my own... so I could keep it to remind me how I looked when I'm old and wrinkly' said Jane with a laugh.

'Me too... let's see what she's done' I said as I jumped up and made my way to the canvas. Jane was with me as we stared at the charcoal outline sketch of us.

'She's very good' I said approvingly.

'She's made our boobs bigger than they are...'

'Don't complain about that' I said hastily.

'And she's made my legs longer than they really are...'

'But she's caught your face beautifully' I said as I realised how Jane's page boy hair style enhanced her long neck and lovely appearance.

'I wonder how it will look when it's finished?' she asked.

'Well judging by her paintings of Evette, I'd say it will be very good' I replied.

'Then it will be worth a bit' said Jane as Christine arrived carrying a tray with three large glasses of mint cordial.

We finished our drinks and were ready to pose again, Christine made a few minor alterations to Jane's position then worked hurriedly on the canvas. In a while she stood back and looked at her work for a few moments, then picked up her palette and began squeezing oil colour from tubes on to it. She opened bottles of linseed oil and turpentine before pouring small amounts into little silver pots then, after picking up several brushes, said with a smile 'and now we begin with the colour, ma petites!'

We remained silent and still for what seemed an age as she painted and casually glanced at us with a look of intense concentration on her face. I began to get slightly impatient and hoped that the session would soon end. I wondered how many times we would have to pose before she finished the painting, I was becoming concerned that it would take up too much of our holiday. I was just about to ask if we could have another break when Christine said 'I've finished for the moment' and I sighed with relief.

'May we see?' asked Jane.

'Bien sûr' replied Christine with a smile.

We hurried over to the canvas and were amazed at what had been accomplished. She had painted our faces in detail but our bodies were still great blobs of pink base colour. The likeness was staggering... she had enhanced our eyes, eyelashes, lips and our skin colour to a lovely even tan. I had to admit that we looked beautiful and said 'wow... I would be very happy if I really looked like that!'

'So would I' added Jane.

'But you do ma petites.'

'I wish' I said as there was a knock at the front door.

'Ah, that will be Evette' said Christine before she hurried away.

'Well what do you think about this?' asked Jane with a smile.

'It's much better than I ever expected' I replied.

'I agree... you look really lovely.'

'And so do you' I said.

'When she's finished I bet the gallery will pay a lot for it' said Jane as Christine arrived back.

'That was Evette and I've told her to come back tomorrow' she said.

'When do you want us again?' I asked.

'Oh not for a day or so and I will only need you for a short while next time. I have everything I need to finish... it's all in here' she said with a smile as she tapped her forehead.

'Oh, that's good' said Jane.

'Oui, you must now enjoy the rest of your holiday.'

We dressed, said 'goodbye' to the artist and had one last look at the painting before leaving the studio. As soon as we got indoors I slumped down on the sofa and said 'I think I've had enough excitement for one day and only want a quiet evening.'

'Me too' said Jane as she sat beside me.

'What will we have for dinner?' I asked drowsily.

'No idea... but you can cook it' Jane replied as I drifted off to sleep.

I awoke just before seven and was pleased when I heard Jane busy in the kitchen.

'Hello sleepy head' she said as I wandered in.

'So what's for dinner?' I asked as I sat down at the table.

'Sainsbury's pilchards with tomatoes and plenty of bread rolls followed by as much cheese as you want... all washed down with more wine' replied Jane with a grin.

'Dear God' I whispered.

'It's too hot for anything else and besides, you were supposed to get dinner' she said as she plonked the food down.

Funnily enough it was all quite light and refreshing as well as filling. We giggled as we went through another bottle of Frank's wine and Jane said that we had better buy a few bottles to replenish his stock before we left at the end of the week.

We planned to spend the next day on the beach somewhere, but we didn't know where exactly, so we decided that we would buy a map in Pertuis on our way to the coast. We went to bed and I lay naked on top of the sheets, falling asleep immediately.

After another breakfast of coffee, croissants and honey, we set off in the Fiat to Pertuis. Jane parked in the tree lined square and we wandered along a row of shops looking for a newsagent's. We found one next to a bar and after several attempts at making ourselves understood to the girl behind the counter, bought a map of the region.

'Let's sit here and have a coffee and see where we're going' I said, sitting at a table on the pavement outside the bar. The waiter arrived in a flash and Jane ordered two coffees, he smiled and disappeared. I opened the map and found Marseille and was just looking at the resorts along the coast when the waiter arrived back with the coffee. After putting the cups down, he asked in English 'are you looking for somewhere special?' We both gazed at him in surprise and I replied 'we're trying to find the nearest beach.'

'To swim?' he asked with a smile.

'That's the idea' I replied.

'Then go to Cassis… its lovely and very safe, I always go there myself to swim.'

'Show me where it is' I said as he glanced at the map and pointed to a spot just along from Marseille.

'You go to Aix then down to the autoroute, but instead of going in the direction of Marseille take the slip road towards Toulon and only a few kilometres along you will see the sign for Cassis' he replied.

'Thank you' I said.

'Your English is very good' said Jane.

'Merci, I worked in London for three years at the Marriott Hotel' he replied with a smile.

'We're just here on a short holiday' said Jane.

He smiled and replied 'I guessed… are you staying in Pertuis?'

'No, Grambois' Jane replied and he nodded.

'Well I hope you have good swim today and stop for coffee on your way back' he said.

'What a charmer' I said when he had left us.

Jane drove slowly to Aix so we could enjoy the gently rolling scenery with its abundance of vineyards. We followed the signs that directed us down towards Marseille and looked carefully for the slip road that would take us to Toulon and were relieved when we saw it. After a few kilometres the sign for Cassis directed us off the main road and onto a narrow one, which eventually led us to the picturesque fishing village. Jane parked the Fiat in a small car park near the harbour and we unloaded our bags and set off for the beach.

As soon as we saw it we thought Cassis was a totally charming place. The small harbour had some fishing boats moored up but mostly there were yachts gently bobbing at the walkways. Around the harbour were many bars and restaurants with brightly coloured awnings attempting to keep the customers shaded from the sun. I could see the glistening blue Mediterranean beyond the harbour wall as we made our way towards the beach. We stood looking down at the expanse of sand, which curved away in both directions to rocky cliffs in the distance, giving a perfect bay of safe, clear water. There were few people on the beach as it was now the middle of September and the hordes of holidaymakers would have returned home at the end of August.

'We've practically got the place to ourselves' I said as we stepped down onto the sand.

'Yes... and isn't this fabulous?' asked Jane as she took the lead and headed for a deserted spot near the cliffs. We spread our towels, slipped off our dresses and wearing just our bikini bottoms made for the sea. It was warm and totally glorious! We swam up and down with the sun glinting on the tops of the waves as they broke around us.

'This is almost as good as sex' said Jane between gasps of breath.

'Almost' I replied with a grin.

When we'd had enough of the sea we lazed in the sun, covered ourselves regularly with lotion... factor 15... and talked. Soon it became too hot and we needed some shade so we made our way to a bar on the beach wall and sat under the coloured awning. We drank sparkling water in tall glasses tinkling with ice and lemon slices. It was too hot to eat so we decided to save ourselves and find a nice restaurant for a meal much later in the cool of the evening.

'This holiday is really doing me some good' I said.

'Me too... as long as nobody spoils it...'

'Like who?' I interrupted but thought 'she means Eric.'

'Well... I don't like to mention your angel but...'

'Look, I've told you, I don't know who he really is' I said impatiently.

'But will he turn up again in Grambois? That's the question' said Jane with a grin.

'You're bloody well enjoying this aren't you?'

'Just a bit' she grinned then added 'you must admit he is good looking and I bet you'd not say 'no' if he wanted a little horizontal dancing!'

'He's unavailable!'

'No he's not... because no man is unavailable, believe me.'

'Well if he did come after me I'd have to say no.'

'Why?'

'He's not my type' I lied.

'Oh, yes he is!'

'Can we drop this now?'

'Ohh, touchy, touchy... but if you're sure he's not your type then I'll try my luck with him... I could do with a good long screw' she said with a lustful grin.

'He won't come' I said firmly.

'I bet he does' she grinned and I could have strangled her with my bare hands once again.

We returned to our spot near the cliffs and had another swim before deciding it was really too hot to stay on the beach any longer. We were both beginning to burn and knew that we had to keep out of the sun, even with our factor 15 smothered all over us.

'Let's go home, have a shower and rest until this evening then find a nice restaurant in Pertuis' said Jane.

'That's a good idea.'

The Fiat was like an oven inside so we had to open the doors and wait whilst the breeze cooled it down before we could sit in the car. The journey back to Grambois was hot and dusty and we were glad to get into the cool house. I stripped off immediately I walked through the door and so did Jane, we decided to shower together... we were too hot to wait! Under the cool water I washed her back and she did the same for me. It brought back memories of my intimacy with Tony and I felt very sad. We all need someone we care about to touch us and be close. I looked at Jane and we instinctively put our arms around each other and kissed... it was so spontaneous and beautiful that we both felt very at ease and comfortable. We said nothing because there was nothing to say and I just smiled at my friend and she smiled back. I stepped out of the shower and dried myself and Jane followed moments later.

'You've really caught the sun' she said as she wrapped the towel around herself.

'Oh, God... I hope I don't look like a boiled lobster' I replied.

'No, you look fine.'

We sat at the kitchen table with the towels draped over us and had a cup of Earl Grey tea to cool us down. We talked about the holiday and made plans to go to Aix the next day to look around and perhaps do some shopping for anything that caught our eye... like shoes or dinky handbags. Well, as every woman knows... you can never have too many. Jane was in full flow about her last disastrous retail therapy expedition in Romford where she could find nothing to fit or that suited her, when there was a knock at the door.

'Whoever can that be?' she asked.

'No idea, shall I go or will you?'

'You go' she replied so I wrapped the towel around myself and headed off. When I cautiously opened the door I was pleased to see Christine standing there.

'Hello' I said.

'Hello, ma petite... if you have a moment I would you like to come and meet someone very special' she said with a smile.

'We'll have to get dressed first' I replied wondering who it was that was 'special'... was it Eric?

'Bon... I'll see you both when you're ready' she said and I nodded then closed the door.

Twenty minutes later we had dressed, roughly tidied our hair and were knocking at Christine's door wondering who this 'special' person was that we were about to meet.

She led the way into her lounge where a tall, strikingly handsome, casually dressed man stood up and smiled when Christine introduced us as her 'beautiful English models'.

'And this is Monsieur Michel Duprey, his father owns the gallery in Monaco' she said with a smile.

'How do you do, Monsieur' I said holding out my hand.

'Very well, thank you, Mademoiselle' he replied in a deep, sexy, broken biscuit accent that made me go all funny inside as he gently shook my hand. Jane held her hand out and gave him her 'rabbit in headlights' open mouthed, amazed look. She said nothing whilst he murmured 'enchanté, Mademoiselle, enchanté.'

'Please sit down... and what would you like to drink?' asked Christine as we tried to compose ourselves whilst still gazing at this gorgeous man.

'Just a sparkling water for me' I said hesitantly.

'Très bien... and you Jane?'

'I'll have the same please.'

Michel sat down opposite and I couldn't take my eyes of him

as he picked up his glass of wine from a small table. He was about thirty five or so, had a truly handsome face topped with dark wavy hair going just a little grey at the edges and large brown eyes that seemed to delve into your soul... I had seen that look before!

As Christine handed us our sparkling water, she said 'Michel has seen your painting.' I could have dropped through the floor when I heard that and nearly spilled my drink but said calmly 'oh really?'

'Oui, and I think Christine has captured you both very well' he said with a smile.

'Thank you, Monsieur' I murmured, thinking 'so this sexy Frenchman has already seen us naked' whilst Jane just sat motionless like a wide eyed statue.

'Please call me Michel' he said.

'Oh' I whispered and nodded.

'Michel is only here today by chance' said Christine.

'Oui, I was delivering a painting to a client in Aix and decided to call on Christine to see what she would be bringing to the gallery soon.'

'Oh, how nice' I said.

'What did you think of our painting?' Jane blurted out suddenly.

'It is very... how shall I say?' he began and I thought 'just say we look bloody gorgeous and I'm yours!'

'...artistic... Christine has a wonderful eye for detail and that makes her work highly sought after by our clients' he replied but I wondered if the clients actually bought her paintings because they liked the large boobs with cherry nipples and long legs in all her nude studies.

'Are you going to buy our painting?' asked Jane.

'But of course... if it is for sale' Michel replied as he glanced at Christine for confirmation.

'I'm sure we can come to some arrangement when it's finished' she said with a smile and I thought 'goody, goody... that's the holiday paid for!'

'Then that is very good news, so we have something to celebrate tonight' he said with a smile and I wondered what was coming next.

'What do you have in mind?' asked Christine.

'Dinner with me at the best restaurant in Aix… it is owned by a client, who is also a good friend of mine, and he will be delighted to see you all, especially when I tell him about the painting… knowing him he will probably want to buy it!'

'That's absolutely fantastic!' I said.

'Oui, thank you Michel' said Christine and Jane just smiled.

'I have some business to attend to in Pertuis, so if you will excuse me, I will come back for you all at about eight o'clock… is that alright?' he asked with another captivating smile.

'Of course' replied Christine.

'We'll be ready' I chipped in and Jane smiled again.

Once back in our house we were struck by the blind panic brought on by unexpected invitations to dinner with handsome strangers.

'What the hell are we going to wear?' I asked.

'We'll think of something… but only God knows what!'

I finally decided on my white halter neck backless dress, which might be a slight problem as I didn't have a suitable bra with me so it meant my boobs would be free to wander! I had brought several belts and chose one, which almost matched my red shoes with the bows, the ones that Mother said made me look like a transvestite. I somehow didn't think Michel would mind if I did. Jane wore her blue, see through, 'flouncy' dress with a white belt and shoes to match. We spent time concentrating on our makeup and hair and at last we thought we looked passable considering the few hours that we had to get ready.

It was a quarter to eight when we knocked next door. Christine looked gorgeous in a little red number and she was beautifully made up. We sat on the sofa and drank more sparkling water whilst we waited for the handsome one to arrive.

'Michel is so charming, just like his father… and of course, very rich' said Christine with a smile.

'I'm sure he is.'

'Has he got a wife?' asked Jane.

'Non, not anymore, she went off with some playboy millionaire from Argentina a few years ago' replied Christine and I thought 'silly girl.'

'How sad' said Jane with a half concealed contented smile.

'Michel was heartbroken at the time' said Christine but I

wondered how he was now.

'Has he anyone special in his life at the moment?' I asked, Christine smiled before she shook her head and replied 'non, but there is a queue waiting anxiously for him to choose!'

'I'm sure.'

'And I'm first in the queue' said Christine firmly.

'I wouldn't mind being second' said Jane as there was a knock at the door.

'That'll be him' said Christine as she leapt up.

Moments later Michel strode into the room and as we stood to greet him his eyes widened a little.

'Mon Dieu! I think I must be in heaven!' he said with a smile and we laughed.

'Perhaps' I said then thinking 'you could be if you played your cards right this evening.' Christine gave me an old fashioned look before she asked 'shall we go?'

'Bien sûr' said Michel as he stood back to allow us to go first then gave a bow... what a perfect gentleman.

Michel's black Mercedes limousine was parked by our little Fiat and it made it look ridiculously small. He clicked open the car and held the back door open for Jane and me to slide into the opulent grey leather interior. He obviously wanted Christine to ride with him in the front, which was understandable, seeing that she was first in the queue of hopeful women, but I wondered if he really thought that about her. He may only have seen her as the talented artist who supplied erotic paintings to his father's gallery. In which case there was everything to play for... namely him! And I felt very lucky!

The car wafted out of the village and was soon purring effortlessly along the road to Pertuis. Jane and I looked at each other and smiled as we both thought... was this really happening to us? Posing for nude portraits one minute then invited out to dinner by the wealthy, handsome Frenchman who wanted to buy our painting... I was really beginning to enjoy this holiday and hoped that nothing or, more importantly, nobody would spoil it... like Eric.

Soon we arrived in Aix and pulled up outside the 'Moulin Bleu' restaurant. It looked beautifully quaint and was lit up with little blue windmills.

'The cuisine here is formidable, cordon bleu par excellence!' said Michel.

He escorted Christine into the restaurant holding her arm as we followed on. We were greeted by a smiling, elegant middle aged man, dressed in a white tuxedo with a bow tie. Michel introduced us to Phillipe as his new, beautiful, English models who had just posed for a masterpiece now being created by Christine and I thought 'this is going well.'

'Ah, that I must see, Michel' said Phillipe as he looked at us and smiled.

'And you shall… but all in good time, Phillipe' said Michel and I could practically see the sale price of our painting doubling with every passing second.

'Then promise me that I will have first refusal' said Phillipe.

'Bien sûr… I promise' replied Michel.

'Ah, you all heard that' he said holding up his finger, we nodded and smiled.

Phillipe led us to a reserved table in an alcove at the back of the restaurant. When we were all seated he clicked his fingers and two waiters appeared as if by magic. They handed us menus and the wine waiter gave the list to Michel. Phillipe smiled and said 'I can recommend the Chateaubriand tonight… it is superb!'

'Merci, Phillipe' said Michel.

'But of course the choice is yours… bon appetite' he said before he gave a little bow and left us to wander through the extensive menu. I was overwhelmed by the choice but I did fancy the Chateaubriand as my main course but wondered what to have as a starter. After some careful thought I decided on foie gras truffe, I had never had truffles before so surely now was the right time and place to try.

'Clare, what are you having?' asked Jane in an anxious whisper.

'To start I'm having truffles, then the Chateaubriand steak' I replied.

'Then I'll have the same' said Jane and I realised she had been slightly overawed by the menu and was unsure.

'Have you chosen already?' asked Michel as he glanced at us over his menu.

'We have' I replied.

'Bon… and you Christine?'

'Oui, Michel… I'll start with moules mariniere, then have boeuf bourguignon' she replied.

'Très bien… Clare, what will you have?'

I told him and Jane said she would have the same.

'Bon… now I think we'll start with a petite Burgundy then we'll go onto Champagne' said Michel. I smiled and thought 'this could be a night to remember!'

The waiters were hovering and stepped forward to take the order when Michel raised his finger. After he ordered our dishes he chose moules marinieres and tournedos Rossini for himself then asked for his choice of Burgundy and two bottles of Moët et Chandon. I thought 'wow… no expense spared tonight!'

All through the meal he chatted about his love of art and the success of his father's gallery in Monaco. He made several enthusiastic comments about Christine's work and I guess she was feeling more secure at herself appointed number one position in the queue with every smile and compliment from Michel.

It was very interesting to listen to him and hear his opinions of the art world and his obvious disgust at speculators who bought great masterpieces for investment and hid them in Bank vaults rather than for the appreciation and love of the work.

The first two courses of the meal were absolutely fabulous and I was delighted with my truffles and the steak melted in my mouth. The rich red Burgundy was smooth and I was beginning to feel a bit squiffy when the first Champagne bottle was taken from the ice bucket and opened by the wine waiter with a flourish. After the Champagne fizzed in the high flutes Michel raised his glass and said 'here's to art and every beautiful woman who has posed for a talented artist!' He looked at Christine who smiled and then he winked at me! My expectations rose as I realised that he probably had more than a soft spot for me.

When we had drunk the Champagne the waiter re-filled our glasses and Michel said 'now I have something to tell you my English beauties' and I thought 'whatever next?'

'On Saturday evening we are holding a private viewing of new paintings for a few select clients... and as Christine has guaranteed that your picture will be finished by then, it will be shown and you are invited to the gallery!' I thought 'oh... my... God' and looked at Jane who just sat wide eyed with her mouth open.

'That's wonderful... thank you so much, Michel' I said in my best grateful, sexy, whispered tone.

'Bon... I have already arranged with Christine to bring you and the painting on Saturday afternoon. After the viewing you will all stay at my villa for the night... it is too far for you to drive back to Grambois' said Michel and my eyes lit up at the prospect of this exciting new world opening before us. 'Where will it all end?' I wondered.

'But we're due to fly home on Sunday' said Jane.

'We can catch a later flight' I said firmly, as I did not intend to miss this opportunity to rub shoulders with the rich and famous of Monaco.

'Très bien... now what will you have for dessert?' Michel asked as he looked at me and smiled.

After struggling through a sorbet followed by cheese and the second bottle of Champagne I was now ready for anything. However, the evening finished quietly with Michel driving us back to Grambois and escorting us to our door.

'Bon nuit, ma petites, I look forward to seeing you on Saturday at the gallery' he said before he kissed us on both cheeks. I noticed he lingered a little longer when he kissed me!

'Bon nuit' I whispered then added 'and thank you so much, Michel... for everything.' He smiled and then Christine quickly wished us 'bon nuit' before she went inside her house with him. As I opened our front door I thought 'lucky Christine... she's obviously making sure that she keeps her position at the front of the queue... and who could blame her?' I think she realised that I was also now in the queue and possibly quite serious competition for her. Only time would tell but I was determined to make the best of any opportunity that came my way to get closer to Michel. He was gorgeous, available and rich... the prefect triple combination that every girl looks for in a man!

Jane made some tea and we sat on the sofa and talked about the evening with the handsome one.

'I really can't believe this happening to us' said Jane.

'Neither can I' I replied.

'This is turning out to be the best holiday I've ever had!' she said and I suddenly felt sad as the memory of my best holiday was in Paris with Tony. Then I thought of Eric... perhaps he would arrive and make my stay in Grambois the best holiday ever if he managed to guide Michel to me... then on the other hand... perhaps he wouldn't.

CHAPTER 6

ERIC IS SUCH A DISTRACTION

We lay in bed the next morning until nearly ten o'clock before dragging ourselves into the kitchen. Jane made the coffee and we said very little as we tried to clear our heads from the excesses of dinner with Michel.

'We planned to go shopping in Aix today... but I'm not sure I want to go now' said Jane.

'We'll feel better soon... besides we don't want to miss the opportunity to buy something that will knock 'em dead on Saturday... just remember we've nothing to wear' I said slowly before finishing my coffee.

'I suppose you're right' she murmured.

'You know I am... I can't be seen in my white halter again and you don't want to have to wear your blue dress... whatever would Michel think?' I said. Her face brightened up and she smiled then said 'let's have some more coffee.'

We left Grambois at about half past eleven and drove to the centre of Aix where we parked the Fiat in the tree lined Cours Mirabeau, where all the elegant shops are situated. We were spoilt for choice so we decided to start at one end of the Boulevard and work our way up to the square, which was dominated by an enormous fountain, then down the other side.

I had a good feeling as we walked into the first shop - we were confronted with rows of dresses all tastefully laid out on racks or displayed on mannequins. We started looking whilst the assistants hovered at a distance, watching our every move. I found a lovely red dress that I thought would fit me and when I looked at the nearest assistant she rushed forward and said something.

'Je suis Anglais' I said slowly and she smiled then replied 'would you like to try it on, Madame?'

These French are so damned clever... I bet there aren't many shop assistants in England who can speak French... and these days you're lucky if you can find one in London that speaks English!

I tried it on in the fitting cubicle with Jane looking closely and passing unnecessary comments.

'It makes your hips look fat' she said.

'I do like it though… but does it make my bum look big?'

'No… only your hips' she replied.

'Does the colour suit me?' I asked turning one way then the other as I gazed into the mirror trying to see if my hips looked too big. I decided they didn't so Jane was quite wrong about that and I felt relieved. I bought the dress whilst Jane carried on searching for something special to wear. She found nothing that caught her eye so we left and moved on to the next shop. There she found a white, lacy little number that suited her and fitted well.

'You look fantastic in that' I said.

'Are you sure?'

'Of course I am… so all we need to do now is find the right accessories' I replied.

Three doors along was an elegant shoe shop so we marched in fully expecting to buy the right shoes but we were disappointed because even the cheapest were far too expensive for us. The quality was superb but far beyond what we could afford… who says money doesn't make you happy? Having no money makes you miserable, especially when you're out shopping, that's for sure. I would have been delighted to have bought a couple of pairs of shoes in that elegant shop.

We walked further along and found a small shoe shop, which displayed quite modestly priced shoes in the window. We went in and were pleasantly surprised by the quality, so we each bought a pair of high heeled shoes. I had a black pair, peeped toe, with velvet bows, which fitted well and were comfortable and Jane bought a red pair. Then I noticed several handbags hanging on a corner display. I found a little black leather clutch with a velvet bow similar to my shoes so didn't hesitate to buy it. Jane found a larger red bag and bought that. The young sales assistant spoke good English and was very helpful so I decided that if I had any money left at the end of the holiday I would come back and buy another pair of shoes that I quite fancied. Outside the shop I told Jane and she said that she would do the same. Having had a good session of retail therapy we were now hungry and looked for somewhere to have lunch.

We found a lovely little bar near the square and sat outside at a glass topped table with a large umbrella to keep us from the sun. The ornate fountain in the square gushed cool water and gave a soothing, splashing sound when it dropped back into the surrounding pool. This place was another heaven and feeling very relaxed I thought 'what would it be like to live here permanently?' Then my mind raced with exciting ideas.

The snack menu listed baguettes with various fillings and when the waiter appeared, Jane ordered two coffees and then pointed at baguettes with ham and cheese as her French only runs to 'deux cafes.' The waiter nodded, smiled and hurried away before returning quickly with our lunches.

'Shall we go to the beach this afternoon?' I asked before biting into my baguette.

'Why not... I think we need to top up our tans for Saturday night, don't you?'

'It makes sense.'

'D'you think Christine will want us to pose again?' Jane asked.

'She said that she would, but after painting our faces I doubt it, as I'm sure she'll remember what the rest looks like' I replied.

'Good... I don't want to waste any time posing when we could be on the beach' she said.

'A week down here is just not long enough' I said.

'No... we'll have to stay much longer next time.'

'I've a feeling that if our painting is a success we might get invited to stay in Monaco for awhile' I said with a smile.

'What about getting back to work?' she asked seriously.

'Bugger work, Jane... we could have a chance to change our lives completely!'

'I'm not sure I want to do that at the moment' she said.

'Listen... I've been thinking... what have we got at home that's so important?' I said.

'Well...'

'Little or next to nothing' I interrupted.

'But Clare...'

'I've got a lousy husband, a demented Mother, a stalker and a knicker sniffing pratt who's after me and all you've got is some failed author hanging around you called Rupert... what a name that is... and a flat that's too big for you, plus a boring job that's worse than mine' I said in my firm know-it-all tone.

'I know I'm a bit of a failure' she said with a sigh before looking down at her coffee.

'No you're not... you're my friend and I think you're a lovely, clever person with everything going for you, which I know is wasted in Romford.'

'Oh Clare...'

'But here you're appreciated by an artist and a good looking, rich Frenchman!'

She smiled and said 'yes he certainly is... and he's seen me naked... well not literally... not yet anyway!'

'There you are... we could have a wonderful future down here by selling Christine's paintings of us' I said enthusiastically.

'Do you really think that we could live here always?'

'Well Christine makes a living so why shouldn't we?'

'I suppose it's possible.'

'And if Frank would let us stay in the house for most of the year...' I said.

'We could pay him just a little rent.' Jane interrupted.

'We'd be sort of 'house sitters' looking after the place for him' I said.

'I'm sure he'd say 'yes'... oh... but where would we go when he and Grace come down on holiday?'

'We'd ask Christine if we could stay with her, or better still... ask Michel if he knows somewhere in Monaco...'

'Like his villa' she interrupted brightly.

'Exactly!'

'Oh you're so clever Clare you really are!'

'I know... let's go to Cassis and soak up this sun... we want to look good on Saturday... you never who we'll meet!' I said enthusiastically and thought 'I know Jane has ideas about her second position in the queue and although she is my best friend I have to put what I want first. I've already met the man who's going to be my second husband and his rich father owns an art gallery in Monaco... how perfect is that? So Jane, I'm sorry to disappoint you... but I'm sure you'll get over it and if you like, you can be my maid of honour... once again.'

We chatted excitedly about our future all the way to Cassis and parked the Fiat in the half empty car park near the harbour. We were soon at our spot on the beach and well covered with factor 15. We lay for awhile, turning like sausages to maximise the sun all over, then went into the clear, cool water and swam for some time. When we were too hot and had enough, we went to the bar and sat under the shade drinking sparkling water.

Back in Grambois we showered together and examined each other's improving tan. We were having a cup of tea when Christine knocked at the door and asked us to pose again.

'It will be the last time and will not be for long, ma petites' she said. I was keen to see how the painting had progressed so we hurriedly slipped on some clothes and followed her up to her studio.

She had painted in a background of small waterfalls and beautiful overhanging trees, which were in full blossom. Jane was sitting on a large boulder in the midst of a clear pool of water with me posed behind looking lovingly at her as she glanced up at the mirror. The whole thing was as impressive as it was spectacular and I was sure that the painting would fetch a fantastic price. We both felt very excited.

'Oh Christine… this is wonderful' I said.

'Bon, I'm glad you like it' she replied with a smile.

'You've made us look really beautiful' said Jane.

'Ah, I have only enhanced what is already there, ma petite' she said.

'Well you've made a good job of it!' I said.

'Très bien… now, come and pose again… I want to look at you carefully for the final details' she said. We were soon naked and in our positions once more. Christine worked quietly at the canvas and occasionally glanced at us with narrowed eyes. It seemed like an age before she said 'Bon… I am content, ma petites, it is now finished!'

'May we look?' I asked.

'Bien sûr.'

I could see only a slight difference in our bodies, my boobs were a little more pronounced and Jane's legs appeared longer.

'It's all really lovely' said Jane.

'Do you think Michel's father will like it?' I asked.

'Oh bien sûre… he adores my paintings and when he meets

you on Saturday I know he will want to buy it for himself' she replied.

'What do you think he'll pay for it?' I asked thinking of our possible lucrative future selling nude paintings.

'I think I will ask for ten thousand Euros' she replied and I was stunned at the amount.

'And if you get it, what will you pay us?' Jane asked as I tried to compose myself.

'Twenty per cent of the price' she replied and I thought at two thousand Euros for each painting we would be living in luxury. Christine was obviously no fool and she had tapped in to a rich source of income with her undoubted talent.

'Let's hope he agrees the price' I said.

'I think he will' said Christine and I felt very pleased when I heard that.

'I can't wait for Saturday' said Jane.

'It will be very good, ma petites, Antoine only invites his very richest clients to these private shows and I promise you that we will drink the best Champagne as we tell them all about ourselves' said Christine.

'How wonderful' I gasped because I am my favourite subject to talk about especially when in rich company. I wondered if any of the women from Michel's queue would be there because it would be interesting to see my competition.

'Now, you must enjoy the rest of your vacance and I will finish off some more details in the painting. If I don't see you before, be ready to go at three o'clock on Saturday, as it is quite a long drive to Monaco' she said.

'Oh we'll be ready alright!' I said.

'We wouldn't miss this for the world!' said Jane.

'Très bien, ma petites' she said with a smile, then added 'and bring your Bikini's... Michel has got a large pool at his villa and you'll want to swim on Sunday.'

We nodded and I thought 'this just gets better and better!'

Jane cooked spaghetti Bolognese for dinner... well it wasn't actually a Bolognese, just some spaghetti with Sainsbury's tinned tomatoes on top. Still, we enjoyed it and finished the meal with various cheeses, and of course plenty of wine. We went to bed happy and quite squiffy after planning our devastating social attack on the rich and famous of Monaco.

I struggled out of bed the next morning with a thumping head and decided to cut down on my drinking before our trip on Saturday, which was now only a few days away! Jane was already in the kitchen and had made some coffee... and after gently sitting at the table I added extra sugar to help my aching head.

'What are we going to do today?' she asked slowly.

'I've no idea... go to the beach I suppose' I replied between sips.

'The way I feel at the moment I think we'd best leave it until later' said Jane.

'Yes... I agree.'

We sat in silence for awhile nursing our hangovers before someone knocked at the door.

'Who the hell can that be?' asked Jane impatiently.

'No idea... but you can go this time' I replied.

'I can't... I look awful!'

'I do too!'

'No you don't.'

'Oh bloody hell...' I mumbled before dragging myself up from the table.

When I opened the door I was surprised to see Pierre standing there smiling at me.

'Bonjour, Clare' he said and I just nodded before stuttering 'Pierre! How... how...'

'Did I find you?' he asked and I nodded again.

'It was easy, I just went to the bar and asked where the two English girls were staying and they told me... everybody knows everything in a small village like this... they call this house 'Maison Anglais'' he said with a laugh.

'Well... come in, come in!' I said as Jane called out 'who is it?'

'Pierre' I shouted back before I led him into the kitchen where Jane stood open mouthed.

'Bonjour, Jane.'

'Oh, Pierre...' she sighed and I was glad because his arrival meant that she would soon be distracted from Michel.

'I had to see you again' he said.

'Oh, I'm so glad that you found us' said Jane.

'It was easy' he replied with a smile.

'Would you like some coffee?' she asked.

'Bien sûr' he replied and sat at the table.

'You must excuse us… we weren't expecting any company this morning' I said and he smiled.

'Yes, I'm sorry if we look a bit of a mess' said Jane as she made his coffee.

'Mais non… you look lovely as always' he said and I thought 'oh bless you… keep this up and she'll soon be totally smitten!'

'We do try to look good, we've been swimming at Cassis and working on our tan' said Jane as she placed his coffee on the table.

'Ah, that's a lovely place and I can see that you've both caught the sun' he said with a smile.

'So what brings you here?' asked Jane as she sat opposite him and I winced because she can be so obvious sometimes.

'Why, you of course' he replied and she lowered her head slightly and smiled. I thought 'you dopey cow!'

'That's nice' she whispered.

'And I thought that if you're not doing anything this morning, we could go for a walk around the village and stop for a drink at the bar' said Pierre.

'That would be lovely' she said.

'You don't mind do you, Clare?' he asked.

'No not at all… I've got things to do, so you two go ahead' I replied and they both smiled.

Twenty minutes later, Jane had tidied herself up and they left the house. I made myself some more coffee and found several croissants in the fridge, which I smothered with honey. I had just finished eating the first one and was licking my sticky fingers when there was another knock at the door. I thought 'that's Christine with a change to the arrangements for Saturday… I hope everything is alright.' I went to open the door but it wasn't her standing there... it was Eric!

'Good God! What are you doing here?' I asked in surprise.

'I've come to see you as I said I would' he replied.

'Well I don't think I want to see you!'

'But you must, Clare, I've some important things to tell you' he said with a disarming smile.

'Like what?'

'I want to tell you about the man who you will eventually marry' he replied which got my immediate attention... well, it would wouldn't it? I mean if your handsome, so called guardian angel is about to tell you what you already know, it is comforting... I mean that's what they are there for... isn't it?

'Then you'd better come in' I said and stood back for him to enter. I led him through to the lounge and he sat on the sofa whilst I parked myself on a chair opposite and tried not to touch anything with my sticky fingers.

He smiled at me and said 'now you have already met the man who will be the love of your life...'

'Oh I know' I interrupted.

'That is good, but it is important that you approach him carefully, so whatever you do, don't put him off with your...' he paused before he continued 'your difficult behaviour.'

'What!' I shrieked.

'Your...'

'I'm not difficult... just ask Jane or anybody... Christine next door!' I interrupted.

'Clare...'

'I'm the easiest person you'll ever meet!'

'Clare you must not be so hasty all the time' he said calmly, but I wasn't calm.

'I think you're unbelievable... you say you're my angel but all you ever do is upset me... I don't think that is very angelic do you?'

'Listen to me...'

'I think you're telling me a load of bollocks all the time!' I said angrily and he sighed then gently shook his head.

'Oh Clare... you have free will to think and do what you wish, but you do seem to have more free will than most women... and it does make my task very difficult' he said.

'Well, bloody hard luck!'

'I can see that I'm wasting my time with you at the moment so perhaps I had better leave everything until you are a little more settled, then we can talk again' he said and suddenly my curiosity was aroused.

'Well... now you're here don't you think you should tell me what it is?' I asked.

'Are you sure you want to know?'

'Yes' I nodded.

'And you won't get angry?'

'No... I promise' I replied and he nodded gently then said 'alright.'

I waited impatiently as he gathered his thoughts and wondered if I had time to go and wash my sticky fingers.

'You have met the man who will be the only one for you...'

'I know' I interrupted and he sighed.

'Will you just be quiet for a moment and listen?' he demanded so I smiled and zipped my lips.

'Good... now this person is not who you think he is...' he began but was interrupted by a knock at the door. I thought 'now who the hell is that?'

'Excuse me' I said and made my way to the kitchen to rinse my fingers then to the front door. It was Christine.

'Bonjour, Clare.'

'Bonjour.'

'There is a change to the arrangements for Saturday' she began and I thought 'oh bloody hell... it's all been cancelled... I thought it was too good to be true.'

'Oh?' I said in a disappointed tone.

'Oui, Michel has just phoned me and asked if we can join him for lunch at his villa, so we'll need to leave by nine o'clock on Saturday morning, can you be ready by then?' she said.

'Oh yes, don't worry about us... we'll be ready alright!' I replied with a big smile as my emotions roller-coasted skywards. So I was now to have lunch with my handsome, rich, husband-to-be at his villa... how cool is that?

'Très bien... we'll be going in my car and remember to bring your overnight things' she said.

'I'll remember' I replied.

'Bon... see you on Saturday, ma petite.'

When I went back into the lounge Eric was standing and he looked down at me then said 'this is no longer a good time to talk so I will leave you now and we'll meet again soon.'

'Well that's a disappointment... can't you tell me something?'

'Not really, we need time together, Clare.'

'You've only got a few days because I may be going home on Sunday' I said.

'Yes, possibly... but you'll have to wait and see what happens' he said with a smile before he made his way to the front door. I thought 'he knows that I'll be staying in Monaco' and I felt quite excited.

'I'll see you later then' I called out from the doorway and he raised his hand without looking back as he strode towards the square.

It was almost lunchtime when Jane and Pierre arrived looking suitably happy with themselves. I guessed that love was definitely in the air... which suited me down to the ground. After Jane had told me all about their trip around the village she asked in her curious tone 'was Eric here?'

'Yes, he was' I replied.

'I thought I saw him in the square... so do tell, what did he want?'

'Just to talk to me' I replied lamely.

'About what?'

I glared at Jane and ignoring her question asked Pierre 'are you going to stay and have lunch with us?'

'Oui merci, that would be very nice' he replied.

'We've not got a lot but I'm sure we can rustle up something' I said.

'Anything would be good' he said with a smile.

I cooked mixed cheese omelettes, which Pierre said were 'unusually different' but very tasty, and we washed them down with two bottles of Frank's wine. After lunch we sat in the lounge talking about our painting and the trip to Monaco, whilst drinking tea and eating biscuits. I managed to steer the conversation away from Eric's visit every time Jane attempted to bring it up and I was getting a little angry with her when Pierre came to my rescue.

'I've invited Jane to have dinner in Aix tonight' he said.

'Oh lovely' I enthused.

'Yes, I told Pierre about the 'Moulin Bleu' and he's taking me there' said Jane with a big smile.

'That's wonderful' I said and thought 'this cosy affair could be really going places and soon she'll forget about Michel as well as Rupert... thank God!... I've never trusted men with beards.'

Pierre left soon afterwards saying he was going to see a college friend in Aix and he'd be back at seven to pick up Jane.

'Isn't he just fabulous?' said Jane when we were alone.

'He is.'

'He's so, so charming, and attentive, he seems to know just what I want all the time' she said with a sigh.

'That's wonderful... now you must look your best so I suggest that you get started now' I said.

'Oh yes... I'll wear my new white dress tonight... that should please him' she said.

'I'm sure it will.'

'It would be really fantastic if we could stay here... and...'

'And you could marry Pierre' I interrupted.

'Oh Clare... you've read my mind.'

'It was easy because I know you so well' I said with a smile and thought 'this is going much better than expected!'

By the time Pierre called for Jane at seven she looked absolutely gorgeous. Her white dress showed off her tan and her makeup and hair were just so. Pierre looked totally blown away when he saw her and he kissed her on the lips.

'Mon Dieu! You are so beautiful' he whispered as she blushed, fluttered her eyelashes and whispered 'thank you' and I thought 'it's nearly leg over time!'

I spent the evening watching the television and luckily, after channel hopping every ten minutes, found a film in English with French sub titles, that was different!

I made sure that I was in my room before the lovers returned, just in case Jane decided to ask Pierre to stay the night. I mean I didn't want to embarrass them... it is so much easier to meet someone new at the breakfast table, don't you think?

I was just dozing off when I heard them come in but I fell

asleep soon after. The next thing I remember was waking up to hear Jane busy in the kitchen. I got up, dressed, in case Pierre was there and went through. Jane was alone but smiling, like a contented cat that's been at the cream.

'Well?' I asked.

'I had a wonderful night with him' she said with a sigh.

'So where is he now?' I asked.

'He went home' she replied.

'And?'

'He's just wonderful... he stayed until after two...' she sighed.

'And did you?' I persisted.

'Need you ask?' she smiled.

'No not really... so when are you seeing him again?'

'He's taking me out for the whole day tomorrow' she replied.

'That's fantastic... now I think I need some coffee.'

Jane said that she wanted to go shopping in Aix again, which suited me, and after breakfast we set off for some more retail therapy. She was anxious to buy the shoes that she had seen previously and her attitude now was 'hang the expense because I've got to look good for Pierre.' And who could blame her? I mean to say, he's a very good looking man and provided he didn't have any wives or serious girl friends in tow he certainly was a suitable catch for Jane. I didn't bother to ask her what he did for a living but I suppose it doesn't matter as long as they're happy together and have enough money to live on. If my plans work out the way I expect, then money will not be a problem for either of us in the future.

Jane parked the Fiat in Cours Mirabeau and we went immediately to the little shoe shop where she bought the pretty, delicate high heels. We stopped for coffee at the bar before wandering along to look around the myriad of shops lining the narrow streets off the Boulevard in the centre of Aix. I was really beginning to enjoy being in France because the attitude to life is very different to England. They really appear to enjoy their lives, I suppose that's because the weather is so good. The French seem to live outdoors where we live in, hunched over our television sets all the time, whilst eating too much fatty food! At lunchtime we found a bar and sat outside under a sun shade and ordered coffee and baguettes full of cheeses.

It was mid-afternoon when we arrived back at Grambois so we decided to sit at the bar in the square, have some more coffee and admire the view. We talked about the trip to Monaco and lunch with Michel at his villa before the gallery viewing. I began to think that we were becoming very French all of a sudden and my problems at home seemed far away. I thought briefly about Tony, Mother, Tina, Wilkes and pratt Hammond and I didn't care if I never saw any of them again. I was pleased that Eric had confirmed my new husband to me and I was now mentally preparing myself for a life of luxury in Monaco. What an experience to go shopping there with all the boutiques catering for some of the richest people on earth. Dear God… life is so good and I intend to enjoy every moment of it from now on. I thought that my past troubles and unhappiness were all behind me now.

The next morning we got up early and had breakfast before Jane went off to prepare herself for the day out with Pierre. When she was ready she looked cool and quite lovely. I knew that she was really in love with this handsome Frenchman and of course it suited my plans for us to stay in France.

Pierre arrived at ten and I said to Jane as they left the house 'don't be too late this evening… we've an early start in the morning.'

'Don't worry, I'll be back' she replied with a smile as she took Pierre's hand and they wandered off towards the square.

I planned to go to Cassis to top up my tan to an 'all-over perfect golden glow' for Saturday. I was sure that Michel would find me absolutely irresistible… it's so lovely to be beautiful.

It was the first time I had driven a left hand drive car and I found it really odd, but I managed in the Fiat and other than a few unnecessary honks from mad, impatient French drivers, I arrived safely in Cassis. The Mediterranean looked as inviting as ever and I laid out my towel on the warm sand. I covered myself in lotion and lay on my back listening to the sound of the sea. I decided that I would only lay face down for ten minutes at a time as I couldn't cover my back with oil and certainly didn't want to burn. I had just turned over for the first time and closed my eyes when I was aware of somebody standing close to me.

'Hello Clare.'

I recognised the clipped tones and didn't bother to open my eyes.

'You're just in time, Eric' I said.

'For what?' he asked.

'To rub sun cream on my back' I replied.

'I'm not supposed to do that' he said.

'Why not?'

'I'm forbidden to touch you.'

'Why? Are you going to melt or something?'

'No… but…'

'Or is the Archangel going to strike you down if you touch me?' I giggled.

'No, of course not but…'

'You're a dead loss, Eric, do you know that?' I asked as I opened my eyes, raised my head up from the towel and looked at him.

'I hope not' he replied with a smile, as he sat down beside me.

He stripped off his white shirt and I was impressed with his tanned, muscular body and his 'six pack' was very pronounced. I noticed that he was covered in fine blonde hair and suddenly I was quite attracted to this strange man with the sparkling blue eyes.

'So… are you going to oil me or not?' I asked with a smile.

'If you wish' he replied with a grin.

'I wish… there's the bottle' I said pointing at it.

I laid my head on my towel, closed my eyes and waited. Then I felt drops of warm oil falling on my back followed by such a gentle pressure as his hands slowly massaged the oil into me. This was truly heaven and I thought that if the laying on of hands could really heal sick people then he would be a fantastic healer and I would certainly be a hopeless hypochondriac.

After several wonderful relaxing minutes he asked 'is that enough?'

'No… I think you've missed a bit' I lied.

'Where?'

'I'm not sure, so you'd better do it all over again… just in case… I don't want to burn you know' I said firmly.

'No, of course not' he said before repeating the process and sending me into heaven once more. After about five minutes of gentle massage he said 'I think that's enough now.'

'Are you sure?'

'Absolutely.'

'So now I suppose you want to talk to me seriously?' I asked.

'Yes I do, but I only offer you guidance for your future happiness…'

'No need to bother, I'm happy and I've got everything well sorted out, thank you' I interrupted with a grin.

'You may think so…'

'I know so, Eric, believe me' I interrupted and I heard him sigh above the sound of the waves breaking on the shore.

'Clare, you are too hasty…'

'That's what you think, but I know what I'm doing and for once I am very happy with my life' I said.

'Clare…'

'How about rubbing some oil into my legs?'

'I don't think so…'

'Oh go on, I'm sure that the Archangel isn't looking and if he is, I am sure he won't mind' I said with a laugh.

'You trouble me deeply' he said with a sigh then I heard him pick up the oil and I waited for the drops to fall. He oiled one leg at a time and gently rubbed the lotion from my ankles right up to my bum. This was absolute heaven and I didn't care about anything for the moment as I soaked up the sun in this paradise.

'Now I've done what you have asked so will you please listen to me?' he said firmly. I do like a man who is firm.

'Yes' I murmured.

'Good…'

'Providing that you don't go on for too long' I said with a grin.

'Clare…'

'Because it's getting too hot to listen' I said then there was a prolonged silence so I opened my eyes and glanced at him. He was gazing out to sea with a faraway look and I waited for a few moments then said 'well?'

He looked down at me and replied 'I'm afraid that you will experience some disappointments if you choose to take the wrong path now.'

'Like what for instance?'

'You must return to England where your future happiness lies…'

'Oh no, it doesn't!' I interrupted.

'Clare…'

'D'you know something, Eric… you're very good at rubbing oil and popping up un-expectedly but…'

'Listen! You will be very unhappy if you stay in France' he said firmly and I believed him for a moment because he really sounded quite sincere. However, I have to look after myself and just knew that I would be very happy with Michel in Monaco.

I said 'I know you mean well, whoever or whatever you are, but I have to make my own choices in life the way I see them, so you'll just have to write me off as a hopeless case and go and guide some other poor soul.'

'Clare you are very difficult…'

'So you keep saying' I interrupted.

'I'm only trying to guide you…'

'Well I'm getting too hot now so I suggest you guide me to the bar and buy me a drink!'

'I don't carry any money' he said.

'Typical!' I murmured as I sat up.

Eric refused a drink so I bought myself a sparkling water at the beach bar and we sat in the shade looking out at the glistening blue Mediterranean. When I had finished my drink he gazed at me for some moments before he said 'you are a very beautiful woman and I would have taken you for my wife in my earthly life, if you were not so difficult…'

'There you go again!'

'But I will leave now and not bother you until I think you need me again' he said with a smile.

'Well goodbye and I don't think I'll need any more of your guidance because I know exactly what I'm doing' I said.

'I hope you do, Clare.'

'Oh, believe me I do.'

'Then I will just watch over you and make sure that you come to no harm' he said with a smile.

'Thanks, but you needn't bother.'

'It is my duty' he said as he stood up and walked away.

I was confused for a few minutes but I cleared my mind and thought of the trip to Monaco in the morning and lunch with Michel, followed by the viewing at his gallery in the evening. I drove the Fiat at speed back to Grambois and begin getting ready for the exciting weekend ahead.

CHAPTER 7

CLARE MEETS THE COUNTESS

On Saturday morning we were both up just after six, sipping coffee, eating croissants and having showers followed by full facial 'slap' application. By nine we were dressed and ready to go with our overnight bags packed.

'God, this is exciting' I said as Jane knocked at Christine's door.

'I think Pierre's a bit jealous' said Jane.

'He'll get over it' I said as Christine opened the door.

'Bonjour, ma petites, come in a minute, I'm almost ready.'

We followed her into the lounge where two pictures were wrapped in brown paper and propped against the sofa.

'I've decided to take my portrait to show Antoine… Michel has seen it and thinks his father would be interested' said Christine and I thought 'I bet he would.'

'Are you going to sell it?' asked Jane.

'Oui.'

'How much will you ask?'

'Oh… I'm not sure yet… perhaps ten thousand Euros' she replied. If this clever woman managed to sell both paintings she would end up with eighteen thousand Euros after paying us our fee. Not bad for a few days work followed by a weekend away in Monaco living in luxury!

'I'll just get my case then we'll go… perhaps you will carry the paintings to the car for me?' she asked.

Within minutes we were heading for the square where Christine's Renault Estate car was parked. We loaded the paintings carefully into the back, along with our bags, and I sat in the front with her. She drove quickly down the familiar route to Pertuis and then to Aix before joining the autoroute that would take us past the turn off to Cassis and on to Monaco. As we sped along in the sun, the names of all the famous places on the Riviera appeared on the overhead signs, Toulon, followed by St. Tropez, Cannes, where we stopped for a coffee at a service station, and on to Nice.   It seemed an age before the sign for Monaco appeared but when it did I felt a tingle in my spine. My life was about to change for the better and soon Tony and all the other annoying things that caused me tears and sleepless nights would be gone forever. From now on it was all going to be Champagne parties with the rich and shopping in expensive boutiques. It just shows what a holiday can do for you when you're down... it completely changes your outlook on the future!

I glanced at my watch and saw it was almost midday when we left the autoroute and reached the outskirts of Monaco. We would arrive at his villa in time for lunch with Michel and I just knew it would be fantastic. The villa had a pool and I wondered how big it was... and would we have lunch on a patio with a view of the sea?

Christine turned left off the Route Nationale and on to a minor road that led uphill.

'Michel's villa is high up and has a wonderful view of the harbour' said Christine as she skilfully drove the car round several sharp bends. As we climbed higher I looked at the town and harbour below with all the luxury yachts at their moorings, glistening in the sun. Within minutes Christine slowed the car and turned in through open gates to Michel's villa. Well... it was absolutely fantastic! I could not believe my eyes and just kept staring at the elegant biscuit coloured villa at the end of the drive with its open green shutters and white pillared entrance. Christine pulled up outside and a woman came out to meet us. As we climbed out of the Renault she spoke to Christine who smiled, nodded and opened the back of the car to give our bags to the woman. We helped Christine carry the paintings into the cool interior as Michel appeared in the spacious hallway.

'Bonjour ma petites, bonjour' he said with a smile before he embraced Christine and kissed her on both cheeks for a little too long I thought... which I didn't like for one moment. Then he kissed Jane before it was my turn and I was disappointed as I seemed to get the same quick kisses as Jane. However, he did look at my revealing low cut, red dress and gave it a second glance, which pleased me.

'Let me take the paintings, Christine and I'll look at them after lunch before Papa arrives' said Michel with a smile.

'Of course' she replied as he took them from her before propping them side by side against the hall table.

'Do come through' he said and we followed him through a large, elegantly furnished room to the far end, which led out onto a patio. The first thing that struck me was the fantastic view of the harbour and the blue sea beyond.

'Oh Michel, this is absolutely wonderful' I said and Jane nodded.

'Oui, it is and I know I'm very lucky to live here' he said as he joined us at the wrought iron railings that surrounded the raised patio. I glanced down at the shaped pool, set amongst a beautifully laid out garden, before gazing at him and thinking 'if I play my cards right all this could be mine.'

'Now what would you all like to drink?' he asked.

We told him and once he had poured our drinks he invited us to sit at the table at the end of the patio under the shade of an awning. The cutlery gleamed on the white tablecloth and the wine glasses sparkled in the bright light.

'Here's to you beautiful women who make art the very servant of your beauty' he said as he raised his glass. Was he a romantic or what? I melted as he smiled at each of us and I thought he lingered a little longer when he looked at me. We raised our glasses and just smiled back at this handsome Frenchman before sipping our drinks.

'Papa will arrive at about three to meet you and view the paintings then he will take them back to the gallery for display this evening' he said with a smile.

'I do hope he likes our portrait' I said.

'Oh I'm sure he will' he replied as the woman appeared carrying a silver tray with our starters.

'I have chosen a light lunch and hope you approve' Michel said as she served the first course of egg mayonnaise. Michel poured a rose wine into our glasses as he wished us 'bon appetite.' I knew the food would be delicious and so it was. Jane and I ate quietly as we listened to Christine chatting to him about her next painting.

'I will get Evette to pose as Joan of Arc laying almost naked amongst a table full of food... she will be partly dressed in some small pieces of armour but her breast plate will be on the floor...

it's as if she had just come from the battle at Crecy and was too tired to eat... I will call it 'The weary Maid of Orleans'.

'That will be very poignant picture which will touch the hearts of all true Frenchmen' said Michel in a serious tone.

'Do you think you'll find a buyer for it?' she asked.

'Bien sûr' he nodded and I thought 'she's a clever one, selling her work before she's even painted it.'

The main course was a light prawn salad with everything in it and covered with a delicious mayonnaise sauce. Michel poured more wine and I tried to be good, sipping it slowly and drinking just a little, but I failed and soon felt a bit squiffy. We had soft ice cream topped with chocolate chips for dessert, followed by coffee. I had several cups in an attempt to sober myself up for the evening. We had only just finished lunch when Antoine arrived. He was an older, elegant version of his handsome son and smiled when Michel introduced us to him.

'So don't keep me waiting any longer, Michel, let me see Christine's painting of these two petites Anglais' said Antoine.

'Be patient, Papa, I've not had a chance to see the finished paintings myself!' replied Michel.

When Michel unwrapped the paintings Antoine just stared open mouthed at them and we waited for his comments. It seemed an age before he said in a whisper 'c'est magnifique, ma petites.' Christine smiled and Jane looked at me then winked. We knew that our two thousand Euros was as good as ours... so that's the holiday paid for and more shopping in Aix then!

Michel helped his father carry the paintings to his Mercedes limousine and after they were placed safely in the boot, Antoine kissed us and told Michel to be at the gallery by seven thirty for the Champagne reception. We stood in the sun waving to Antoine as he pulled away in the Mercedes and I suddenly felt the need to lie down... the wine had really got to me.

'Gabrielle will show you to your room' said Michel when I said I wanted to rest.

We were shown up to a bright, spacious double room with a large ensuite bathroom.

'This is too good to be true' said Jane as I slipped off my dress and flopped down on the bed whilst she went into the ensuite to look at all the soaps and perfumes.

I fell asleep and woke up to hear Jane singing and splashing away in the shower. I lay still for a moment gathering my thoughts then glanced at my watch… it was almost six o'clock. I struggled up, found my overnight bag and searched for my makeup.

An hour later we had just about finished getting ready when there was a knock at the door and Gabrielle came in with some tea on a tray.

'Monsieur Michel says that you need to be ready to leave in fifteen minutes' she said.

'We'll be ready' replied Jane and Gabrielle nodded and left after putting the tray on a small table. We drank the tea, checked ourselves for the last time in the full length mirror and agreed we looked good before going downstairs. Michel was waiting with Christine in the lounge and he looked absolutely fabulous in a white Tuxedo with a frilly dress shirt and big bow tie, she was wearing a slinky black dress that accentuated her figure and showed off her deep tan. Around her neck was a black velvet choker with a large glittering diamond stud, which matched her ear-rings. She looked very sophisticated and I knew I had stiff competition if I wanted to take her place at the head of the queue. Michel kissed us both, told us that we looked stunningly beautiful and wished us all a wonderful evening… oh, how I do love all this romantic fuss.

Michel drove his Mercedes at speed to the 'Gallerie Duprey' in the Boulevard de Mimosa, just off Casino Square and parked in his space in the private courtyard behind the gallery.

I was quite overawed when we went into the viewing room. Our picture was in pride of place and lit from above by a spotlight. It looked stunning and several couples were gazing at it and talking loudly as a waitress toured around offering flutes of Champagne whilst another wandered about carrying a large silver platter of canapés. I thought 'this is the way to live… so bugger Romford and everything connected to it!' as I took a flute of Champagne when it was offered by the passing waitress.

Christine's nude self portrait was hanging on the adjacent wall and was also lit by a spotlight. It looked as good as ours and several men were peering at it from a distance.

Antoine saw us, broke away from a group of people and said enthusiastically 'bonsoir, ma petites, bonsoir' before he kissed us all.

'Bonsoir' we chorused.

'May I say how fantastic you all look tonight' he said with a big smile.

'Merci Monsieur' I replied, trying to sound sophisticated and hoping to impress my future father-in-law as I sipped Champagne.

'If I were twenty years younger I would have great difficulty in choosing which one of you I would invite to dine with me on my yacht' he said.

'Well you could forget how old you are, Antoine, and invite all three of us' said Christine with a mischievous grin.

'Ah... so true, but what would my other mistresses say when they found out?' he asked with a smile then added 'now come and meet some of my clients.'

We were introduced to several grey haired, tanned men of inestimable age and their much younger women, who all appeared as if they had just stepped out of the Vogue magazine's centrefold as model of the month. Diamonds glittered from necklaces, ear rings and fingers, proving that they are a girl's best friend when all the kissing is finally over.

I was suddenly aware of Michel looking at our picture with a tall blonde who was nodding as he spoke. Antoine noticed my glance and said 'ah, I see the Countess has arrived, let me introduce you, ma petites.'

As I got closer to this blonde I thought she looked like a cross between a transvestite and an old porn star. She was well 'slutted up' with too much thick makeup, overdone blue eye shadow, ruby red lipstick and wrinkles around her neck. She was wearing a diamond necklace that looked like it belonged to the Crown jewels! Her dress was a low cut, blue satin effort, which didn't suit her, and her boobs were almost too big and pointy to be real. She half smiled as Antoine introduced us as his 'petites Anglais' and then announced loudly that she was 'the Countess Nina de Volmaire.'

Jane and I nodded at this creature as she put her arm through Michel's and clung on as if claiming he was hers... I was not happy about that and vowed to scrape this old barnacle off 'my intended' as soon as possible.

'Michel tells me that you are on vacation' she said in a thick accent.

'Yes we are' I replied.

'When are you going back to England?' she asked, looking at me with her piercing grey eyes.

'We're not sure at the moment' I replied.

'Oh, won't your family be concerned?' she asked.

'No not at all' I replied and Jane added 'we have nothing to go back for really... so there's no hurry.'

'I see...' began the old star but I interrupted her and said 'we thought we'd stay for awhile and pose for some more paintings.'

'How nice' she said through clenched teeth and I thought that she must be in the queue and saw us as competition for Michel.

'That would be very good as I'm sure Papa agrees with me that we can sell everything that Christine paints at the moment' said Michel and the old star's face fell.

'Bien sûr... I have already some clients who are collecting Christine's work... and paying good prices for the privilege' said Antoine with a broad smile and the old star's face fell even further. Oh, I love seeing this mental torture of old tarts! And in public too!

'So what do you think of our painting, Countess?' I asked with a grin and watched her struggle to find the right answer in front of Michel and Antoine.

'Well... I, er...'

'Yes?' I interrupted and she blushed, just a little, then suddenly another creature arrived and kissed Michel on his cheek. He looked surprised for a moment and then said with a smile 'ah, bonsoir, Danielle, bonsoir.' She said something in French as I looked at this latest apparition. She was about forty five, with dark hair swept up in a roll, too much makeup on over her well tanned face, stupidly long false eyelashes that she kept fluttering and she was covered in diamonds. She was wearing a white, low cut dress that looked as if she had been poured into it by someone who hadn't the heart or the courage to tell her that she looked ridiculous. She had the same large, pointy boobs as the old star, so I guessed that they must have gone to the same plastic surgeon for their implants.

Danielle totally ignored the old star and just jabbered away to Michel as she clung to his other arm. I looked at Antoine and thought 'is she one of yours by any chance?' He glanced at me as if he knew what I was thinking and saved the situation by suggesting that we circulate and meet some more of his clients.

Jane and I took Antoine's arms and we wandered off like prize young mistresses either side of the man with the money... I was really beginning to enjoy all this and I sipped my Champagne, nodded and smiled at everyone.

Antoine introduced us to Russian multi millionaires with unpronounceable names who had large yachts moored in the harbour and were accompanied by their diamond covered mistresses. We met seriously rich Americans with private jets and holiday homes in Monaco as well as Chinese businessmen with substantial interests in Hong Kong... whatever they might be... and I thought 'best not to ask!'

After a full tour of the gallery looking at all the other paintings on display we stopped in front of Christine's self portrait.

'She not only is an accomplished artist, she's very beautiful... don't you agree, ma petites?' asked Antoine.

'Yes she is' I replied and Jane murmured 'yes.'

'She will make a lovely wife' he said with a sigh and wondered if he had her lined up, which suited me because that would knock her out of the queue for Michel. I wondered how I would get on with Christine as my mother-in-law and thought 'alright I suppose... providing she didn't see Antoine as her fall back husband until she could get her hands on Michel.' I didn't know if Antoine was still married after his earlier comment about his mistresses, so I had to ask.

'And are you free to propose?' I asked as diplomatically as I could. Antoine glared at me for a moment and replied 'ma petite, you don't ask questions like that in France!'

'Oh sorry, I'm sure' I said lamely, realising I had put my foot in it... just like my Mother would... oh dear God help me... I really am turning into her!

I felt blind panic and thought that I should say something but thankfully Michel arrived with the two old crows hanging on his arms and would you believe he had another one hovering close to him.

'Ah, Genevieve, bonsoir, bonsoir, ma petite' said Antoine with a broad smile as this additional creature pushed forward and offered herself for kisses on both cheeks.

'Bonsoir, Antoine, ma cherie' said Genevieve as I looked at her carefully. She was younger than the other two and was an attractive blonde without too much makeup. If she was in the 'Michel queue' she would be serious competition for me. She wore a green dress that fitted nicely and her boobs were obviously all hers, although her low neckline showed a bit too much flesh for my liking. Another inch and you would see her nipples!

'So, Antoine, when are you going to ask Christine to paint me?' she asked with a smile.

'After he's told her to paint me' said the old star and I thought 'God... she'll need to erect scaffolding to hold up your tits and saggy flesh when you get undressed!'

I believe the truth is often cruel.

'Now, now, ma petites, I'm sure that you will all pose for Christine eventually and I'm sure that your portraits will be sold instantly they are displayed in the gallery... there's always a demand for paintings of beautiful mature women' said Antoine which smoothed everyone over very nicely.

'Papa is right of course... you will be invited for sure' said Michel and his father beamed.

'Genevieve, ma petite... I'd like you to come and meet some very special clients' said Antoine as he took her arm and led her away, leaving us looking at Michel and the old crows. Before anybody could say anything Christine arrived with a tall, silver haired man with a deep tan and said 'this is Marcel... and he wants me to paint you two.'

'Us?' I queried.

'Oui, mademoiselle, on my yacht' said Marcel with a broad smile.

'Well, that'll be a new experience' I said with a grin, wondering if I would be sea sick. Then I thought about the money and was sure that I could buy some tablets to cure it.

'You will pose in my studio first then I will paint in the yacht afterwards' said Christine as if she read my mind and Marcel looked a little disappointed. I'm sure he'd like to watch Christine painting us as we posed naked on his yacht... but you can't have everything you want in life. Then Phillipe, the owner of the 'Moulin Bleu', arrived.

'Ah ma petites, bonsoir, bonsoir' he chortled before he kissed us.

'Bonsoir, Phillipe' I said.

'Mon Dieu… you both look fantastic!' he said.

'Merci, Monsieur' I replied.

'And I have some good news for you' said Phillipe.

'Yes?'

'I have just agreed a price with Antoine for your painting' he said and I was completely surprised as I thought that one of the other clients would have made an offer that Antoine couldn't refuse.

'How nice' I said with a smile.

'And I will hang it in the 'Moulin Bleu' for everyone to see' said Phillipe.

'Well I hope that your customers are not put off their meal by all that naked flesh on display' said the old star.

'Non, Countess, I assure you they will not be 'put off'… because the 'Moulin Bleu' is famous for its cuisine and nothing will deter customers from eating in my restaurant' said Phillipe firmly and I wanted to shout 'hip, hip, bloody hooray!'

'So you may believe…' said the old star with a sniff.

'It's what I am certain of Countess… because love and good cuisine go hand in hand, as any romantic person knows and the painting of these two petites represents love' said Phillipe. Oh how I do love the French!

'I'm glad that you came to an arrangement with Papa for the painting, Phillipe… it means I can look at it every time I have dinner at the 'Moulin Bleu'' said Michel with a smile. I thought 'oh goody, goody, he likes to see me naked when he eats!'

By now the old star looked really fed up and started gazing around for someone else to latch onto.

'Ah, there is Ricardo, I must see him about my autumn collection, excusez-moi' she said as she released Michel's arm.

'I hope you'll join us for dinner later, Nina' said Michel and I felt shattered by that.

'But of course, ma Michel' she purred before stepping away to join Ricardo. So, we were going to have to suffer her at the dinner table... and Michel called her 'Nina'... my heart sank.

'Am I invited too?' asked Danielle.

'Bien sûr, ma petite' replied Michel and then I suffered a mini panic attack! Just as I was recovering from the attack, Antoine arrived back with Genevieve.

'Now, ma petites, I have reserved a table at the Casino for dinner and you are all invited' said Antoine with a smile. I tried to get this straight in my mind... did he really mean to take all these old women along with us? I hoped not... but I was wrong... God help me... Please!

After a lot of noisy laughter, back slapping and wishing 'bon nuit' accompanied by kisses from Antoine, all the clients eventually left the gallery. Orders were given to the staff to clear away and lock up before we made our way out into the warm night.

We walked across Casino Square to the famous place where fortunes have been won and lost, we were greeted at the entrance by two smooth looking men in dinner suits who greeted Antoine as if he were a long lost brother. We all trooped behind Antoine to the restaurant, where we were met by the maitre 'd, who, after smiles and little bows, showed us to a table reserved for eight in the middle of the dining room. Antoine sat at the head and Michel sat at the other end whilst Jane, Christine and me faced the old star, Danielle and Genevieve. I was not looking forward to this! I had hoped for an intimate dinner with Michel and Antoine aboard his yacht. At this point I felt as if my emotional roller coaster was rapidly going downhill!

The waiters arrived and passed us menu's before the wine waiter handed a list to Antoine, he chose whilst we wandered through the extensive menu.

Jane whispered to me 'what are you having?'

'I don't know yet, there's so much to choose from' I replied.

'Why don't we have the same as we had at the 'Moulin Bleu'?' she asked.

'That's a good idea' I whispered back and searched for truffles and Chateaubriand. When I found them on the menu I pointed them out to Jane who nodded, then looked at Antoine as he glanced at me and smiled. I gave him our order first and the old ones followed on with various dishes that I wouldn't have liked. The conversation was a bit prickly to begin with but as the wine flowed and we started on the first course, the atmosphere improved. I began to quite enjoy Genevieve's little jokes at the expense of the other two sitting beside her and I noticed that Michel laughed a lot at her comments. The food was absolutely fabulous and our Chateaubriand steaks were so tender they just melted as we ate them. When we had eventually finished the main course the sweet trolley arrived just as the wine waiter opened the first bottle of Champagne with a loud pop. I was spoilt for choice and decided to have a huge slice of chocolate gateaux, which the waiter covered with too much cream.

'You'll be sick' whispered Jane.

'Probably' I whispered back and grinned as the Champagne was poured. When we had our glasses full, Antoine proposed a toast.

'Here's to you all, ma petites, and the appreciation of art by sophisticated people.'

'To us and art' we chorused and then drank the fizzing Champagne.

'And I'm pleased to tell you that tonight the gallery sold almost every painting on show!' announced Antoine.

'Congratulations, Antoine' said Christine then asked 'and who bought mine?'

'Ah, that was not for sale…'

'Why?' interrupted Christine.

'Because I'm keeping that for my private collection' he replied with a smile as he winked at her. I thought 'if he's free, she'll be the next Madame Duprey and if he isn't then she'll be the favourite mistress… that suited me because in any event Christine would be out of the Michel queue and I would only have to worry about the others'.

Coffee and brandy was served and I began to feel more that a little squiffy, so I hoped that Michel would soon take us back to his villa. I waited a little longer before I whispered to Jane that I thought a trip to the ladies would be a good idea, she nodded and we excused ourselves.

We had just arrived in the carpeted, palatial loo with a pretty attendant and begun to discuss the old crows when, bugger me…

the Countess walked in followed by Danielle. We both hastily dived for empty compartments, which gave me time to think, before having to make an appearance. When I had finished I came out to find the old ones sitting at the ornate dressing table in front of the vast mirror that stretched along the wall opposite. They were attempting to freshen up their makeup and I thought 'both of you might as well try to push custard uphill with a fork for all the good it's doing you!' I mean to say... old and ugly is still old and ugly however you try to cover it up!

I sat down next to Danielle and gave her a false smile in the mirror as Jane joined me and said 'that meal was absolutely delicious, and I'm full to bursting.'

'Mmm... I'm not surprised... I don't suppose you're used to eating cordon bleu cuisine in England' said the old star as she puckered her lips and applied her lipstick.

'No we're not... we still have to exist on boiled cabbage and scraps of horse meat...' I began sarcastically before Danielle looked at me in the mirror and interrupted 'mon Dieu! Surely you have something better than cabbage to eat, non?'

'She is being stupid, Danielle, take no notice' said the old star and I grinned before I put on my lip gloss.

'Oui, perhaps she has had too much Champagne and is drunk' said Danielle.

'Perhaps I am drunk... but in the morning I'll be sober whilst you'll still look the same' I said with a grin and they stopped dead and glared at me in the mirror.

'Mon Dieu! You go too far you rude imbecile!' shrieked the old star.

'Jane... I think Michel and Antoine must be missing us, so let's leave these ladies...'

'You're making a big mistake if you think Michel is missing you!' interrupted the old star.

'And how would you know that?' I asked as I glared back at her in the mirror.

'I just know!' replied the old star with her eyes blazing angrily.

'Besides, he wouldn't be interested in either of you petites Anglais' said Danielle.

'Why not?' asked Jane.

'Because you're too young and inexperienced' replied the old star with a smug grin.

'Well, I can tell you that we've both had our moments with men and so far there have been no complaints!' I said firmly.

'Très stupide enfants' whispered Danielle with a shake of her head as she gazed into the mirror and touched up her mascara.

'Come on Jane, let's go back' I said.

'Yes, I think we're all done here' she replied and we left the old crows to talk about us and repair their makeup.

When we arrived at the table Antoine was busy in conversation with Genevieve and Christine who were nodding. We had hardly sat down when the Countess and Danielle came back and Antoine said 'now I think it's time we all went home.' I thought 'thank goodness for that... I'm knackered and have had enough.'

'Oui, bien sûr' said the old star and Danielle nodded.

'Thank you for a wonderful evening, Antoine' I said.

'My pleasure ma petite' he replied.

'Countess, are you staying with me tonight?' asked Michel and I was shocked then upset.

'Bien sûr, ma Michel' she replied with a smug smile. When I had recovered slightly, I thought 'God, why does he want to have this creature staying at his villa?' Well, there's no accounting for taste!

'And Danielle you are welcome to stay with me' said Antoine.

'Merci, Antoine, that's very kind of you' said Danielle. Then Genevieve said 'bon, we can go shopping together in the morning... there's a new boutique that's just opened along from the gallery.' Danielle nodded and said 'très bien.' I was surprised at the speed in which they had sorted out their sleeping arrangements and I began to wonder what was actually going on. Was Antoine taking care of Genevieve and Danielle? I hoped that Michel was not involved with the old star... but somehow my suspicions were aroused and it was the way she smiled that did it... but surely Christine would not tolerate that? I might be mistaken ... but you know what the French are like!

After numerous kisses from Antoine we left him, Genevieve and Danielle outside the Casino and made our way to Michel's car. The Countess sat in the front with Michel whilst Christine, Jane and I squeezed in across the back seat. No one said a word until we reached the villa and as we climbed out of the Mercedes Michel said 'I think I'll open a bottle of Champagne to celebrate a wonderfully successful night at the gallery.'

'Bien sûr' said Christine.

'Ah, ma Michel you always know how to finish a perfect evening' purred the old star. I didn't like the 'ma Michel' bit… far too familiar. Although I felt very squiffy and wanted to go to bed, I decided to stay and have a drink so I could keep my eye on the Countess.

We followed Michel into the villa and slumped down on the soft leather furniture in the lounge. Gabrielle arrived immediately and Michel asked her to take a bottle of chilled Champagne and glasses out to the patio.

'The view is so romantic… it's the only place to drink Champagne at night' he said and we all smiled. Within minutes Gabrielle had it all set up on the patio and soft lights were switched on which gently lit the warm night air. We all trooped out and Michel started to open the Champagne as we admired the spectacular view of the harbour. Every yacht had its lights on, reflecting in the water, making it all a glorious sight. I thought 'I could live here forever.' I looked at Jane and she smiled at me then whispered 'Romford seems a long way away!' and I nodded as the Champagne cork popped and Michel poured the fizzing drink into the glasses.

'Here's to us… salut' said Michel and we all chorused 'salut!' before taking a sip. Then the old star put her glass on the table and placed her arms round Michel's neck and gave him a long, hard kiss and it looked to me as if tongues were being used! My God… I could hardly believe it! I glanced at Christine who turned away from the disgusting scene and gazed out at the harbour whilst Jane looked at me in horror. I wondered 'what was the attraction of this so called 'Countess'?'

When she had finished with Michel the old star picked up her Champagne glass and wandered over to us standing at the wrought iron balustrade. I was holding on tight and trying to concentrate on the view, thinking that any moment I might fall over… I don't seem to be able to drink much alcohol these days before feeling squiffy. Perhaps I'm getting to old to cope with it!

'It's been a wonderful evening' said the Countess.

'Oui' replied Christine still looking straight ahead.

The Countess looked at Jane and me then said 'and I'm sure you must be tired now ma petites, after so much excitement that you're obviously not used too.'

'We can cope' I replied in a slurred tone.

'Ah, I wonder if you can… but on second thoughts… I doubt it' she said before making her way back to Michel's side and whispering to him as she glanced at me.

'She's a cheeky old cow!' I whispered to Jane who nodded and I thought Christine must have heard me because she smiled a little.

Then Michel and the old star wandered arm in arm down the steps to the garden below and over to the pool, which was lit by concealed lighting and looked very inviting.

'Bloody hell… I hope she's not going to swim' I said to Jane as the old star bent down and put her hand in the water.

'I think she is' said Jane.

'This will be a sight to see and remember' I said.

'Or forget!' said Jane and Christine laughed.

'So tell us, Christine, what's her fatal attraction?' I asked and Christine looked at me for a few moments as if she was unsure what to say but replied in a hesitant whisper 'she… is a man.'

I thought 'oh…. my…. God… No!' All my hopes and desires were shattered into a million pieces when I heard that and I felt completely numb… the old star was a transvestite and obviously Michel liked sex with a partner who was able to offer a little something extra. Suddenly I was aware of Jane looking at me in disbelief and she asked 'did I hear what I think I heard?'

'You did!'

'Bloody hell… the old crow is a bloke! Well, I'm not surprised… she had to be a man with that amount of makeup slapped all over!' said Jane and at that moment something snapped inside my head. I rushed down the steps to where Michel and his bloke were standing and with a mighty push I shoved 'her'…'him' into the pool! I watched as 'it' disappeared under the water whilst I screamed 'you disgusting, ghastly old creature!'

Michel shouted out 'mon Dieu!' then his bloke surfaced next to his floating blonde wig and as Michel reached out his hand to help the 'Countess' I also gave him a good push, shouting 'how could you, Michel? How bloody well could you?' He followed 'it' into the pool with a huge splash and I struggled back up the steps to the patio. On the way I twisted my ankle, breaking the heel of my shoe, so I had to limp into the villa with tears streaming down my face. Jane followed me up to our room saying silly things, trying to comfort me, but it was no use and I sank down onto the bed and sobbed. I thought 'why, oh why, does everything happen to me? Why can't I meet a nice, reasonable guy who will love me and want to get married, stay faithful and have a family? Is it too much to ask? Other people seem to manage it so why can't I?' Then I thought about Eric and wished he was here to comfort me and give me some guidance... I wondered if he really was my angel. It's quite a thing to have your own angel.... then I fell into a deep, unconscious sleep.

CHAPTER 8

CLARE RETURNS HOME

I was aware of being shaken and struggled to open my eyes.

'Come on, Clare, wake up' said Jane as she persevered to bring me round.

'Alright' I mumbled.

'Gabrielle has brought us some tea… and says that Christine wants to leave soon, so you'd better get up' said Jane.

'I don't suppose I'm flavour of the month after last night' I murmured.

'No you're not, so let's get out of here before something awful happens' said Jane anxiously.

'Like what?'

'I don't know do I?'

I nodded, slowly arose, went into the ensuite and had a shower, which woke me up, so I was feeling much better when I drank the tea. We had just finished getting our things packed, including my broken shoe, when Christine knocked and entered. She smiled at me and said 'I think we'd better leave now… before Michel is up.'

'Right' I nodded but my head was full of questions and I thought it best not to ask her anything at the moment.

We followed her downstairs then out to her car and as we climbed in, Gabrielle appeared. Christine spoke to her briefly then she nodded and waved at us before we drove out into the road. We did not speak until we had left Monaco and were heading towards the start of the to Marseille.

'Well… I must say that I've had better evenings' I said lamely.

'Michel told me last night that he never wants to see you again' said Christine.

'I'm not surprised' I replied then asked 'but how do you put up with it?'

Christine sighed and said 'I've known Michel and Antoine for many years… they both like gay men as well as women, so you have to understand and accept that if you want to be part of their lives… I've told you that there several women after Michel…'

'And you're first in the queue' I interrupted.

'Oui.'

'But why?'

'Because I love him… also the money and power he has is an extra helpful attraction' she replied with a smile.

'And you're prepared to put up with him carrying on with that ugly old thing?' I asked.

'Oui, I am, because I know that it will not last for long.'

'But after the 'Countess' has gone, they'll probably be another ghastly creature in his life' I said righteously.

'I'm sure there will be, but he'll soon get tired of them… he always does' said Christine.

'Well, I'm buggered if I can understand why you'd want to put up with it all' I said as I imagined a queue of 'trannies' plastered with thick makeup shuffling slowly towards Michel's bedroom.

'Ah, it's a compromise that you have to be French to understand completely' she said.

'Oh really?'

'Oui, it's so you can get what you want in life… and I always do' she said with a smile.

'And you still want Michel' I said lamely.

'Oui, most certainly' she replied.

'Well you're welcome to him' I said firmly.

'Merci, Clare.'

'I suppose that you knew that I never had a chance with him?'

'Oui, it was impossible from the start' she replied with a smile.

'That makes me look a right fool' I said and Jane piped up 'here, here' from the back seat.

'You weren't to know' said Christine.

'That he likes trannies' I said.

'What is 'trannies'?'

'Transvestites' I replied calmly 'men dressed up as tarty old women… like the 'Countess'… you know what I mean.'

'Ah, oui, I do know' she nodded.

We remained silent until we reached Nice, where we stopped in the service area for coffee and croissants. I was now feeling much better and began to think about our future in France. Somehow the outlook didn't seem so rosy now and I was beginning to have doubts. I wondered if the prospect of us posing for Christine

133

would come to complete dead stop after I had chucked Christine's patron into his swimming pool along with his ghastly old 'trannie'. She must have read my mind because as drove out of the service area onto the she said 'things might be difficult with Michel for awhile, he's very sensitive you know, and I can't promise that he will buy any paintings of you…'

'That's understandable' I interrupted glumly, thinking that Mother was quite right… I was always too damned hasty for my own good.

'And I only paint what I can sell to the gallery' she added.

'That makes sense' I said, realising that my planned new life in the sunny South of France was about to end because I let my silly emotions get the better of me instead of playing it cool. I thought 'there's no hope for me… none whatever… so, ho hum, it's back to Romford… and Mother… and divorce… and work… God help me… please… I think I'm now going mad!'

'Well I'm glad my Pierre is straight' Jane piped up from the back, interrupting my desperate thoughts of impending insanity.

'Yes, I'm sure' I said in a flat tone and thought 'I'd forgotten all about Pierre… I guessed that Jane would want to stay in Grambois to be with him… so it would just be me on the flight back to Luton… oh what a mess I'd made of everything again!'

It was almost one o'clock when we eventually arrived home and I was so pleased to say goodbye to Christine, get into the cool house and sink down onto the sofa.

'I'll make us some tea before we have something to eat' said Jane as she went out to the kitchen.

'I'm not hungry' I called out.

'Well I am' came her reply.

I sat gazing out of the picture window and thinking about everything that had gone wrong when suddenly I realised that we were due to fly back this afternoon. Panic made my mind go into a twizzle and all I could think was what time did I have to be at the airport and would Jane actually come back to England? On second thoughts, I was certain that Jane would want to stay so I had to get to Marignane in time on my own. I got up and went into the kitchen.

'Jane, we're supposed to fly back to Luton this afternoon' I said.

'I know, but aren't we staying here now?'

'Well we were until I buggered it all up... you heard what Christine said, Michel didn't want to see me again and he certainly won't buy any pictures of us and Christine won't paint anything she can't sell... so that's it... it's all over for me.'

'But I want to stay with Pierre' she said.

'I know you do, so you can stay but I think I have to go home...'

'After all you said about a new life here?'

'Well I must admit that I was probably a bit hasty and didn't think it through' I said as someone knocked at the door.

'Now who can that be?' asked Jane.

'I'll go... you make the tea.'

When I opened the door there was a young woman standing there and I wondered if it was Evette because she looked a bit like the girl in Christine's paintings.

'Bonjour' I said.

'Bonjour, are you the Anglais having an affair with Pierre Dalmas or is it your friend?' she demanded angrily.

'And who are you?' I asked somewhat taken aback... but realising instantly there may be trouble ahead.

'I'm Madame Dalmas, Pierre's wife!' she replied and I thought 'oh... my... God! There's a surprise'

'Who is it?' called Jane.

'It's Pierre's wife' I called back and heard Jane scream before the teapot crashed to the floor.

'I think you'd better come in' I said to Madame Dalmas with a smile and a nod. She flounced passed me and into the lounge just as Jane appeared from the kitchen. The angry woman looked at us in turn with hard eyes and demanded 'is it you... or you ... or both of you?' I shook my head as Jane whimpered 'I'm so sorry... I didn't know he was married... he never said...'

'He never does' interrupted Madame Dalmas.

'How did you find out?' I asked going on the attack.

'His Auntie told me that he brought you into her restaurant and that you were staying here in Grambois, so when he didn't come home until late the other night I knew he was up to something and I guessed he was with you... it was easy to find you, I only had to ask at the bar where you were… everybody knows everything in a small place like this' she replied.

'Well I can tell you Madame Dalmas that it's all over now, because we are going home today, so you won't see either of us again and you can tell your lying, cheating husband that we think he is a disgusting, unfaithful bastard!' I said firmly and she looked shocked at what I'd said.

'Oui… oui, mademoiselle' she stammered.

'So if you'll kindly leave now because we have to pack and get to the airport' I said.

'Oui, bien sûr… I am sorry Pierre deceived you' she said calmly.

'And I'm sorry you're married to him' said Jane as tears began to stream down her cheeks.

'Oh, ma petite' said Madame before she put her arms around Jane, who sobbed a little and I thought 'God… these bloody men!'

Madam Dalmas left immediately and after showing her out I came back to find Jane flopped out on the sofa and crying like a baby… I knew exactly how she felt… her world had just crumbled before her very eyes… just like mine.

'Come on, we both know that no man is worth it… so let's have some tea and get packed' I said in a gentle, resigned tone.

'We can't have tea because I dropped the pot and it's broken' she whimpered.

'Then we'll have coffee' I said with a smile.

I checked our flight details and realised that we had only two hours to get packed and to the airport in time to check in. We rushed about, flung all our clothes into our cases, tidied up the kitchen, left a note for Frank apologising for his half empty wine rack and locked the front door after us. I knocked at Christine's and when she opened her door I told her that we were leaving right away and handed her Frank's keys. She smiled and said 'I think it is for the best, ma petites.'

'We think so too' I replied.

'Now, just one minute' she said before she hurried away returning moments later holding some Euros.

'Here is your share of the money for the painting… two thousand Euros' she said as she handed me the notes.

'Well thank you, Christine, I must admit I didn't think you'd pay us after last night' I said.

'That had nothing to do with it, Phillipe bought the painting and I know that Antoine will pay me' she said with a smile.

'Well, thanks again' I said.

'And I'm so pleased that you pushed the Countess into the pool last night... it was wonderful to watch!' said Christine with a smile.

'Well I'm glad you approved and I must say that it felt good' I replied with a grin and she nodded, saying 'au revoir, ma petites, au revoir' as she kissed us.

I drove the Fiat back to Marignane airport at speed, Jane was not up to it as she was still weepy eyed over Pierre... the love rat!

We returned the car to the hire company, they seemed to take their time checking for any damage and taking a note of the mileage. We hurried into the airport and were relieved to see that we had arrived in just time. After checking in, we made our way through to the departure lounge where we sat down to draw breath.

'This has been a holiday to remember' I said.

'I'll never forget it... or Pierre... he was so romantic and uncomplicated' replied a tearful Jane.

'And married' I added.

'Yes' she whispered.

'He's just another predatory prick!' I said and thought 'men... they are all the same' but suddenly Eric came into my mind and he wasn't the same... he was different... very different.

The flight back to Luton was quite quick and uneventful. I spent most of the time gazing out of the window thinking what might have been. Now I was going home to face all my problems and I wasn't looking forward to any of it. We landed just before eight in drizzling rain and made our way out of the Terminal and across seemingly endless miles of car park to my car. We were wet, tired and generally fed up when we started the drive back to Romford. Our mood only got worse the nearer we got to Romford and occasionally we had a few words of blame for each other, so I was glad when I dropped Jane outside her flat. We said a frosty 'goodbye' and I drove off to Mother's.

'I'm home' I called out as I opened the front door but there was no answer although I could hear the television blaring in the lounge.

'Have you had a good time?' she asked after I had flopped down in my chair.

'It was alright' I replied.

'Did you meet anyone?' she asked as she popped a chocolate into her mouth.

'No... I didn't' I lied.

'Oh, that's a shame. '

I thought 'yes it is a shame!' as she glanced at me.

'But you've caught the sun' she said before returning her gaze to the television.

'Yes, I have.'

'Well I hope this holiday will put you in a better mood and make you easier to live with for awhile' she said.

'I'm sure it will.'

'That's good... now have you eaten?' she asked.

'No, I'm starving... I'll make a sandwich and some tea, would you like a cup?' I asked and she looked at me in surprise, pushed her glasses up her nose and replied 'yes please, dear.' I thought the 'dear' was a little sarcastic in tone so I knew that things would be difficult with Mother as usual. I realised that it would be a never ending battle with her until I moved out... I sighed and went into the kitchen.

It was almost eleven when I fell into bed and lay thinking about the holiday. It was hard to believe that only the previous night I had been in Monaco, sipping Champagne with the rich and infamous, looking at a nude painting of my best friend and me on show to an appreciative audience. Michel was my dream man and my whole future happiness revolved around him so I was completely shattered by his behaviour with the old star. On the other hand he never actually said how he really felt about me so I was a little foolish to let my imagination run riot, but I was in need of love and romance. How depressing it is when things quickly change for the worse in your life. Then reality dawned on me and I wondered what to wear for work in the morning but couldn't decide... then I thought of Eric... perhaps he would help me get some perspective in life and guide me in a new direction... I certainly needed it! And I would listen this time... promise.

I could hardly drag myself out of bed when the alarm went off the next morning. It was a great effort to actually get dressed and ready for work. After tea and a slice of burnt toast I struggled out to the car and drove to work in a sort of haze of disbelief at my situation. It started to rain and looked like a late November day, which depressed me even more. Was I really going to the office to spend the day with silly Tina and Mr 'Efficiency' Wilkes instead of going to the beach at Cassis to swim and then off to Monaco for Champagne with Michel and his Father? My God... how I hated the 'Countess'! If it hadn't been for 'him'... her... or 'it', I would still be in France, enjoying the sun, food and Champagne and posing for Christine whilst earning loads of cash! What a life I could have had if hadn't been for that old tart! I was still distracted with my angry feelings when a cyclist pulled out in front of me and I swerved to miss him and nearly hit a car coming the other way... the driver hooted and waved angrily at me. That left me a little shaken and added to the day, which had started badly and was not going well... I felt that my emotional roller coaster was speeding down hill at a faster rate than usual. The rain was still falling quite heavily when I parked the car and made a run for it... I just got into the office, looking like a drowned rat, when... bugger me, it stopped!

'Oh, morning, Clare... had a good holiday?' asked Tina brightly as I slumped down on my chair.

'Yes thanks' I mumbled.

'You've got a tan.'

'Yes...'

'Meet anybody nice?'

'No!'

'Shame, still never mind, there's always next year' said Tina with a grin.

'I look forward to it' I replied sarcastically.

'You've been missed here' she said.

'Oh?'

'Oh yeah, old knicker sniffer has been in and was asking after you.'

'Oh dear God' I whispered as my heart sank further down.

'I bet he'll be back this week to see how you are' she grinned.

'Did you tell him that I was on holiday?'

'Yeah, of course, and I told him that you'd be back today' she replied.

'Thanks a bunch... couldn't you have said I was away until next Monday?'

'Why would I want to do that?'

'So I could have a week's peace before...' I began but stopped as Wilkes came in.

'Morning Clare... good holiday?'

'Yes thank you, Mr Wilkes' I replied trying to smile convincingly.

'Good... now, Mr Hammond said that he would be back this week to check on the system as he is concerned that it may be affecting the cash flow unnecessarily and we can't have that' said Wilkes.

'Oh, dear' I said... as if I was interested or cared.

'So try and get up to speed as quickly as possible and I will catch up with you later to find out where we may be going wrong' said Wilkes.

'Yes, Mr Wilkes.'

'And Tina... make sure you have the figures for last week on my desk by lunchtime.'

'Yes, sir.'

When we were alone Tina said with a grin 'I bet you're glad to be back!' I could have strangled her!

The rest of the day went slowly by and Tuesday was only marginally better but things brightened up on Wednesday evening when Jane phoned and invited me out for a drink. I picked her up at her flat and we went to 'The Red Lion' where she bought the first round of large gin and tonics needed to steady our shattered nerves.

'God... it's been awful at work this week and I'm dreading tomorrow' I said sipping my gin.

'Why?'

'I think the knicker sniffer will be back to worry me' I replied and she rolled her eyes and said 'that's all you need.'

'Men are such bastards' I said with feeling.

'True… but we couldn't do without them' she said wistfully.

'Why can't they be more like us?' I asked.

'Heaven knows, but they aren't… so we just have to put up with them as they are' she said firmly.

'I suppose so' I muttered and thinking what my life might have been with Michel.

'Now, I've had an idea that would make us feel a lot better' she said with a smile.

'Go on.'

'If we were to turn things around and instead of us getting dumped we did the dumping… it would balance things up a little don't you think?'

'Yes' I said slowly and cautiously.

'So how about we have a dinner party at my place and invite Rupert and Simon!' she said brightly.

'And after leading them on all evening… we'd dump them?'

'Exactly… they deserve it and they would be the 'dumpee's' instead of us… it would make a nice change and I think their time is up… after what we've been through our revenge will be so sweet!' said Jane with a grin.

'Let me get you another drink!' I said with a smile.

We made plans for the coming Saturday and were certain that the two loons would take the bait and come to Jane's flat.

'I'll phone them both tonight… I'm sure they'll come, if only to see our tans and be fed' said Jane.

'Right… what'll we eat?'

'I'll do a chicken curry… you bring something for pud and a couple of bottles of plonk' she replied.

I was feeling much brighter when I arrived home and guessed the gin had played its part in raising my spirits but the thought of egging on the two 'no hopers' did a lot for my morale. It was boosted when Jane phoned just after eleven and told me that the 'no hopers' would be there on Saturday… and they were looking forward to it! I went to bed a happy woman.

It was just after three on Thursday afternoon when, as I expected, Hammond arrived in the office with Wilkes… he was all smiles and silly compliments.

'My word... you have caught the sun, Clare' he said as Tina grinned and sniffed loudly... I couldn't look at her.

'Yes, the weather was good' I replied lamely.

'Where did you go?' he asked.

'The South of France, we had a villa in Provence... but we were invited to Monaco and stayed there at the end of the week with friends' I said hoping to impress him and Wilkes, who hovered by the knicker sniffer, looking pleased with himself.

'How fantastic... you must tell me all about it sometime' he said with a smile and I thought 'not likely my little pervert!' but replied convincingly 'Yes, I will, Mr Hammond.'

'Oh Clare, please call me Jeff, we're all on the same side you know' he said with a grin and I could have slapped him.... I wanted to say 'I'm not on your side Captain Chaos, and never will be!'

'Yes, if we work as a team we will improve our efficiency no end' said Wilkes with a beaming smile.

'Of course' added Hammond before Tina sniffed again and I nearly cracked up.

'Have you got a cold Tina?' asked Wilkes.

'No, Mr Wilkes, I think I must be allergic to something' she replied innocently and I had to turn away to hide my grin and fumbled in my bag to find a tissue to cover my face.

'Are you also allergic to something in here, Clare?' asked Wilkes, I shook my head and had to bite my lip not to laugh as Tina sniffed again.

'I think we'll leave you for the moment and come back later' said Hammond firmly, so I guessed he knew something was up and it was possibly him that was the cause!

'Right' I said, holding the tissue to my nose. When they had left the office we almost screamed out loud with laughter.

'Oh do stop it, Tina... you'll get us sacked!' I said between giggles.

They came back about an hour later and droned on about the importance of cash flow. I was fed up to the back teeth by the time they had finished and gave a sigh of relief when they eventually buggered off.

'Only tomorrow to go... then it's the weekend' said Tina brightly.

'Thank God' I murmured.

'So what are you doing?' asked Tina.

'Ah... I'm taking my 'hate all men' revenge out on a stupid, boring pratt!' I replied thinking of silly Simon.

'Anybody I know?' she asked.

'No.'

'Well, it all sounds good to me, let me know how you get on' she said with a grin.

'I will.'

After leaving the office on Friday I went shopping at Marks and Spencer's on my way home. I bought a party size sherry trifle and a large chocolate gateaux, three bottles of white wine and two of red, that were this week's 'special offer'. I wondered what Michel would have thought about the quality! I knew that Simon and the bearded Rupert wouldn't have a clue... as long it was wet and contained alcohol they'd be content.

I was looking forward to Saturday evening when we would play the two 'loons' like hooked fish and then reel them in before chucking them back in the water, never to be seen again! Jane and I were about to become the 'dumpers' instead of the 'dumpee's' and it felt good... there was something delicious about it all!

When I arrived home, Mother asked me what all the food was in aid of so I told her. She sighed and said 'I hope you're not going to get involved with someone before...'

'Get involved? Just a moment ago you were telling to find someone quick as I was now 'hurtling towards thirty!'' I interrupted her angrily.

'Well you are but...'

'There's no 'but' about it... I will do as I damned well please thank you very much!' I said firmly. I hadn't forgotten her unkind remark about 'hurtling towards thirty' and she must have known it hurt. There was a few minutes silence before she said 'there's two letters for you, I think ones from your solicitor, I don't know about the other.'

She was right, the first letter was from Mr Clarke asking me to make an appointment to discuss further complications in the divorce settlement... I sighed and opened the second letter. I was completely dumbstruck... my jaw must have dropped as I read it because Mother asked 'who's it from?'

'I can't believe this... it's from that creepy manager at work' I said.

'Mr Wilkes?'

'No... that pratt Hammond!'

'Well, what does it say?'

'He wants to meet me for a drink!'

'That's nice...'

'No it isn't!' I interrupted.

'What's wrong with him?'

'He's awful... and Tina thinks he's a knicker sniffer...'

'A what?'

'He's a divorced bloke who lives alone and has funny sex habits' I said firmly.

'How do you know?'

'I don't... but it just seems as if he might' I replied.

'Well all men are a bit like that... and if he's divorced he could be ideal for you' she said lamely.

'Mother!' I screamed.

'You're getting too fussy as well as too hasty... if he wants to take you for a drink, where's the harm in that for goodness sake?'

'You don't understand...'

'I never will' she interrupted so I decided to shut up and go to my room as it was useless to carry on the conversation.

I sat on the bed and read the letter again. He said he was sorry for what happened on our day out and that he'd like to be just a friend and have an occasional drink with me. He asked me to phone him at home any evening if I wanted to meet him, but if not, he'd understand and never bother me again. I thought for a moment and decided to add him to my list of men that I intended to dump before I moved on! As Jane said 'how sweet is revenge?' and the answer is 'very sweet!'

On Saturday evening I wore my red dress, the one I was wearing when Greg dumped me, and arrived at Jane's flat just after six. She looked good in her blue 'flouncy' dress and we chatted as I unpacked the desserts and wine before putting them in her crowded fridge.

'The curry smells good' I said looking at it simmering in the pan.

'I think it should be okay' she smiled.

'Did you put any poison in?' I asked.

'No... I thought we'd probably do that later' she laughed.

'Oh yes... without doubt!'

'I'll bet they'll never forget tonight' Jane said.

'That's for sure... now, let's have a drink to get us in the 'dumping' mood' I said.

'Right!'

Simon arrived first, just after seven, with a bottle of wine and a bunch of red roses.

'Well I must say that you both look fabulous' he said as he gave us each a little kiss on our cheeks. I caught a whiff of his after shave and thought it was quite pleasant.

'You look good tonight' said Jane and I had to admit he did. He wore a neatly ironed light blue shirt and black trousers.

'I do try sometimes' he grinned.

'Thanks for the roses' said Jane.

'And the wine' I added.

'You're welcome' he said with a smile.

'Now... what would you like to drink?' asked Jane.

'A glass of wine, please' he replied.

'Red or white?'

'What are having for dinner?' he asked.

'Chicken curry.'

'Then I'll have white if I may and stay with that' he replied.

No sooner had Jane finished pouring the wine for Simon and refilling our glasses when Rupert arrived bringing a bottle and some flowers. He also looked very good, dressed in a dark red jacket over a high collared white shirt. He had trimmed his beard neatly and smelt nice.

'Hello Jane' he whispered before giving her his gifts and a quick kiss on her cheek.

'Hi Rupert... you remember Clare and Simon' said Jane.

'Yes, you were both at Melanie's party' he said with a smile.

'We were and I was boring Clare silly going on about cars as usual' said Simon.

'You certainly were' I said.

'I didn't get a chance to apologise because you disappeared with your future husband' said Simon with a smile and I thought 'you're really enjoying this but wait until the end of the evening!' then he added 'so I apologise now… am I forgiven?'

'Only slightly' I said with a rueful grin.

'Oh that's good' he said.

We sat and talked about our holiday and the 'no hoper's' seemed really interested in what we'd been up to. They asked many questions and Simon finished by asking 'would you both like to live in France someday?'

'Oh yes' I said and Jane nodded.

'So would I' said Simon which surprised me.

'And me' said Rupert.

I looked at Simon and asked 'why?'

'Because I love the French way of life' he replied.

'So do we' I said and Jane nodded.

'I've often thought of buying something in Provence and doing it up so I could rent it out when I wasn't there… an investment as well as a holiday home where I would spend more time after my business takes off' said Simon.

'And I would like to live there to write' said Rupert.

'It's the ideal place' said Jane enthusiastically.

'I know… and the good news is… I have just sold my first novel to a publisher… so I'm very happy and might actually move to France!' said Rupert.

'Oh congratulations, Rupert… you clever thing you!' said Jane.

'Thank you.'

'What's your book called?' I asked.

'The Disappointed Man' replied Rupert.

'What's it about?' asked Simon.

'An artist who is constantly dumped by the women in his life until he sells a modern art painting for a huge sum to an American and goes to live in Hollywood where he meets all the stars, paints for them and becomes a multi millionaire' replied Rupert with a smile.

'And then what happens?' asked Simon.

'The woman in his life who dumped him, just before he sold his painting, follows him and tries to make it up, but he turns her down and remains single, enjoying every sinful pleasure imaginable in his luxury mansion' said Rupert.

'There's a moral in there somewhere' said Simon with a grin.

'Yes, most definitely, never be unkind to anyone, especially those who have the potential to be very rich and famous!' said Rupert with a laugh and I glanced at Jane who looked quite bemused. I guessed like me she was having second thoughts about dumping the 'no hoper's' tonight in case maybe, just maybe, it would be a decision we'd live to regret.

'I didn't know you had a business, Simon' I said brightly.

'Yes, I'm in computer software and now branching out a little into manufacturing bits and pieces, nothing too grand at the moment but things are going pretty well' he said.

'Do you employ anybody?' I asked.

'Yes, about thirty, but I am looking for more help with the manufacturing side' he replied.

'Oh… how nice' I said suitably impressed.

'I think it's time we ate… would you come and help, Clare?' asked Jane.

'Right' I replied before I followed her out to the kitchen and whispered 'I think we should just play it carefully tonight, Jane.'

'I agree… we won't do anything too hasty for the moment.'

The chicken curry was delicious and we all enjoyed it. Over the meal Rupert said that his agent was trying to sell the film rights of his book to a major Hollywood studio, which would make him very wealthy and Simon told us that his computer accessories were being considered by several Government departments. The future for both of them appeared very rosy so I thought we should stay cool as agreed and just have a good evening then see what happens next. I thought that Simon was beginning to look very attractive as the night wore on or perhaps I was wrong and it was the wine lulling my senses again. Then I thought about Michel and although he was devastatingly attractive to me, he was a man whom I could never trust, not that I would ever be able to get near him because of all the 'trannies'. Then there was my Tony… so handsome and loving but another bloody man I could never trust. Simon, however, looked calm, reliable and was the sort of person who you could settle down with… true, he'd need some training, but what man doesn't?

By the time we were having coffee I had made up my mind about Simon and hoped he would ask me out so I could get to know him better. It was just before eleven when Simon said he had to go home as he had a meeting the next morning with his sales director.

'On a Sunday?' I asked.

'Oh yes, we have to have meetings most weekends because we're too busy in the week' he replied.

'Goodness… you must be doing well' I said and he smiled then nodded.

. 'It's been a lovely evening and I've really enjoyed it, perhaps we can do it again sometime' said Simon as he was about to leave.

'Yes, that would be good' said Jane as I stood up to give him a quick kiss.

'Goodbye, Simon' I said as I made a lunge towards him and he replied 'goodbye, Clare' before giving me a quick, disappointing peck on my cheek before Jane showed him out.

I had hardly recovered from Simon's quick and unromantic departure when Rupert said 'I think I should go as well, it's getting late and I've things to do tomorrow.' Jane looked surprised and said 'please don't rush off, Rupert… have some more coffee.'

'No thanks, Jane… perhaps I'll call you sometime… and if you're free we could meet up' said Rupert with a smile.

'Okay… that would be good' replied Jane.

After she had shown him out and returned looking glum I said 'well, what did you make of all that?'

'I think we've just been dumped!'

'So do I… let's have another drink!'

CHAPTER 9

ERIC APPEARS

The next morning I got up quite early, which was unusual for me on a Sunday and went for a walk in the park hoping to meet Eric. I needed to talk to him about my latest personal disaster, but on second thoughts... everything in my life. The time had come for us to have that deep conversation about me and my future happiness... it is my favourite subject after all. He said he was my guardian angel so, if he is, it was up to him to do something for me and as they say 'the ball was in his court!'

I sat on the bench where we had met before and glanced around the empty park. There was no sign of Eric or even a jogger. An elderly man with a sweet little dog appeared and as he slowly passed by, he wished me 'good morning'. I smiled and replied before glancing back at the entrance hoping to see Eric, but there was no one there. I sat calmly and gazed at the trees, they had now turned to a beautiful autumn gold. After about twenty minutes I got up and made my way over to the lake to watch the ducks splashing about amongst the reeds. Looking at them, I thought 'how wonderful to have such an uncomplicated existence with nothing to do except search for food and breed... that would certainly suit me for the rest of my life.' I sighed and decided to go home and face a difficult day with Mother before trying to mentally prepare for another tiresome week at work. I turned away from the lake and glanced back at the bench where I had been sitting and was overjoyed to see Eric standing there. I rushed towards him and he smiled at me. I felt warm inside and so comforted at seeing him... my angel, my own angel... if he is one that is... I hoped he would let me kiss him!

'Eric!' I gasped.

'Hello, Clare' he said as I clasped my arms around his neck.

'Give me a kiss!' I demanded.

'I'm not supposed to...'

'I didn't think Vikings were shy!' I interrupted and he laughed, shook his head slightly, then gave me a real 'plonker'... I made it last.

'There… that wasn't so difficult was it?' I asked in a whisper when our lips parted.

'No, but I'm on duty and...'

'You're not supposed to do that… I know' I said with a big smile then asked 'will God be cross with you or is it the Archangel you're frightened of?'

He laughed and shook his head. 'Let's sit for a moment and talk'.

'Yes, let's' I replied and sat close to him on the bench as close.

'So…' he began but I interrupted saying 'put your arm around me first' and he did. I looked up into his open face and fascinating blue eyes and asked 'tell me honestly, Eric… are you really an angel?'

He gave a little nod and replied 'but I'm not supposed to tell you.'

'I'll keep it a secret' I replied with a smile.

'I'm not a very good one yet, I'm afraid.'

'Well, if you really are one, I think you're good for me.'

'I'm glad to hear it! Now, I've decided to try and guide you little by little because I don't think you'll stay on the right path for long…'

'Really?'

'You tend to wander about, like one of our longboats in a wild ocean's cross current' he said firmly.

'So does that mean I'll see you more often?' I asked.

'Yes…'

'Oh good.'

'I think it is the only way.'

'I'll enjoy being guided a little bit at a time, it means that we can keep meeting for a quick kiss and cuddle' I said with a smile.

'That will have to stop, Clare.'

'Ohh…'

'I mean it' he said firmly.

'Right, but I want you to know that it's a big disappointment to me because I need some TLC and I'll complain to God about you when I eventually meet him' I said.

'What's TLC?' he asked.

'Tender... loving... care.'

'Ah, everyone needs that and I have to try and guide you to the person who will give you TLC for the rest of your life on Earth' he said with a smile.

'Well, why don't you do it and cut out the middle man?' I asked in naïve hope.

'Clare…'

'Answer me' I interrupted.

'That's not how it works…'

'Well it should do!' I said and he sighed then remained silent for a few moments.

'What I want you to do, first of all, is open your heart and mind to everyone you meet…'

'I do already' I interrupted.

'No you don't.'

'Oh, yes I do!'

'Clare!'

'What?'

'Just be quiet and listen to me, will you?' he said angrily so I zipped my lips.

'Good. Now if you will open your heart and mind to people, don't pre-judge them and give them a chance, you will find that they'll respond to you with kindness and love…'

'What about those who don't?' I asked.

'Clare!'

'Alright, alright… I'll just shut up and listen.'

'You will see people that you know in a new light and if you treat them properly you will be very happy with the outcome.'

'So, is one of them really going to be mine for always?'

'Yes…'

'Who is it?' I asked excitedly as I tried to think who it might be.

'You must find out yourself but if you follow my guidance one of them will soon be part of your life' Eric replied with a smile.

'I will' I said.

'Good…'

'Is there only one perfect person for each of us?' I asked.

'No, there are several that will match you very well, so you always have a choice' he replied.

'Oh good.'

'Always remember, there was only one truly perfect person and we crucified him two thousand years ago and the rest of us have to struggle on as best we can to follow his example…'

'I know that, but what about me?'

'What about you?'

'Will one of these men I already know make me happy?'

'Yes, but as I've said, he's not perfect!'

'That's a pity… but I'm sure I can lick him into shape!' I said and Eric sighed as he glanced up to heaven.

'Now we'll meet again…'

'When?' I interrupted.

'Soon' he replied before standing up.

'Are you going now?'

'Yes I am… goodbye Clare.'

Before I had a chance to say anything, he strode away towards the small wood beyond the lake. I watched him until he disappeared amongst the golden trees. I felt happy and content that I had seen him and knew that he would appear again to guide me. As I walked home I intended to be calm and nice to everyone in future… including Mother!

After I made tea for us both I decided to phone Jane then Simon and finally Jeff Hammond.

'You're being very pleasant this morning' said Mother.

'Am I?'

'Yes, it seems a walk in the park does you good' said Mother as she bit into a chocolate biscuit.

'I think you could be right' I replied before taking a sip of tea.

'That's good.'

I felt that I had been polite enough to her for the moment and said nothing more… just in case I fell by the wayside and said something I shouldn't… you understand!

I finished my tea in silence then went to my room and called Jane.

'Hi, I was just about to call you!' she said in a happy tone. 'You'll never guess…'

'No, so do tell!' I interrupted.

'Simon phoned this morning and asked for your number… I think he's going to ask you out' she replied.

'The day is getting better' I said.

'Has he called yet?' she asked.

'No, but I'm sure he will.'

'Well I'll get off the phone now, just in case he's trying to get through… call me and tell me what he says.'

'I will.'

'Catch you later' she said before she hung up.

I sat looking at the phone and wondered if I should phone Jeff Hammond. I mean he really isn't my type… but Eric said be nice to everyone and don't pre-judge. So I would give him a chance… after all, if we were friends, he could help me get promoted at work. I mean, it's who you know in this world that counts… promotion would mean a raise and perhaps enable me to afford a place of my own… what heaven that would be!

I opened his letter and dialled the number. It rang for some while so I guessed he was out playing golf or something equally silly and I was just about to hang up when he answered.

'Hammond here.'

'Oh hello, how are you today?'

'Clare… Clare is that you?' he asked excitedly.

'Yes…'

'Well, hi there, how are you?'

'Fine, just fine, thanks.'

'Good, so… have you decided to accept my invitation for a drink?' he asked.

'Yes, why not?'

'Fantastic, when are you free?' he asked.

'Oh, any evening' I replied.

'Fine, what about tomorrow night? I could pick you up at work…'

'No, I think it would be better if you came here… say about eight, if that's okay' I replied.

'Yes, yes, of course, so I'll see you tomorrow, Clare.'

I said 'yes… goodbye' then hung up. A moment later the phone rang and it was Simon.

'Hello, Clare, it's Simon here.'

'Oh Simon… what a nice surprise!' I lied convincingly.

'I'm glad you think so. I had a lovely evening with you at Jane's and I wondered if we could do it again? Just the two of us, that is.'

'Yes, why not… what have you in mind?'

'A romantic dinner at a little French restaurant I know… the food is really superb!'

'Romantic dinner… that sounds nice.'

'So when are you free?' he asked.

Thinking quickly that I was out with Jeff on Monday night then hair wash and gossip with Jane on Tuesday and an evening in on Wednesday to recover, I replied 'any time after Wednesday.'

'Fine… let's make it Thursday then, say I pick you up at about eight… is that okay?'

'That'll be good' I replied.

'See you then.'

'Oh, have you got my address?' I asked.

'Yes, Jane gave it to me' he replied and I thought 'she's a busy little match maker on the quiet!' So I phoned her back, told her all the news and we had a good gossip.

Finally she said 'I think Simon's the right one for you.'

'Possibly' I replied but thought 'not very likely!' We said 'goodbye.'

Over lunch I told Mother that I was going out for a drink with Hammond on Monday and dinner with Simon on Thursday and she was all smiles at the news.

'That's nice, dear, I'm sure you'll have a good time' she said.

'Hope so' I mumbled.

'Are you bringing them back later for coffee?' she asked in a genial tone.

'I hadn't planned to.'

'As you wish, but it would be nice to meet them' she said and I wondered why was she being so nice? Was Eric's advice working already? Had I suddenly become a paragon of virtue? Don't think so… she just planned to get rid of me as soon as possible and wanted to decide which of these two 'muppets' would get her vote as my next husband! Then I remembered I had to make an appointment to see Mr Clarke to discuss problems about my divorce. I made a mental note to phone from work the next morning.

Monday morning at the office was pretty slow as usual and other than Tina wittering on about the new bloke she'd met whilst clubbing on Saturday, nothing much happened. His name was Desmond, she kept calling him 'Dezzie' for short and as far as I was concerned he might well have been called 'Dizzie' after listening endlessly about his antics in the club. Tina didn't ask about the dumping of my 'no hoper' on Saturday night and I decided not to say anything.

I phoned the solicitors and made an appointment to see Mr Clarke at three o'clock on Wednesday... I was dreading it because every time I visited his drab office it brought back all the unhappy memories.

We were just about to have our lunch break when Wilkes walked in with Jeff Hammond. I was surprised to see him and hoped he wouldn't say anything about our date arranged for that night.

'Jeff has called in on the 'off chance' to see if we had any problems he could help us with' said Wilkes.

'No, I think everything is okay, thank you' I replied with a smile.

'Good... and are you alright, Tina?' said Wilkes

'Yes' she replied.

'Well the system seems to be working well, Jeff' said Wilkes with a smug grin.

'I'm pleased to hear it' said Hammond with a smile. They said nothing more and left the office.

'What was that all about then?' I asked.

'He just called to see if you were here and give you a quick sniff' Tina replied, we both laughed and I thought it was probably the truth, more likely than not.

In the evening I was ready to go when Hammond pulled up outside the house spot on eight o'clock. I hadn't bothered to get dressed up in a posh frock and had just touched up my makeup... I thought I looked good enough for a 'friend'.

'I'm out now' I called to Mother, who was still busy in the kitchen fussing about.

'Have a nice time, dear' she called back. It's the way she always says 'dear' that bothers me and I think the constant message is 'find someone quick and move out.'

Hammond stood by the BMW and smiled as he opened the door for me.

'Hello Clare, I must say you look good tonight' he said

'Thanks' I replied as I slipped into the passenger seat and caught a strong whiff of his after shave or something else that men use to cover up unpleasant personal smells.

'So was he trying to impress me or did he have a serious body odour problem?' I asked myself.

On the way to his 'pretty village pub' he chatted aimlessly about nothing in particular and I was beginning to wish I hadn't agreed to go out with him. Still, I thought of Eric's advice and gritted my teeth to survive what was already becoming a boring evening. I decided that I should try to make the best of it, open my heart, give him a chance and not pre-judge this 'muppet' and perhaps persuade him to help get me some sort of promotion at work. So I began talking about Hamilton Motors and it seemed as if he was completely overawed for a moment then he came alive and launched enthusiastically into his plans for his future career, but I couldn't have cared less about his intended climb up the slippery management ladder. My conversation wasn't supposed to be all about him… it was all about me! He eventually finished by telling me that he intended to become the UK Finance Director as we pulled into the 'Barley Mow' pub. I was glad to get out of the car for some fresh air and waited whilst he clicked the central locking with his key before he took my arm and led me into the quaint little pub.

'I'm sure you'll like it here because it has such an old, rustic atmosphere' he said as we approached the bar.

'Yes' I replied, glancing at the old 'rustic' locals scattered around the place who stared at me.

'What'll you have?' he asked and decided on a large gin and tonic… I needed some alcoholic help!

We sat at a table near the roaring log fire and I listened patiently whilst he droned on about business. I tried to look interested and occasionally mentioned that I was looking for promotion but realised that he was only concerned with himself. He bought another round of drinks and when he was at the bar I glanced at my watch. It was only nine o'clock but it seemed as if I had been with him for days! I decided to give him another hour then tell him I had to go home because of a busy day at work on Tuesday.

He drove me home and we arrived outside just after ten... my ordeal was over at last, thank God!

'I've had a lovely evening, Clare, I hope we can do it again sometime' he said.

'Yes, why not' I replied and was surprised that I had actually said it and wondered if Eric was guiding my thoughts... can angels do that?

'Can I call you at home?' asked Hammond.

'Yes' I replied and gave him my number. We said 'goodnight' and I was relieved that he didn't try to kiss me or anything. He ran round and opened the car door for me so I thanked him and said 'goodnight' again and was sure I heard him give a little sniff, which made me giggle all the way up to my front door.

Mother was still watching the television and asked lots of questions about Hammond whilst keeping one eye on the box. I stayed calm and polite before deciding I'd had enough and went to bed.

Tuesday slipped by and I left work early on Wednesday afternoon to keep my appointment with Mr Clarke. I thought his office seemed to smell mustier than the last time I visited. I sat in silence as he peered at the paperwork in front of him and occasionally glanced at me. He looked totally bemused and I listened carefully as he went through the list of demands made by Tony's solicitors. I couldn't be bothered with it all and just agreed to everything that they wanted.

'You don't have to agree to everything you know, Mrs Franklin' said Clarke with a smile.

'I just want to get it all over with' I said dismissively.

'I'm sure, but please take my advice and contest some of this' he said and I sighed.

'Alright I will, so what do you suggest?' I asked thinking about the ever increasing bill for all this legal nonsense. Mr Clarke went through all the paraphernalia once again and made suggestions which I readily agreed to. I didn't care about anything anymore and just wanted to get out of his musty office. At last the interview was over and he stood up and wished me 'good day', adding that he would be in touch after he had heard from 'the other side'. These legal worms really think it's some sort of war they're involved in, not a dreadful, unhappy experience for two people who were once in love... my God, what parasites they all are!

I drove home feeling very sad and after parking my car in the drive decided to go for a walk in the park as I couldn't face a long conversation with Mother. I hoped Eric might come along and that would cheer me up no end.

I sat on the usual bench thinking of Eric and glanced at several children playing noisily by the trees and some mother's with toddlers in push chairs gossiping by the next bench. Then, after a little while, the elderly gentleman with the sweet little dog came along and wished me 'good afternoon' so I smiled and replied. I thought he mumbled something else as he passed by, which sounded like 'he'll be here soon.' I watched the man and his dog for some time as they made their way across the park and wondered who he was. I had my suspicions and perhaps Eric would tell me if he knew... and I would certainly ask.

I tried to think which man I knew who would be the one to make me happy. Hammond was certainly not the man of my dreams but Simon... now he had real potential. I mean, as Eric said, he wasn't perfect, but I thought in time I could make him into someone I would be happy to live with. Perhaps we would grow together into a comfy mould of complacency! Then I thought of Rupert... I know he is officially Jane's long term 'on and off' boy friend but that could all change in the future, especially if he became a famous author and moved to France or even... Hollywood!

Suddenly I was aware of Eric standing next to the bench.

'Hello, Clare' he said before he sat down next to me.

'Hello my angel, what are you doing here?' I asked with a happy grin.

'Trying to look after you and guide you as always' he replied with a smile.

'I'm pleased to hear it... now, before you start, tell me, is that elderly man with the little dog one of yours?' I asked and Eric smiled then nodded slightly.

'I thought so' I said and he laughed.

'Yes, we're everywhere... and most people don't realise' he said.

'That's probably a good thing!' I said and he laughed again.

'You may be right! Now, I know that you're unhappy at the moment but the problems you are going through with the divorce will be over soon and you can prepare yourself for a nice surprise' he said.

'Oh tell me what it is, I don't like surprises of any kind... even nice ones' I said.

'I'm afraid you'll have to wait and see because as you have free will, you may take another path which might lead you away from the surprise for the moment' he replied.

'What should I do then?'

'Just treat everybody with kind consideration and don't pre-judge anyone' he replied.

'Is that the top tip for today?' I asked.

'It is, so follow my guidance and the surprise will be yours' he said.

'Then I will.'

'Good.'

'So, what else have you got to tell me?' I asked.

'Nothing at the moment... I just wanted to give you that guidance for your future happiness' he replied.

'Well that's a bit of a disappointment' I said.

'It's enough to be going on with' he replied.

'So when will I see you again?'

'Soon.'

'Here in the park?'

'Not necessarily.'

'Where then?'

'It will always be somewhere appropriate' he replied with a smile.

'Oh, you are a mystery' I said.

'And that's how it should be... I must go now as I'm wanted elsewhere, goodbye Clare' he said as he stood up.

'Bye, Eric.'

I watched as he strode towards the golden trees and eventually disappeared from view. I wondered what my nice surprise was and hoped I didn't have to wait long for it. I certainly could do with a bit of a lift at the moment.

Thursday dragged by slowly at work and I was glad to leave the office. When I arrived home, I reminded Mother that I was going out for dinner with Simon that evening and she looked quite relieved.

'Are you bringing him back for coffee?' she asked with raised eyebrows.

'Possibly' I replied.

'Oh good, I'd like to meet him' she said sweetly.

'Yes of course... now I need to go and get ready' I said.

After a quick shower, a 'slap' makeover and touches of Givenchy 'L'amour' in all the right places I slipped into my 'killer' little black dress, matching shoes and clutch bag. I wanted to make a good impression and was already to go with Simon to his French restaurant.

He arrived just after eight, so I grabbed my coat and went out to meet him standing by his silver Audi sports car.

'Hi Clare, you look good tonight' he said as he opened the door for me.

'Oh, thank you, Simon' I replied in my new 'nice to everyone' tone.

As we drove away he asked 'what's that perfume you're wearing?' but before I could answer he said 'I bet it's French.'

'It's Givenchy 'L'amour'... it's my favourite' I replied.

'Ah... I was right then.'

'You were' I replied with a smile, and thought 'this evening has started quite well and let's hope it stays that way.'

'The restaurant is called 'Le Pomme D'or', and it's quite near my office in Brentwood' he said.

'Oh really.'

'Yes, and I hope you don't mind but I have to just call in and check something with my Technical Director before he goes home... I won't be long.'

'No, I don't mind... can I come in with you?' I asked, thinking that it would be interesting to see what sort of business set up he had.

'Yes of course, and I'll introduce you to Mike, he's busy

working on the Government contract at the moment' Simon replied and I thought 'this is good news for the future if Simon is the chosen man!'

We chatted all the way and I had to admit I found him quite charming in an old fashioned way. All the lights were on when we arrived outside his two story office block in the new industrial estate on the outskirts of Brentwood. I followed him in through the glass doors and up the stairs to the office as he explained that his workshop was on the ground floor. I was introduced to Mike and then glanced around as he and Simon talked about the work in hand. I was impressed with the office as it was neatly laid out, well furnished and tidy. Within minutes we said 'goodbye' to Mike and were on our way to the restaurant.

'Sorry about that, but it was important that I spoke to Mike' said Simon as we pulled out of the estate.

'That's perfectly alright... is everything okay?' I asked.

'Oh yes, Mike's a good bloke and we're well ahead of the schedule' replied.

'Oh good.'

We were soon in Brentwood and Simon turned off at the end of the high street and pulled up outside 'Le Pomme D'or.'

'The food is very good here and I'm sure you'll enjoy it' he said.

'I'm sure' I replied with a sweet smile.

We were shown to our reserved candlelit table by Henri, the manager, who had welcomed Simon as if he were a long lost brother. Sometimes the French are a bit OTT, but it's quite nice and brought back happy memories of my recent holiday in Grambois.

I wandered through the extensive menu whilst Simon glanced at the wine list and chose a light, sparkling rosé. I decided to have mushroom soup followed by Tournedos Rossini and when I told Simon he raised his eyebrows slightly.

'I didn't think you were into steak' he said.

'More of a fish person perhaps?' I asked with a smile... I was being nice and not pre-judging him as I thought he may have believed I was a vegetarian for some reason!

'Yes.'

'Well it shows that you don't know much about me then' I said sweetly.

'That's very true, but I hope I can find out much more... given time' he said with a smile. I just smiled and looked away as the wine waiter brought the rosé and poured a taster for Simon. He nodded and the wine was poured into our sparkling candlelit glasses.

'Here's to us and a happy future' said Simon, I smiled as we touched glasses and murmured 'to us.'

Simon chose prawn salad as a starter and he also ordered Tournedos Rossini.

The first two courses were excellent and I was quite full and slightly squiffy when the sweet trolley arrived. I chose pear belle Helene and Simon had Black Forest gateaux. When we had finished he asked 'would you like some coffee now?'

'I think it would be much nicer if we had coffee at my place' I replied and his eyes lit up. I guess he thought he was in for some 'smooching' or possibly a 'leg over' but I had no intentions of going that far and of course Mother dear would be there, no doubt stuffing herself with chocolates and asking inane questions... if that didn't put him off, nothing would!

'That's a nice idea, I'll get the bill' he said with a smile.

On the drive home Simon was amusing and I felt that, given time, he may indeed be the man whom I could settle down with and have a family. He seemed dependable, likeable and easy going, which meant I could soon change anything I didn't like about him. I must admit I had misjudged him at the party, but then I hadn't given him much of a chance as I had been so dumbstruck by Tony.

When we pulled up outside my house I said 'I must tell you that my Mother will probably still be up watching some silly film on TV.'

'Oh, not to worry and in any case I'd like to meet her' he replied and I wondered if I should warn him about her, but decided not to... it would be interesting to see how he coped with Mother.

The television was blaring out as usual when we entered the house and I called out from the hall 'we're back!' She heard me and suddenly there was silence as she clicked off the set and waited for us. I led the way into the lounge and introduced Simon as she hurriedly closed a box of chocolates and smiled.

'I'm pleased to meet you at last Simon, I've heard so much about you' she lied.

'Really?' he asked with a hopeful smile.

'Yes, Clare's always talking about you' she carried on lying... God she's awful and I know that she wants to get rid of me but she was going too far and too fast! How to stop her, that's the thing.

'Well, I hope she doesn't bore you too much' he said in a polite tone.

'Oh I couldn't possibly be bored with news about you Simon' she said and I cringed.

'That's nice to know' he said nervously after a moments dither.

'So, is it coffee all round?' I chipped in.

'Of course' said Mother and Simon nodded.

I left them to it, went out into the kitchen and put the kettle on wondering what she was saying about me. I thought 'well, he'll either sink or swim and knowing Mother, he'll probably sink... which means he's not the right one for me but on the other hand if he survives and still wants to see me, then he possibly is the right one. I was becoming confused and then the kettle boiled so I had to forget everything for the moment and concentrate on making the coffee.

Mother was in full flow and Simon looked slightly bemused but relieved when I went in with the coffee on a tray.

'I've been telling Simon about the time you fell into the duck pond when we were on holiday in Devon... do you remember, dear?'

'No, I can't say I do' I replied as I handed Simon his coffee.

'Oh you must remember, you'd been so naughty... and your Father had to smack you because of your silly tantrum, then you ran off and didn't look where you were going and ended up in the pond... you looked so funny all covered in weed...'

'I'm sure Simon isn't that interested' I said as I placed her cup on the coffee table.

'Oh, I am' he volunteered and I looked at him with a stony expression as I sat down opposite.

'See, he wants to know all about you, dear' Mother purred before picking up her coffee cup.

'So... what embarrassing thing are you going to tell him next?'

163

I asked in a truculent tone.

'What would you like me to tell him, dear?' she countered.

'Anything you like... I've no secrets' I replied, she raised her eyebrows and scoffed, murmuring 'dear God... I wish.'

'I fell into a pond once, not a duck pond, just one in my uncle's back garden' said Simon, attempting to come to my rescue.

'Oh, what happened to you?' asked Mother, as if she was interested.

'Well, I'd been playing with a friend from school and we'd been mucking about and I fell backwards into it' he replied.

'Oh dear, were you hurt?'

'No, just wet, and uncle wasn't amused as he had just put in some water lilies' he replied with a smile.

'We had a superb dinner this evening' I said, wanting to get out of ponds of all types as soon as possible.

'Oh how nice, what did you have?' asked Mother so I told her and when I'd finished she said 'obviously Simon has such good taste... and that's so rare to find in a man these days.'

'You're too kind' he said with a smile and I thought 'she's doing her very best to flatter him into submission... poor thing, he doesn't stand a chance with her. Then to my surprise she stood up and said 'it's past my bedtime now, so I'll say goodnight, Simon and hope to see you again soon... you must invite Simon for Sunday lunch sometime, Clare'

'Yes, I will' I replied as she left the room, calling out 'goodnight' once again. Simon replied to her and then came and sat by me on the settee.

'I've had a wonderful evening, Clare' he whispered then kissed me on my cheek as he put his arm around me.

'So have I.'

'I'm glad, can we do it again soon?' he asked.

'Yes why not... but first, I think you should come to lunch one Sunday, when you're free.'

'Oh I would like that' he replied.

'Good' I said before he kissed me on my lips and made it last.

'Oh Clare, I think you're gorgeous' he whispered.

'And you're so nice too' I replied.

We kissed and cuddled for awhile, which was very pleasant and I really began to believe that this could be the man of my dreams, but what was the surprise I wondered?

Simon left about an hour later and I turned everything off downstairs and went to my room. I was just about to go in when Mother appeared on the landing in her nightie and said 'he's very nice, Clare, I really like him and I think he'd be absolutely ideal for you.'

'Yes, I think you may be right' I replied with a smile and then she hesitated for a moment.

'I don't want to interfere or anything...' she began and I thought 'not much!' before she continued 'but a very well spoken man phoned this evening, while you were out, and asked if you could ring him... he left his number and said his name is Rupert.'

CHAPTER 10

JEFF RECEIVES AN UNWELCOME CALL

Try as I might I couldn't get Clare out of my mind. There was always something there to remind me of her and I decided that I should keep on trying no matter what... even if she said 'no' to me a thousand times.

I called in at Hamilton Motors as often as I could, without being too obvious and when I discovered that she had gone on holiday to France I thought that this was the moment I'd been waiting for. I reasoned that she would be in a relaxed mood when she returned and so this was my chance to try something different and persuade her to say 'yes'. I found out when she was due back at work and went in to see her on some pretext. She looked so lovely with a tan and I was tempted to ask if it was all over, I didn't of course, but I did wonder. She said that she had enjoyed her holiday and spent some time in Monaco with friends and I wondered who they were... perhaps one of them was Eric, her mysterious labourer who was at the pub. I felt a tinge of jealousy... no, on second thoughts it was more like a big wedge of jealousy!

I said that I would like to hear all about her holiday in Provence and to my surprise she said 'yes'. This was my chance, so when I arrived home that evening I began to think how I could persuade her to come on a date. It was too difficult to say anything at work with Tina there and Wilkes hovering, so I decided to write her a little note. The Personnel Department at Hamilton's gave me her home address along with other members of staff when I told the manager that I planned to invite some of them to a private function. I made several attempts at writing the note, the first few were too direct and had some sloppy bits, but I was finally satisfied when I finished up with a more casual and friendly invitation to call me at home. I kissed it before placing it in the envelope and hoped that it would do the trick.

It was Sunday morning when she phoned and I could hardly contain my excitement on hearing her voice. She agreed to come out for a drink the next evening and asked me to pick her up at eight. I arrived outside her house spot on time and when I saw her she looked lovely as ever. I drove to the 'Barley Mow' pub and we chatted all the way there about work and I was really pleased that she seemed so interested in my future plans. We sat by the fire, had a few drinks and I realised more and more that she was definitely the one for me.

Suddenly she said it was time to go as she had a busy day ahead at work tomorrow and I understood. When we arrived back at her place I asked if she would come out again and she said 'yes' so I told her that I would call her soon and she gave me her number... I was overjoyed!

I drove slowly home to Brentwood listening to the radio and wondering many 'what if's' about our blossoming relationship. I was so happy and began to plan our future together. We would have to get married in a Registry Office of course but that wouldn't be too much of a problem. Then we could honeymoon either in Antigua or the Seychelles, or whatever other paradise she chose. Nothing would be too good for her and fortunately I had enough money saved from my Army gratuity to spoil her. When I arrived home I poured myself a large scotch and sat like a contented cat... very relaxed listening to some of Chopin's piano masterpieces.

I was busy all week and had to make many follow up calls to the Dealerships who had been flagging up various problems. I had intended to phone Clare on the Thursday but I didn't get home until quite late that evening so decided to call her on Friday and invite her out for dinner on Saturday. I phoned her just after eight and her Mother answered before passing me over. We had a chat about work and I apologised for not calling sooner but she understood when I explained how busy I had been... she's always so wonderfully understanding. She agreed to have dinner with me on Saturday... I said I'd pick her up at seven. We said 'goodbye' and I kissed the phone before putting it down.

I planned to take her to 'The Royal Hotel' in Chelmsford where the food is superb and then, if I could persuade her, back to my place for coffee. I felt lucky at last and believed that my years of loneliness were coming to an end. I phoned the hotel and booked a table for two at eight on Saturday. I had just poured myself a celebration scotch and added a little ginger when the phone rang.

'Hammond here' I said then there was a few moments silence so I repeated 'Jeff Hammond here.' Then my heart froze as a voice I recognised instantly said slowly 'Jeff… it's me… Evelyn.' I didn't know what to say for a moment then blurted out 'what do you want?'

'To talk to you.'

'Why?'

'I'm in a lot of trouble…'

'So talk to Ashford' I interrupted.

'I can't…'

'Why not?' I asked angrily.

'Because he's dead' she replied… that shook me and I heard her begin to cry. I thought 'God, this bastard broke up our marriage and now has made my lovely ex-wife unhappy… will this evil never end?'

'So tell me, what sort of trouble are you in?' I asked in a sympathetic tone.

'Oh, Jeff, everything has gone wrong for me' she replied and I heard her sobbing gently.

'Well, I realise that you must be upset but I can't help if you don't tell me' I said gently.

'He died last week from a massive heart attack…' she began, but started sobbing again so I waited patiently for her to compose herself before saying gently 'please go on.'

'He was only sixty four you know' she blurted out as if I cared a damn about his age. To me he was an unscrupulous adulterer who had ruined my happy life and I couldn't have cared less about him. In fact I was quite glad he was dead but I knew that Evelyn was now in trouble as a result and I would have to help her. This could not have come at a worse time… just as I was hoping to start a new life with Clare I was being dragged back into my dark unhappiness by events caused by Ashford.

'So how can I help you?' I asked.

'Oh Jeff, can I come and see you?'

Slightly alarmed, I asked 'when?'

'Tonight…'

'It's very late' I replied.

'I must see you, Jeff... I'm in terrible trouble, I really am...'

'Well first off, I think you'd better tell me what's wrong' I said firmly realising that this was going to be lengthy and difficult. I waited for a few moments before she said 'I've got to move out of my flat straight away...'

'Why?'

'It's a long story' she replied wearily.

'Well start near the end!'

There was another pause.

'This flat is owned by the business...' she began and I guessed what was coming next.

'... and the business was in deep trouble, well I knew it was before he died... but I didn't know how much trouble... it's... it's now finished, totally bankrupt.'

'Go on' I murmured.

'It's in the hands of the Receivers and they have given me notice to move out within fourteen days and I've nowhere to go' she replied and started to cry again.

'Well you can't stay here with me' I said.

'I just want to see you, Jeff, because you're always so sensible and I'm sure if we can just talk it'll help and I'll know what to do for the best, I'm in such a muddle at the moment' she pleaded and I felt sorry for my lovely ex-wife.

'Okay' I sighed.

'Oh, thank you, Jeff.'

'Have you my address?'

'Yes, I'll be there as soon as I can... goodbye, darling.'

I didn't much like being called 'darling', as it sounded like some sort of opening shot to something that I wasn't prepared for... like having her back. I finished my scotch and poured another one... I made it extra stiff!

It was just before ten when she arrived and rang my sonnet. I clicked the front door open and waited until she came up the stairs. My first impression was that she had aged quite a lot since I saw her last but I smiled and she smiled back before I put my arms around her and gave her a quick kiss then said 'come on in.'

'Thanks, Jeff' she whispered.

I waved her to a seat and asked 'would you like something to

169

drink?'

'Yes, please, a scotch would be nice' she replied as she sat on the settee.

I poured two large scotches, sat beside her and said 'here's to you and may heaven help you!' She smiled and touched my glass before taking a good gulp of the golden reviver.

'So, start at the beginning and I'll listen carefully' I said and she nodded.

At the outset of their relationship everything was wonderful with many trips abroad on so called 'business', which actually amounted to very little in the way of firm orders for the paper making machinery that the company manufactured. It soon became obvious that Ashford was on some sort of prolonged 'holiday abroad' enjoying himself at his shareholders expense whilst Evelyn spent money that the business didn't have. His spendthrift actions were tolerated by the Bank because he was able to offer up his home and Evelyn's flat as security whilst he talked vaguely about large orders that were just about to drop into his sales portfolio. This nonsense eventually had to come to an end and so it did. The business collapsed very swiftly, the Bank seized everything they could then sent in the Receivers for the remains. All the staff were made redundant and salaries were paid up to the end of the month with nothing more to come. In the midst of all this Ashford had his heart attack, leaving many unanswered questions. As a result Evelyn had lost her home, her job and her old lover… what an unhappy mess this wretched man had made of our lives.

When she had finished her tale of woe I asked 'why don't you stay with your Mother for awhile whilst you sort things out?'

'I can't.'

'Why not?'

'We had a terrible row when I left you…' she hesitated then continued 'she said that she disowned me for what I'd done to you and she hasn't spoken to me since.' A tear ran down her cheek as she looked down into her glass of scotch. I sighed and looked away then nodded.

'You could ask her, I mean you're her only daughter and you are in trouble…' I said.

'It's impossible... she'll never agree' she interrupted.

'Well, that's that then' I said slowly after a few moments.

'Oh Jeff, I know that I was a fool to leave you but...'

'There are no 'buts' Evelyn, this could have all been avoided because I remember begging you on my bloody bended knees not to leave me for that old bastard and you were having none of it!'

'I know' she whispered.

'All you said when you marched out the door was 'that's how it is!' and left me in lonely misery for years!'

'I'm so sorry, Jeff' she whispered.

'Well it's all over now and because I still love you I will try and help, but I can make no promises' I said fairly calmly.

'Oh thank you darling... I always knew that you still loved me.'

I ignored that and said 'so the first thing is to find you somewhere to stay when you leave the flat.'

'Can't I stay here with you?' she asked.

'Certainly not!'

'Why? I thought you just said that you loved me and would help me' she said with an imploring wide eyed look.

'I do love you but could never trust you again no matter what you say' I replied.

'But Jeff...'

'Listen carefully to me, Evelyn. I've lived alone for years now, worrying and thinking about you, but those days are over forever. If I let you back into my life for just one moment you might do the same thing again with someone else and I just couldn't stand it... it would kill me and I really can't take that chance. So, I will help you this time, but once you're gone and I know that you are okay, I never want to see you again, is that clear?'

She burst into tears began to sob and I felt like a real callous monster.

'Oh Jeff' she whispered between sobs but suddenly I was feeling better about myself.

'You must understand how it is now... there's no going back' I said firmly and she nodded slightly before taking a large sip of her scotch.

'Well, can you give me some money?' she asked tearfully.

'How much?'

'A thousand would help me a lot' she replied.

'What's it for?'

'Oh, bloody well everything... help the bank overdraft, something for the credit cards, food and some petrol to get home' she said gloomily.

'Have you nothing at all?' I asked.

'No, my salary is all spent, my cards are all maxed out and my car has to go back on Wednesday...'

'It's a company car then?' I interrupted.

'Yes' she replied and I just shook my head. She really had nothing left so now was the time for action.

'Right, I'll give you a cheque for nine hundred and I've got about a hundred in cash that you can have now...'

'Oh thank you Jeff' she smiled.

'And when I get to work on Monday I'll try and find you a car of some sort before Wednesday.'

'That's wonderful!'

I wrote a cheque, gave her the cash then poured another much needed drink for us. We sat and talked for what seemed quite a short time and I gave her my advice on what she should try to do next. It was obvious that she had to get a job and find somewhere to live, both top priorities but not easy at the moment. I glanced at my watch and saw that it was well past midnight.

'I think we'd better call it a day now' I said.

'Yes, of course, you must be tired, darling... now where am I going to sleep?'

I was stunned for a moment and replied 'well not here!'

'But Jeff darling it's far too late for me to drive home, besides I've had too much to drink!' she said with a grin and I sighed, knowing that I had to give in.

'Okay, you can sleep in my room and I'll kip down on the floor in here' I said, whilst thinking that I had to get rid of her before Saturday evening when I planned to bring Clare back for coffee. If Clare knew Evelyn was here, it would be all over forever! Oh dear God... I hoped that nothing would go wrong!

When I woke up on the floor the next morning I felt pretty awful and promised myself that I wouldn't drink so much in future, especially late at night. As I came round, still in a haze of alcohol,

I could hear Evelyn in the kitchen, then smelled the coffee. It brought back memories of having my wife living with me and I felt so bitter at what Ashford had done to us.

'Morning darling' she said as she came in with two steaming mugs.

'Morning' I mumbled.

'I thought you could do with this' she said as she placed a mug next to me on the floor.

'Thanks' I said glancing up at her. She was wearing one of my shirts and just her panties! It was a lovely sight and I had to look away when she sat down on the settee.

'I thought that after breakfast I would do some food shopping and then buy the petrol' she said.

'A good idea' I mumbled.

'Where's the nearest garage, darling?'

'At the end of the high street... going back towards the motorway.'

'So it's on my way home then?'

'It is' I replied thankfully before sipping my coffee.

'Good. Now what would you like for breakfast?'

I had arranged to play golf with Richard that morning but I was unhappy about leaving Evelyn anywhere near my flat. I didn't want her turning up unexpectedly again when I was with Clare and knowing Evelyn that could easily happen! For my own peace of mind I had to make sure that she was well on her way home before I left to meet Richard at the club.

After we had pulled ourselves together, showered and dressed, Evelyn told me that she was ready to leave and I breathed a sigh of relief.

'Now promise you'll give me a call, here's my number' she said as handed me a business card.

'I will' I replied looking at the pretentious, embossed card which said she was the PA to the CEO, R. Ashford.

'And when you find a car, can you deliver it to me?' she asked.

'I'll try, but I can't make any promises' I replied, taken aback by her nerve.

'Well if you can't, it'll mean I'll have to find my own way over here on a train or something' she said.

'It may come to that, Evelyn.'

'That doesn't suit me at the moment!'

'Surely you must realise that you have lost everything and you'll have to start all over again... your life will be very different from now on' I said and she pulled a face.

'We'll see' she replied.

'That we will' I said before giving her a quick kiss on her cheek and opening the door.

'Goodbye, Jeff.'

'Bye.'

'Thanks for the money and everything' she said as she stepped down the stairs to the front door.

'You're welcome' I said and thought 'I've a feeling that's not the last I've seen of you my darling!'

I told Richard about Evelyn's visit as we approached the fifth and he was about to chip to the green.

'I hope that you're not going to do anything silly, Jeff' he said as he squared up to take the shot.

'Like what?'

'Give her money or, God forbid, take her back' he replied.

'I've already done that' I said and he sighed before striking the ball.

'Done what?'

'Given her some money.'

'You're a fool, do you know that?' he asked, glancing at me.

'Well I prefer to think that I'm helping my ex-wife who's in deep trouble through no fault of her own' I said firmly.

'Bloody hell, Jeff, the woman had an affair... then deserted you for no good reason to be the mistress of an old married man... she deserves nothing!'

'No one gets what they deserve in this life, Richard... you should know it's too bloody unfair for that!'

He shrugged his shoulders and wandered off towards the green where his ball had landed, about five yards from the pin. As we putted for the hole, I said 'but I'll never take her back, you know.'

'Glad to hear it.'

'I'm seeing Clare now and hope it'll lead to something permanent' I said and he stopped his putter in mid swing then

174

smiled 'good for you' before sinking the ball with his next stroke.

He won the round as usual and after a quick drink in the clubhouse we said 'goodbye' and he wished me luck with Clare.

I spent the afternoon tidying the flat, hoovering throughout and dusting where necessary. I arranged my music discs for easy listening and checked all my drinks. I decided to pop out and buy a bottle of Gin as mine was almost empty and I knew Clare liked it with tonic. Armed with the Gin and several packets of nibbles of various kinds from my corner shop I made my way back to the flat and was horrified to see Evelyn standing by the street door.

'What's wrong now?' I asked anxiously.

'Would you believe my bloody car has broken down' she replied angrily and I murmured 'Oh dear God.'

'Where is it?'

'They towed me off the motorway and now it's stuck at some garage somewhere' she replied.

'Why have you come back here?' I asked.

'Well you were nearest, so where else could I go?'

'I don't know' I replied.

'I can't get home unless you take me…'

'Oh I will, I will!' I interrupted thinking what the consequence might be if she remained… I couldn't even think of it.

'Come in for a minute and I'll get organised then run you home' I said, hastily unlocking the door.

'Thanks.'

I hurried up the stairs and opened the door to my flat and she followed me in. I put the bag with the Gin and nibbles on the table and the bag opened up enough for her to see the bottle.

'Oh, having a party tonight are we?' she asked with a grin and my heart sank.

'No, it's just in case a business friend calls unexpectedly'.

'Does she work for you?'

'That's none of your business, Evelyn.'

'Oh darling, please don't go all 'po' faced about it' she said with a mischievous smile.

'I'm not, I will be ready to go in a minute' I said and I was!

I drove my BMW as fast as I dare to the M25 motorway and

headed towards St Albans, where she lived in the soon to be repossessed company flat. I told her to leave her car with the recovery garage and just tell the Receivers where it was and let them sort it out.

'You will make sure you get me a car then' she said.

'I promised you I would, didn't I?'

'Yes, but I need it now... I can't wait 'til Wednesday, I have to get about, Jeff.'

'I'm afraid I can't do anything until Monday...'

'Can't you call one of your garages or something and get them to deliver one today?' she interrupted.

'No, it's not as easy as that' I replied.

'Surely they must have hire cars or...'

'Evelyn, no!' interrupted angrily.

We remained quiet until I reached the turn off for St. Albans then she directed me to the road where her flat was situated. When I pulled up outside the two story building she asked 'are you coming in, Jeff?'

'No thanks' I replied as I was not curious to see where the old man had slept with my wife.

'Please yourself then.'

'I will thanks.'

'Phone me on Monday about the car' she said frostily as she undid her seat belt and climbed out.

'Yes, I will' I replied. She slammed the door shut and flounced up the path to the front door without looking back.

I drove to Brentwood feeling very relieved knowing that she wouldn't turn up unexpectedly and spoil my evening with Clare.

I put all thoughts of Evelyn behind me as I drove to Romford to pick up Clare. I also decided not to talk about work or anything remotely connected to it and instead would ask her about her holiday in Provence.

Clare looked lovely as usual and was smiling when she came out of her house. I smiled at her as she walked down the driveway towards me waiting by the car.

'Hello, Jeff.'

'Hello, you' I said before I opened the door for her.

As we drove away I caught a glimpse of her Mother looking out of the window and wondered when I was going to be invited to meet her… I would like it to be sooner rather than later.

'I hope you're hungry tonight because the hotel restaurant we're going to not only serves good food, but the portions are pretty enormous' I said and she laughed.

'Oh dear, that's not good news because I'm trying to lose weight' she said.

'What on Earth for?'

'Well, I overdid it a bit in France… one way or another' she replied with a smile.

'That's hard to believe, so you'd better tell me all about it' I said and she did.

She was very open about it all and I was quite fascinated by the events surrounding her posing for the artist, Christine and then the unceremonious ducking of the 'Countess' in the pool. I laughed a lot during her tale of woe and felt very attracted to this lovely, spirited young woman.

Clare finished telling me about her 'interesting' week's holiday with Jane just as we arrived at 'The Royal Hotel.'

Our reserved candlelit table for two was at the back of the elegant restaurant and we were shown to it by the attentive Maitre d'.

'Well this is very nice' said Clare.

'I'm glad you approve' I replied as the waiter arrived with the menus.

After a quick perusal Clare chose prawn cocktail followed by Beef Wellington and I decided to have the same. The wine waiter appeared, presented the list and I ordered a light Burgundy to complement the meal.

'So tell me all about yourself and the positive things in your life' I said.

'Do you really want to know?' she asked.

'Of course… but if you wish you can leave out all the disappointing relationships and let downs… if there are any' I said with a grin and she laughed before replying 'believe me, those would take all night to go through!'

'I've all the time in the world and I'm listening' I replied and she smiled.

We chatted and laughed all through the meal and I got the impression that she was beginning to find me quite attractive, which pleased me no end but I wondered if it was the wine talking. There's nothing like success to encourage you on to better things, even if it is wine induced! As the sweet trolley approached I thought that I could get her back to my flat without too much resistance.

Clare had a sherry trifle whilst I chose the fruit salad. When we had finished I asked 'would you like to have coffee here or perhaps at my place where we can talk some more?' I waited anxiously in hope for a moment before she replied 'that sounds inviting, so why not?' My heart beat faster and I waved to the waiter for the bill.

I drove at a leisurely pace back to Brentwood with the stereo background music on low volume as Clare chatted away. I could sense her relaxing as the journey continued and I was so very happy and feeling content.

I opened the street door for her and she went up the stairs with me following. I unlocked my flat door, went in and switched on the hall light.

'So welcome to my humble abode' I said with a smile as she walked in and that was when it all suddenly changed. As I helped her off with her coat she caught sight of my painting. She stood motionless, pale faced, staring at it.

'Do you like it?' I asked anxiously but she didn't reply so I hesitated for a moment before saying 'I like to think it's a portrait of my guardian angel... do you believe in angels, Clare?'

She turned, looked at me and whispered 'make the coffee, Jeff then you can tell me all about this picture.' So I did.

CHAPTER 11

CLARE HAS A SURPRISE

I laid in bed thinking about my very pleasant evening with Simon but wondered why Rupert had phoned. Why did he want to talk to me? Perhaps he wanted to find out more about Jane's antics on holiday or was there something else? I decided to call him from work during my lunch break the next day when I knew that Tina would be out of the office and I would have some peace. She does go on about 'Dezzie' all the time now!

I hurried to work and began to go through the outstanding list of accounts but my curiosity about Rupert was becoming more aroused as the time went on and I could hardly wait for lunch time to call him. At last it came and Tina wandered off to gossip with the other girls in the rest room and to eat her slimline, fat free yoghurts. I dialled the number that was on the scrap of paper that Mother had given me and waited. It seemed to ring out for an age before I heard his voice.

'Hello, Rupert Carter here.'
'Hi Rupert it's me…'
'Oh, Clare! I'm so glad you called' he said.
'Yes, so tell me, what's this all about?' I asked in my polite but curious tone.
'Well, it's a long story, so could we meet?'
'Yes, I suppose so…' I replied hesitantly.
'Excellent, how about lunch tomorrow and I'll explain everything?'
'Tomorrow?'
'Yes.'
'Is it urgent then?'
'I think so and it's very important to me' he replied.
'I hope it's nothing serious.'
'That's for you to decide.'
'Oh my God, then it is serious… is it about Jane?'
'No not really.'
'Well, what then?' I persisted but realised I was getting

nowhere with him.

'I'll reveal all when I see you tomorrow.'

'Right.'

'I'll collect you at your place at about twelve if that's okay' he replied.

'Yes, okay, see you at twelve then' I said and he hung up.

I sat for a few minutes wondering what he wanted to tell me and my emotions went into roller coaster mode but I didn't know whether I was travelling up or down.

Then Tina came back from the rest room early and my mood changed as she waffled on about 'Dezzie' for the remainder of the break.

The rest of the day dragged and I was glad to get home for the weekend, which on the face of it, looked like it could be quite interesting. Mother was in a good mood and I suspected that her meeting with Simon had much to do with it. She could now see me married and away in the near future.

'Did you have a chance to call that nice man Rupert?' she asked as she made a pot of tea.

'Yes.'

'Well, what did he say?'

'He didn't tell me over the phone but he's taking me out to lunch tomorrow to explain everything' I replied.

'Oh that sounds interesting, dear' she said and I guessed she thought that the more men hovering around me, the better chance she had of waving me 'goodbye.'

'Whatever it is he said it was very important to him' I said as she poured the tea.

'And by the sound of it… it might include you' she said.

'Me?'

'Yes, he may have a nice surprise for you.'

'Like what?'

'I don't know dear, but you'll find out tomorrow… that's for sure' she replied and I sat silently sipping my tea thinking 'whatever could it be?'

We had just finished our evening meal and were about to watch the television when Hammond called, Mother answered and passed the phone over to me. I was surprised when he invited me out to dinner and thinking quickly about Eric's advice to be nice and open my mind to everyone, I said 'yes'... hoping I wouldn't regret it.

After I put the phone down, Mother looked smug and said 'it sounds as if they're queuing up for you, dear.'

'Yes it does' I replied and thought 'I'm in for a busy weekend and if Eric turns up, it will be the icing on the cake!'

Rupert arrived just after twelve on Saturday and I was all ready to go with my curiosity now at fever pitch. He smiled as I walked down the drive to him waiting by his car. It was a gleaming black Mercedes sports car with cream trim and he opened the door for me. I was suitably impressed and thought 'he must have been paid a hell of a forward royalty for his novel to be able to afford this little beauty.'

'Hello Clare, I'm so glad that you could make it today' he said.

'So am I' I replied as he closed the door.

The Mercedes wafted effortlessly away down the road and I asked 'This is very nice, Rupert, is it yours?'

'No not yet, I've got it on approval for the weekend' he replied.

'And do you approve?'

'Well it seems okay so far... but what do you think of it?'

'It's very nice and swishy' I replied thinking 'why should he ask me... or was I being naive?'

'I'm glad you like it' he said as if it really mattered to him and my curiosity went up another notch. I decided to let him tell me what was on his mind rather than asking, so I sat back and enjoyed the fast ride out to wherever he was taking me. On the way he chatted about his novel and the adventures he was having with his publisher trying to organise a book signing tour. I was very interested but wanted to know what progress his agent was making selling the screen rights to a film studio but remained silent... my questions would come later!

He drove out to Stapleford Abbotts and pulled into the car park at 'The Lamb' pub.

'The food's good and I often come out here to think' he said as he guided me into the picturesque, oak beamed pub. We ordered drinks, sat down near the open fire and said 'cheers.' I had a sip of gin and then looked at him closely. Without a doubt he had changed, become more mature, worldly and he somehow now appeared distinguished or was it my imagination? As I was now giving everybody the benefit of my 'open minded' approach I wondered if it was allowing me to see them in a new light... perhaps it had been lit by my angel Eric.

At Rupert's suggestion we ordered shepherds' pie for lunch and I waited impatiently for him to tell me what was on his mind as he prattled on about his publisher. The food was delicious and it was after he bought another round of drinks that he started on the big important story.

'My life has been in quite a whirl since I signed the contract with my publisher and received the advance royalty cheque' he said with a smile.

'I'm sure it has.'

'And I've had a chance to re-evaluate everything in my life and I know what I want for the future' he said in a serious tone and I thought 'oh oh, here it comes!' but asked helpfully 'a move to Hollywood?'

'No, not just yet... but to France... with you!'

'With me?'

'Yes, Clare with you!'

'But what about Jane?' I asked.

'I fell in love with you the first moment I saw you and have been in love ever since' he replied and I was slightly bemused but quite happy to know that I was so attractive to men.

'Really?' I asked with a mischievous smile.

'Oh yes, Clare.'

'But what about Jane?' I persisted.

'I've never really seen Jane as my life's companion, she is just a good friend in reality' he replied and I thought 'so she's been wasting her time then.'

I stayed silent for a moment whilst that sunk in, then asked 'so how would this work, Rupert?'

'We'd buy a villa somewhere, anywhere you like in the south, and move there right away... leave everything behind, all the unhappiness... all the day to day harassments, everything... and start a new life together' he replied.

'Sounds too good to be true' I said.

'Listen Clare, I have enough money now to last us for years and if the film contract comes off, we could live like millionaires for the rest of our lives.' It sounded more than 'too good to be true' but I wasn't sure if he was the right one for me. I had to have time, much more time before I could make such a leap into a new life with a comparative stranger. I thought about Jane and knew how upset she would be if I wandered off to France with Rupert. It would be the end of our friendship forever and I would be very sad about that.

Then I thought 'what if he is lousy in bed? That would never do... because I need it daily, perhaps that was why I was so edgy at the moment. I needed to talk to Eric first, so I planned a walk in the park on Sunday morning and hoped the old gentleman with his sweet little dog would let my angel know that I was waiting for him.

Rupert carried on talking as if I had agreed to live with him in France but I wasn't paying much attention and just nodded now and then.

He was waffling on when I suddenly got fed up, decided to call his bluff and asked 'so are we getting married before we go to France or when we get there?' He stopped mid-sentence, blushed a little and replied 'er, er, I hadn't planned that far ahead yet...'

'And why not?' I demanded.

'Well, as you know all artists are great lovers but authors are the best...'

'What makes you say that?'

'Because, Clare, they have empathy' he replied with a smile.

'But never marry' I added.

'They can't for years and years, you have to realise that they're free spirits... only limited by their own imagination and marriage must wait until that dims...' he said with a silly little wave of his hand upwards. At that moment I decided I had seen and heard enough so didn't bother to pursue anything further with this stupid man who had just become very well off, which was a total surprise to him. I was fairly sure that he was not the one for me and I had doubts that he was ever right for Jane, but time would tell if she became more than a friend.

After I told him that I would consider his proposal to be his mistress and live with him in France while he churned out bestsellers, but needed time to think, he seemed to loose interest. I mean, I could have said 'no' to him right away, but I didn't want to burn my bridges if it wasn't absolutely necessary... just in case!

He drove me back home in relative silence and I was glad when we eventually arrived. After he stopped the Mercedes he said 'please give it all some careful thought, Clare.'

'Yes, I will, Rupert.'

'I wouldn't want you to be unhappy with me...'

'Neither would I' I interrupted.

'But I'm sure we'd be great together and having you with me would spur me on to write such wonderful things that I feel deep inside' he said with a touch of passion.

'Well I'll think about it' I said in a flat tone.

'Let's talk some more... I'll call you sometime next week' he said.

'Okay' I replied before opening the car door.

We said 'goodbye' and I went in to face Mother's questions before getting all 'glammed' up for Hammond. When I went to my room to get ready I wondered if I should tell Jane what Rupert had proposed but I decided to think about it and perhaps ask Eric before I said anything to her.

In my new spirit of 'open heartedness' and my previous unkind 'pre-judgments', I made a conscious effort to look good for Hammond. I didn't think he was my type but I stuck to Eric's advice and did my very best for the knicker sniffer. After a shower, hair dry and full remake of my makeup, I slipped into my red dress, put on my transvestite shoes, piled everything necessary for the evening into my clutch bag and dabbed my Givenchy 'L'amour' in all the right places. I was now ready to meet him and hoped this time I would enjoy myself a little, but I wasn't expecting too much from Hammond except more 'work talk'. I hoped the food was going to be good.

Hammond arrived on time and we set off to 'The Royal Hotel' in Chelmsford where he assured me the food was excellent. To my surprise he never mentioned work but chatted about my holiday in Provence and asked all the right questions. I told him everything in detail and he laughed in all the right places and seemed really interested. It is so good when a man listens to what a woman says because so often they just bang on about what they've done all the time and it's so bloody boring!

The hotel restaurant was very swish and I was quite impressed when we sat at our reserved candlelit table for two. I decided on prawns for my starter then Beef Wellington as my main course. Jeff ordered the same and a bottle of Burgundy to go with the meal. It was all very pleasant and I felt myself relaxing with this man who had appeared so boring on our last date. He laughed easily, smiled a lot and was really entertaining. I finished my meal with a trifle from the sweet trolley and had extra cream poured all over it! Then Jeff asked if I wanted coffee here or back at his place where we could talk. I hesitated for just a moment before saying 'that sounds inviting, so why not?' and he looked delighted.

We drove back to Brentwood listening to his music and chatting about nothing in particular. I was now feeling very relaxed and warming to Jeff in a positive way which surprised me. After he parked the BMW he opened the street door and followed me up to his flat on the first floor. He unlocked the door then switched on the hall light and I followed him in. As he took my coat I saw the painting and was completely dumbstruck! It was of an angel with folded wings and had a face that I instantly recognised. Jeff said something about his guardian angel but I wasn't listening and told him to make the coffee then tell me all about the picture... so he did.

I tried to compose myself while Jeff was making the coffee. My mind was turning somersaults but I tried to think clearly as there were so many questions to be answered. He appeared with a pot of coffee and cups on a tray and placed it on the low table before sitting beside me on the settee.

'How do you like it?' he asked.

'Black please with plenty of sugar' I replied and he poured then spooned in two heaped brown sugars.

'I hope that's okay' he said with a smile and I just nodded.

I sipped the coffee for awhile before asking him to tell me all about the painting.

'Well, it's quite a long story and you may find some of it a bit strange' he said.

'Somehow I don't think so' I replied.

'Right then, well it goes back to when I was serving in Iraq...'

'You were in the army?' I interrupted.

'Yes, the Seventh Armoured Brigade... I was a tank commander' he replied.

'Really?'

'Yes, and I had a life changing experience out there which is why I ended up buying that picture of an angel.'

'Please go on... I'm listening' I said and he smiled.

'We had been ordered forward on a 'recce' to try and pin point Saddam's tanks as the weather had closed in with low cloud cover and on top of that, sand was blowing all over the place, which made impossible for our aircraft to spot any movement on the ground.'

'Dear God' I whispered.

'We had stopped and I was standing up in the turret with my binoculars trying to spot anything, but it was no good, the bloody sand was making it impossible. After a few minutes I called down to my gunner, a wonderful chap called 'Ozzie', to come up and take my place because I wanted to contact Command HQ on the radio and report our position. We changed places and I slipped down to make the call. I had just started when I heard the sound of incoming small arms fire hitting the tank then a terrible 'thwack' and I realised that we had been hit by something pretty substantial' he said then stopped for a moment and I could see his eyes misting up.

'Then what happened?' I asked gently.

'I called out to 'Ozzie' several times but he didn't reply, so I knew he'd been hit' he replied and I saw his tears.

'Sorry, I'm so sorry, Clare' he whispered as he took out a handkerchief and dabbed at his eyes.

'Don't tell me any more if you don't want to' I said.

'No, no, it's okay, I'd like to... if that's alright.'

'Yes, of course.'

'Well, I tried to get 'Ozzie' down from the turret but couldn't manage it on my own so called Mike, my driver, to help. He scrambled up from his seat and somehow after a struggle we got him down through the hatch into the tank. I didn't know whether he was alive or dead when I first called out to him but when I saw the terrible shrapnel wounds in his face, I knew he was dead. I can't remember much else... except saying over and over again 'oh, Jesus Christ, oh, Jesus Christ!'' he said as the tears ran down his cheeks.

'How awful' I whispered.

'We could do nothing for him, he was gone... gone forever and I never felt so bloody helpless in my life. If I hadn't asked him to take my place I would have been killed... and not him, which haunts me still... I thought I must have a guardian angel.'

'I'm sure that's true.'

''Ozzie' had served with me for years and I got to know him very well. His name was Alec Osbourne but he preferred to be called 'Ozzie', and so that's what we called him.'

Jeff stayed silent for a moment and had a sip of coffee before he said 'then I called HQ with the sad news and we were ordered to pull back, which we did, but only after I fired our .50 calibre machine gun in an arc of about 45 degrees in the direction of the incoming fire, which stopped. I couldn't see anything through the sand and dust but for 'Ozzie's' sake I just wanted to do something to show that his life had not been taken in vain.'

We sat quietly for a moment or two before he said 'then 'Ozzie' was repatriated for burial at his home near Lincoln and I had a replacement gunner.'

'So tell me about the painting of the angel' I said, hoping that changing the subject would make him feel better. He smiled and said 'now this is the strange part of the story, so I hope you won't think I'm mad or anything.'

'No, I won't' I said knowing that this was going to be very interesting and what I half expected.

'When I got back from Iraq I left the army but was still suffering from post traumatic stress and had many sleepless nights, sweats and nightmares. So I went to the Doc numerous times but there was little he could do for me, then a friend suggested that I go with them to a Christian Spiritualist Church service where I might find some peace of mind through their healing.'

'And did you?' I asked and he looked at me for a moment as if he was hesitating with an answer that might put me off.

'Yes, I did… thinking, I'll try anything that helps and something quite remarkable happened.'

'Go on.'

'I wasn't sure what to expect the first time but everybody seemed very friendly and the young Minister was quite an extrovert character and made the congregation laugh a lot. We sang hymns and had readings by some of the regulars and I was impressed with these people's kind thoughts towards others, then we came to the medium. This lady was quite remarkable and spoke to various members of the congregation, telling them that she was in touch with their close family and friends who had died. I listened to the messages coming through and thought 'oh yeah' but was totally surprised when she came to me. She asked if she could work with me and I said 'yes', then… you won't believe this…'

'Oh yes I will' I interrupted.

'Have you been to a Spiritualist Church then?' he asked.

'No never, but I think I know what's coming next' I replied and he looked surprised.

'Well, she said she could see a man standing near me in an army uniform and said that his name began with 'O', at that moment I went cold but she carried on, saying that I was with him when he passed over to the spirit world and he wanted to tell me that everything is alright now and not to worry about him… I was quite overcome and then she said 'O' is glad that 'Daisy' was alright…'

'Who's Daisy' I asked.

'That's what we called our tank, 'Daisy Doolittle', and nobody, other than the three of us, knew that' he replied.

'That was a surprise then.'

'It was and from then on I went fairly regularly and have felt so much better as a result of the healing that was given to me at the church after the service' he said.

'But you still haven't told me about the painting' I said with a smile.

'Ah well, when I arrived back from Iraq I went up to Lincoln to visit 'Ozzie's' family and see his grave. Afterwards, when I was walking through the town, I saw the painting in the window of an antiques shop. I was very moved by it and something inside of me said that I should buy it, so I did. I've hung it opposite the mirror, so when I check myself out before I leave in the morning, I can see the reflection of my angel looking at me over my right shoulder. I realise how lucky I am to be alive, think of 'Ozzie' and always feel much better.'

'Do you recognise the face of the angel?' I asked.

'No... I don't' he replied.

'Well I do!'

'Really?'

'Yes... it's the man you saw when we when we stopped at the Windmill pub for lunch' I replied.

'You mean that tall labouring fella, who was following you, er, what's his name...'

'Eric' I said helpfully.

'Are you sure?'

'Quite sure, don't you recognise him now?'

'No, not really, I mean I didn't take much notice of him at the time, all I can remember is that he was tall' replied Jeff.

'He certainly is.'

'Have you seen him since then?'

'Often...'

'Oh my God!' he interrupted.

'...and he says he's an angel' I said and Jeff looked stunned.

'Do you believe him?'

'Yes, I do.'

'What makes you say that?'

'Things he tells me when he appears unexpectedly... like in France' I replied.

'Was he on holiday with you?'

'No, he just appeared sometimes when I was alone and we talked' I replied.

'What about?'

'Me... and my future happiness.'

'So tell me then' he said with a smile.

'Well he said that I would be happy with someone I already knew and marry him' I replied.

'That's hardly a shattering observation' said Jeff.

'True, but what you don't know is that there are several people in my life at the moment and anyone of them could be the man' I replied.

'And do you know which one it is?' he asked.

'I think I do now' I replied.

'And?'

'That would be telling' I replied with a grin.

'So is it the fickle finger of fate or Eric that will decide who the lucky man will be?'

'No, it'll be me, but I know I've been guided to him' I replied.

'Presumably by Eric?'

'Yes.'

'Well good for you and when will the man of your dreams be told that he has to marry you?'

'Soon' I giggled.

'That's a relief then' he said with a smile.

'It is.'

'Then I think I should like to have a drink to Eric's health and good guidance... so would you like to join me?' he said with a smile.

'Yes why not.'

'Brandy or scotch?'

'Brandy please' I replied and he nodded.

When he had poured the drinks he said 'I think we should toast him by his picture, don't you?' and I nodded.

In the hallway Jeff stood looking at the picture for a few moments and said 'you're right, my angel does look a bit like that chap Eric.'

'Trust me... it is him' I said.

'But the painting is very old, just look at it closely... and I don't know who painted it.' The dark background was all cracked with age but without doubt the face was Eric's and the unknown artist had captured the fascinating sparkle in his blue eyes.

'I'm sure it's him' I whispered.

'Well, here's to Eric then' he said as he raised his glass.

'To Eric' I said before sipping the brandy.

Jeff put his arm around me and kissed me gently on my cheek before saying 'I think it's time I took you home, Clare.'

I didn't argue for once and just nodded as I gazed at the painting for a few moments and thought 'there's a time and place for everything... but now is not the time to say or do anything more but go home and think carefully about the future.'

We remained quiet on the journey and I was content to listen to the background music whilst I thought about the evening's events. When we pulled up outside my house, Jeff asked 'can I see you again, Clare?'

'Yes of course.'

'That's wonderful, I'll call you on Monday evening if that's okay' he said with a smile.

'It is.'

'Well, goodnight, Clare, I hope you've enjoyed most of the evening.'

'Oh I have, thanks... including the sad story about 'Ozzie' and the medium in church' I replied and gave him a quick kiss on his lips before I opened the door. I called out 'goodnight, Jeff' before I made my way up to the front door then turned to wave before he drove off.

Would you believe that Mother was still up watching the television when I walked into the lounge?

'Have you had a good time, dear?'

'Yes, thanks.'

'Why didn't you bring him in for coffee?'

'Because we already had it at his place' I replied.

'Ohh... was it nice?'

'Do you mean the coffee or his place?'

'Well both.'

'Yes, his flat is very nice and so was his coffee' I replied as I tried hard to be pleasant.

'Are you seeing him again?' she asked with a grin.

'Yes, he's calling me on Monday to arrange a date.'

'Oh good, but he'd better be quick because that nice man Rupert phoned this evening and asked if you would call him tomorrow' she said and my heart sank. I hoped he wasn't going to be a nuisance just as I was trying to sort out my feelings.

'Right, I'll do that' I said lamely.

'I think he's got a soft spot for you, dear' she said.

'Possibly... I'm up to bed now, goodnight.'

'Goodnight.'

The next morning I pulled myself together, had a quick cup of coffee and went off to the park in the hope that Eric would turn up. I needed to talk to him as soon as possible. I sat on the usual bench and watched several sweaty, red faced overweight joggers stagger by before I spotted the old gentleman with the little dog, walking towards me from the other end of the park. I waited excitedly for him to approach and when he did, he smiled and said 'good morning.'

'Good morning.'

'He'll be along later' he said as he passed by.

'Thanks.'

'You're welcome' he nodded and I thought 'it's lovely to be surrounded by angels and I wonder how many more are wandering about?'

I sat quietly for the next half hour looking at each person who passed by and thinking 'is he one? No, too fat and not good looking enough! Or, perhaps she's one... no, her face is too severe and her jogging bottoms look ridiculous! Some people have no taste!

I was miles away when suddenly I heard Eric's voice say 'hello, Clare' and it made me jump because I hadn't seen him arrive.

'Hello, my angel' I replied with a smile as he sat next to me.

'So, you wanted to talk to me' he said gently.

'Yes, I suppose you know what it's about?'

'Of course' he said with a smile.

'Well, tell me, who is it?'

'It's your choice, Clare' he replied.

'But I want you to guide me' I wailed.

'I have, up to this moment, and now the final choice is yours, remember what I told you... you always have free will' he said.

'Well I don't want to have free will this time... just in case I make a mistake again, so I want you to guide me!'

'I'm afraid I can't do that... you have to be responsible for the decisions you make in this life and now the time has come for you to do that, or... you can walk away from this decision and wait until another opportunity for a happy marriage comes along, perhaps later in your life' he said.

'But I don't want to wait.'

'Then make your decision' he said calmly with a smile.

'Ohhh, men! You're all so bloody difficult!' I said and he laughed before he asked 'and you're not?'

'I don't think so!' I said and he laughed again so I decided to change the subject for a moment and asked 'should I tell my friend Jane that her bloke, Rupert, has asked me to live with him in France?'

'Yes, because friendship and loyalty are based on love and respect, it was not you who proposed this, but Rupert. He knew that it would upset Jane when she eventually found out and he should have told her himself before he said anything to you... but he didn't' he replied.

'Right, I'll tell her then... now will you at least give me a clue about...'

'No, Clare, you have to make your choice and I think you have already done that in your heart of hearts' he interrupted firmly and I knew he was right... I had made up my mind but just wanted him to confirm I was making the right decision. I didn't want another 'Tony' episode... one divorce was enough for me to last my lifetime!

'So tell me about the painting of you that Jeff bought in Lincoln' I asked and he just smiled, replying 'ah... that was painted a long time ago.'

'I could see that, but how long ago and who was the artist?' I asked... well a girl's got to know these things for her own peace of mind because there's nothing worse than not knowing something... is there?

Eric paused for a few moments and gazed at the lake before he looked at me and replied 'the artist was a young Dutchman who had tragically lost his wife in a house fire while he was away in the Dutch navy fighting the English.'

'So what's his name, when did he paint it and what happened to him afterwards?' I asked.

'Do you ever stop asking questions?'

'No, never' I replied and he laughed.

'I suppose that's to be expected... his name was Hans de Graff and he painted it after I met him.'

'Obviously, but when was it?'

'I went to him in 1652 with another angel…'

'In 1652?' I interrupted in total disbelief. 'I thought you were new to this?'

'Yes, I am. That was my first training mission but soon after that I had to help with other work and so have only recently returned to work as a guardian angel. Back then I was with an Archangel who was teaching me how to guide and give Hans some comfort in his despair by letting him know that he was never alone.'

'And what happened to him?'

'After a few years he found happiness with a widow, who loved him very much and they had four children, they prospered and lived a long life together' he replied.

'Oh that's a lovely story and I do love happy endings.'

'So do I, but sadly, not all lives end happily' he said.

'And what happens to those poor sods?'

'They are happy when they return to the spirit world. They chose the life they would lead before coming to the earth plane to enable them to learn a particular lesson. You are all here to learn lessons, that is the purpose of life on earth. But because of free will, things do not always work out quite as intended!' he replied with a comforting smile. 'It's too complicated to explain everything now, but I promise that one day all will be revealed to you.'

I decided to remain quiet and not ask any more questions... for the moment. We sat together in silence looking at the lake and admiring the golden trees for awhile. I was deep in thought when Eric said 'I think that you have made your decision and now there is no further need for me, so other than watching over you, I will not apear again unless I feel it is really necessary.'

'Ohhh, Eric…'

'I have much work to do, as I'm sure you can imagine, but I would like to give you something of mine because I think that you are a very special person and, as I told you, in my previous life I would have taken you as my wife.' I looked at him wide eyed and for once didn't know what to say.

'So take this ring with my love' he said as he produced a small band of gold from his leather jacket and, as if in a trance, I held out my left hand and he slipped on my little finger. I gazed at it and whispered 'oh, Eric… it's beautiful, thank you…'

'It belonged to my only real love, a young Saxon woman called Rowena' he said.

'What happened to her?'

'No questions, please… just take care of it and one day give it to your daughter' he said gently.

'Oh, Eric…'

'Goodbye, Clare' he said before he took me in his strong arms and kissed me very passionately for a long time… I didn't know angels could do that!

Then he stood up and strode away towards the golden trees leaving me breathless! He never looked back and I watched him until he disappeared… wondering if I would ever see him again… then I looked at the ring and started to cry.

CHAPTER 12

THANK GOD FOR ERIC AND HAPPY ENDINGS

I eventually stopped crying and sat for about an hour in the park, occasionally looking at the beautiful little gold ring that Eric had given me. It had a lightly engraved pattern on it and glistened in the bright autumn sun. I realised that he must care for me very much to give me such an intimate possession and I wondered what Rowena had looked like. Perhaps she was tall and a brunette like me or was she a petite blonde? Judging by the size of the ring I guessed she was petite, or… if she wore it on her little finger she was probably my size, because it fitted me perfectly. Was she a Saxon Princess or someone lowly born who he had fallen in love with? I wondered how they met and was it love at first sight? I had so many questions and so few answers to everything that had happened to me this year so I gave up thinking and wandered home for lunch. I didn't know where I was on my emotional roller coaster ride but hoped that it would soon settle down and level out so I could think clearly for awhile.

When I sat at the kitchen table, Mother took one look at me and said 'you've been gone a long time this morning and you look awful… have you been crying?' and I nodded.

'What about?' she asked in a sharp tone.

'It's a long story' I replied and there was a moments silence before she said 'well go on then… tell me!'

'I've been seeing another man and…'

'Now this sounds interesting' she interrupted as she sat down opposite.

'He says he's my guardian angel and gave me this ring' and I held up my hand, she gazed at it then said 'I've never heard such silly nonsense, so where did you get it? Tell me, because you know I'll find out in the end!'

'Oh bloody hell, I really can't be bothered with you at the moment' I said.

'Well it's no good having secrets, Clare, the truth will out one day' she said firmly and I sighed then gave in.

'His name is Eric…'

'And where did you meet him?'

'I first saw him at the wedding…'

'Was he one of the other side's guests?' she asked dismissively.

'No… he came alone.'

'Why?'

'I've told you… he said he was my guardian angel!' I replied angrily.

'Did you invite him?'

'No of course I didn't!' I replied.

'Well why should he come to your wedding for goodness sake?'

'I don't know do I?'

'So have you been meeting this Eric regularly?'

'Yes, we met when I was on holiday in France' I replied.

'Oh, I see and I suppose you're now involved with him.'

'Well no… at least not the way you mean' I said.

'And how do I mean?'

'Having rampant sex with him at every possible moment!'

'Well, it would probably do you good if that was the case but seeing as you're so touchy I can believe that he hasn't been near you… on second thoughts, that's probably why you're in such a state!' she said and I just shook my head. 'So is he gay?' she asked.

'No!'

'How do you know?'

'I just know… that's all.'

'Married?'

'No.'

'Are you sure?'

'Yes, I'm sure.'

'So when did he give you the ring?'

'This morning.'

'When you were in the park?'

'Yes.'

'And I suppose he's dumped you now and that's why you have been crying' she said in her 'know it all' tone.

'He hasn't dumped me because…' I started then hesitated.

'What?'

'He said that he loved me' I whispered and my eyes moistened.

'I can hardly believe what you're telling me' she said slowly.

'It's true.'

'You've got that nice man Simon after you and your boss, who you don't like... goodness knows why, and Rupert who keeps calling and you have to go off and start something with this Eric, words fail me, Clare!'

'That'll be the day!'

'So are you going to bring this Eric home so I can meet him?'

'He says that I won't see him again unless I need him' I replied.

'Well I think what you need is for him to make up his mind... does he love you or not? And why did he give you a ring?'

'It's something to remember him by... it belonged to the only other woman he loved' I replied.

'Oh, so he's gone back to her and now you're the other woman?'

'No... she's dead!'

'Oh, good God.'

'She was a Saxon...'

'I think you're becoming mentally disturbed and you should see Doctor Jennings as soon as possible' she said in a serious tone. At that precise moment the phone rang and I was glad of the interruption.

'That's bound to be for you' said Mother and I nodded before I went into the lounge.

'Hello.'

'Hello, Clare, it's Rupert here.'

'Oh hello, Rupert I was going to call you but I've only just got in' I said.

'Right, okay... now have you had a chance to think about things?' he asked.

'No not yet, but...'

'That's a shame' he interrupted.

'Is there some hurry now?' I asked.

'Well, there might be.'

'How so?'

'Look... it's a bit difficult to explain over the phone... so can we meet?'

'Yes… why not' I replied, now that my curiosity was aroused.

'Right, I'll call for you in about an hour if that's okay.'

'It is.'

'See you then, bye.'

'Bye, Rupert.' I hung up and wondered what it was all about.

After telling Mother I was going out with Rupert in an hour, I had a quick lunch of soup and a cheese sandwich in case he just wanted to talk in his car.

He arrived in his Mercedes and I was already to go with my curiosity level up a notch before I hurried out to meet him. We said 'hello' and then wafted away in his sleek sports car.

'I'm glad that you were able to come out' he said as we approached the end of my road.

'No problem, I was just having a quiet day as usual' I replied before I glanced at Eric's ring.

'Good.'

'So, what's this all about, Rupert?' I asked.

'Well… something unexpected has come up…' he said then hesitated.

'And?'

'It effects us' he replied and I wondered what was coming next!

'Go on.'

'Can we leave it until I can park up somewhere?'

'Yes, if you need to stop before you can talk' I replied a touch sarcastically. I mean to say, he phones me up and asks to see me within an hour because something urgent has come up and then he's struck dumb whilst driving! Men… I ask you!

I stayed silent, which was very hard in the circumstances, until he pulled into the car park at Hainault forest. It brought back childhood memories of when my parents were together and we all came here as a family to picnic… happy days!

He switched off the engine and we sat in silence for a few moments before I asked 'well, Rupert?'

'I don't how to tell you this…'

'I thought you were an author and good with words' I interrupted in a firm tone as I had now decided to give up my 'open minded' approach to him.

'Well I am…'

'So get on with it then!'

'Well… last night, I was invited by my publisher to a new author's 'do'… drinks and things.'

'And you met someone' I said, guessing what was coming next.

'Yes… yes I did, how did you know?'

'And you asked her to live with you in France' I replied.

'Oh, yes Clare, she's so in tune with me…'

'It's good to have met someone so in tune, Rupert' I said with a relieved smile knowing he wouldn't bother me anymore and my list of potential husbands was narrowing down to the chosen one.

'I think that's possibly true… her name is Sophie and she's just had her first book of poetry published' he said with a smile.

'Good for her.'

'Yes, it is and we spent last night after the 'do' at my place talking about my novel…'

'Then you're obviously made for each other' I interrupted.

'Yes, I think so too.'

'Well in that case everything is fine' I said and he gave me a serious look then said 'I'm glad that you've taken it so well, Clare.'

'It's the only thing to do' I replied thinking 'I wonder how long this cosy little relationship will last once they get to France… if they ever do.'

'I think you're wonderful' he whispered and I asked 'so what about Jane?' He looked flustered and replied 'she was only a friend you know.'

'Are you going to tell her about Sophie?'

He hesitated for a moment and then blurted out 'I wondered if you could tell her for me… I mean, I would tell her normally but I don't want to see her upset just now.'

What a bloody cheek! This silly man has no balls at all and as far as I was concerned he was a complete waste of time but thought it best that I should tell Jane she was dumped.

'Yes, I'll do that for you, Rupert, now I think you'd better take me home' I said calmly.

'Oh thank you, Clare, I really do think you're wonderful!'

'So do I.'

We drove back in silence, which I was grateful for, otherwise I might have been tempted to give this useless nobody a piece of my disturbed mind.

After saying 'goodbye' outside my place I felt relieved that I wasn't going to see him anymore. As I walked up to the front door I thought I'd had a lucky escape from a life with him that was definitely too good to be true... I must say I was almost tempted at first... but only for a brief moment!

I called Jane and asked if I could go over to see her at her flat.

'Yes of course, Clare' she replied.

'I've got something important to tell you' I said.

'Can't you tell me now?'

'No, it's a long story and it's better that we sit and talk' I replied.

'Well, okay... is it about Rupert?'

'Yes, he has...'

'Asked you to live with him in France' she interrupted.

'Look, I'll be over soon and we can talk then, so put the kettle on' I said.

'I knew it... he has asked you... the bastard!'

'Jane...'

'And are you going?'

'No I'm not! I'll see you soon' I replied and hung up.

She looked pretty cross when I arrived at her flat and her welcome was a bit subdued to say the least. She made mugs of tea and then we sat and talked. I told her all about Rupert's invitation to live with him in France whilst he churned out bestsellers. I said I wouldn't have dreamed of doing any such thing because whatever I felt about him, she was my best friend and I could never let her down... well sometimes you have to bend the truth a little so you don't hurt people you care about. Jane looked pleased with that but went pale when I told her about Sophie and her new book of poems.

'So he's dumped me for some little tart who can scribble 'the cat sat on the mat!''

'I'm afraid so' I replied.

'My God… what a tosser!'

'He certainly is.'

'And to think he kept me on a bit of string whilst he waited for someone else to turn up!'

'Yes it seems so.'

'Well I suppose it was only a matter of time before one or other of us dumped the other one and he's beaten me to it' she said philosophically with a sigh.

'Of course, but you did think about it when we had the dinner party' I said soothingly.

'So that would have made me first then' Jane said brightly.

'Yes, it's just a shame that we decided not to dump either of them at that moment' I said.

'But we thought it was for the best at the time' she said.

'It was' I replied with a nod.

'Just in case' she said with a grin and I laughed.

We gossiped on for awhile about Rupert before Jane asked about Simon. I told her that we had dated and I expected to see him again. Jane told me that she had no doubts that he was the right one for me and I just smiled. It was quite late when I left her and we parted good friends as usual.

Monday morning at work was boring and I had to listen to Tina going on endlessly about 'Dezzie' whilst I tried to concentrate on the overdue list for Wilkes. I had finished the important stuff by lunchtime and whilst Tina was with the others in the rest room I sat and thought about Jeff. He said he would call me later to arrange a date and I looked forward to being with him again. He seemed to have changed miraculously since we first met and I wondered if it was him or me. Perhaps it was Eric's influence that had brought about the change in both of us. Whatever it was… it was nice and I felt very comfortable with him. I mean to say, I'm not perfect, as you may have noticed… but neither is Jeff, but perhaps we will be perfect together… if he is the man of my dreams!

It was just after eight when Jeff called and invited me to have dinner with him at his flat on Saturday. He said he couldn't see me before then as he'd been called to Germany for a meeting at the factory and wouldn't be back until Friday.

'So what are you going to cook for me?' I asked.

'Whatever you want' he replied... which of course, is the right answer.

'Well... I think I fancy a starter of prawns then a fillet steak followed by trifle with extra cream... but I could change my mind about all of that by Saturday' I said and he laughed.

'So what am I to do then?' he asked.

'Use your imagination and surprise me!' I replied with a giggle.

'Right, I will!'

'Good.'

'I'll pick you up at about eight... is that alright?'

'That's fine, Jeff.'

'Fantastic... take care and I'll see you then, bye, Clare.'

'Bye, Jeff' and as I put the phone down, Mother said 'I hope you're going to bring him in for coffee this time... so I can see what he looks like.'

'Yes, I will.'

'I look forward to meeting this one... but he'll have to be really special to beat Simon... I'm sure he's the right one for you, dear' she said and I nodded half heartedly as the phone rang. It was Simon and after general chit chat he asked me out to dinner on the coming Wednesday. I said 'yes' and he told me to be ready by seven as he was taking me somewhere in London. I asked where, but he said it was a surprise... well I don't like surprises, even nice ones, so I spent the next two days wondering where we were going to eat.

I was all 'glammed' up in my low cut red dress and ready by seven when Simon arrived. As we drove off, I was just about to ask where we were going when he said 'I'm taking you to the Savoy Hotel in the Strand, the food is always fantastic and they have dancing all evening.'

'That sounds good.'

'Oh it is... and it'll be the first time we've danced together' he said with a smile.

I had never been to the Savoy and I must say that I was impressed. When we arrived we were served drinks in the palatial lounge, by a very attentive waiter, before going through to the restaurant. We were shown to our reserved table on the edge of the dance floor by the Maitre d'.

'This is all quite special' I whispered to Simon as the waiter appeared, wished us 'good evening' and handed us the menus before hurrying away.

'They know how to do things properly here' said Simon as a pianist started to play and I glanced at the man in the white tuxedo as he tinkled out a relaxing tune. This was really romantic and I looked back at Simon and wondered if he was the man. The waiter re-appeared and interrupted my thoughts and as I hadn't even looked at the menu yet, Simon asked him to leave us for a little longer. Eventually I chose a starter of smoked salmon followed by Chicken Kiev and Simon ordered the same. He selected a sparkling rosé to go with the meal and we talked about nothing in particular for a short while before I asked him about his business... that was my big mistake!

'It's all going well' he replied with a smile then continued at length. The waiter brought our first course and Simon only stopped talking to eat and only stopped eating to talk. Then our main course arrived with Simon still in full flow! Suddenly I realised that behind his seemingly romantic outlook, lay a driven, boring, shallow man only interested in financial success. He didn't ask me one question about myself or bother to find out what I thought about anything! We finished the meal with Simon still talking about himself and his business and where he planned it to go in the future. I listened whilst he told me about his three year plan then his five year plan and then... I stopped listening as a small orchestra assembled on the stage and started to play dance music... thank heavens!

Eventually I had to interrupt and ask him to dance, but he spoilt the mood by continuing to talk about his plans for the future. I made up my mind on the dance floor that I would not be any part of it! Added to that, he was not exactly the best dancer I've been with!

When we left the Savoy I felt as if I couldn't care less about Simon and my first impressions of him when we met at Melanie's party were right all along. He was simple and silly! He had no depth and he may have appeared the 'ideal one' for me in other people's eyes… like Mother or Jane, but in reality he wasn't the man I could ever settle down with and be happy. I remained quiet on the journey back to Romford and could only think about Eric and Jeff ,whilst Simon prattled on about Government contracts… is it me or is that boring… or what?

We said 'goodnight' outside the house after I told him Mother was not too well at the moment… well she had been a pain! I really couldn't be bothered and was not in the mood to make coffee whilst he and Mother fussed over each other. He nodded and said he'd call me in a few days to make a date. I smiled and thought 'I'll tell him the next time we meet that it's all over.'

The following days flew by at work and other than a few minor skirmishes with Tina and Mother, everything flowed along quite nicely. Saturday dawned and after lunch I started preparing myself for my dinner date with Jeff. I really was looking forward to it and wondered how the evening would end… I hoped that it wouldn't be a disappointment otherwise I'd have to speak to Eric… seriously!

I wore the red dress I'd bought in France and was satisfied with myself when I looked in the mirror. I splashed my Givenchy 'L'amour' and made my way downstairs to wait for Jeff.

He arrived just before eight and I called out to Mother in the kitchen 'I'm out now, don't wait up!'

'But aren't you going to bring him back for coffee?' she shouted back.

'Possibly' I said as I opened the front door and thought 'probably not!'

We chatted all the way to Brentwood and he was quite relaxed, amusing and charming.

'So what are you cooking us for dinner?' I asked as we neared his flat.

'It's a surprise' he replied with a grin.

'I don't like surprises…'

'When I asked you what you wanted you said prawns, steak and trifle but then you said you'd probably change your mind by Saturday!'

'Well, yes, I probably have…'

'So you told me to use my imagination and surprise you!' he interrupted and I laughed.

'Okay… you win!'

'Good… at last a blow for freedom!'

'So tell me… what are we having?' I persisted.

He sighed then replied 'you'll just have to wait and see.'

'Will I like it?'

'I hope so, I'm told that it's the best quick meal that Marks and Spencer's do!' he replied and I laughed again.

We were still giggling when we made our way up the stairs to his flat and we only stopped when we were in the hallway looking at Eric's portrait.

'I must admit he's a handsome guy… my angel' said Jeff.

'He is and he's mine too you know.'

'I know, so let's go in and get something to drink, then you can tell me all about him whilst I unpack the food!' he said with a grin.

When I went into the lounge and sat down I could smell something savoury cooking slowly. I glanced at the table in the dining alcove and saw it was all set up beautifully with wine glasses and silver candle sticks with red candles. Jeff lit the candles then poured us both a gin and tonic, plopped in some tinkling ice before sitting next to me on the settee.

'Here's to us and the future' he said with a smile and I murmured 'to us' before we touched glasses. After I had sipped my gin I asked 'so what's cooking, Jeff?'

'Give me a kiss and I'll tell you' he replied so I did.

'Well that was worth all the cooking' he said with a lovely smile.

'So, tell me.'

'I've been slaving over a hot stove for hours you know…'

'Tell me!'

'Alright… I've braised tender beef in red wine with some herbs.'

'Oh that's lovely' I said and thought 'I do like a man who can cook… it makes such good sense.'

'Then as a starter we've got prawns with avocado pear covered with my special sauce…'

'Your own special sauce… why you clever thing you' I

interrupted.

'And for dessert we've got strawberries and cream, followed by a selection of cheeses, then coffee and brandy.'

'That sounds delicious' I said with a smile.

'I hoped you'd say that' he said and I gave him a lingering kiss.

We sat for awhile and I told Jeff all I knew about Eric and showed him Rowena's ring. He was quite taken aback and held my hand close so he could see the ring more clearly.

'It's very beautiful' he whispered and I just nodded.

He was amazed when I told him that the painting had been done by a Dutchman in 1652 and he just shook his head and said 'well I knew it was old but not that old.'

The meal was absolutely delicious and I was more than a little squiffy after we finished the second bottle of red wine... just before we started on the cheese board. I struggled to finish a large piece of Danish Blue and knew that I had to wait awhile before coffee and brandy.

We sat on the settee and Jeff told me some more about himself and his family whilst listening to my complaints about Mother. He smiled and nodded occasionally and he really seemed to take an interest in what I was saying to him. I realised that he was a kind, thoughtful person who, despite being in the Army for many years, was a very gentle man. Over coffee we talked some more about Eric and guardian angels and he laughed when I told him about the old gentleman with the little dog.

'Well, they must be everywhere and we're just not aware of them' he said with a smile.

'I'm sure that's true... and of course I never believed in angels until I met Eric and he eventually persuaded me that he was the genuine article' I said with a grin.

'I bet he had a job trying to persuade you of anything' he laughed.

'He did... and when I first met him I thought he was only after one thing...'

'I'm sure, but not all men are like that, Clare, some of us care deeply about people we meet and like, so we wouldn't do anything to hurt or upset them' he interrupted and I smiled.

'Glad to hear it.'

'Are you ready for a brandy now?'

'I shouldn't really but I'll be tempted just this once' I replied with a smile and thought 'I think I'm ready for anything with you Jeff.'

He poured the brandy, we said 'cheers' before we sipped and then chatted on for awhile until he said 'It's getting late, so I think I'd better take you home soon.'

'Do you have to?' I asked and he stayed silent for a few moments then replied in a whisper 'Clare, if you want to stay here with me... then I'd be the happiest man in the world.'

I looked at him and replied 'oh I do like a happy man' before I kissed him passionately. I had finally made my choice - Jeff was the right one for me. I wondered how I could have been so wrong about him and it is true that often we can't see what is right in front of us. I thought 'thank God for Eric' as I kissed Jeff once more.

When we had finished our brandy's he led me into his bedroom and closed the door. He undressed me gently, kissing every part of me as he went until I was standing naked in front of him.

'I think that you're incredibly beautiful' he whispered before he laid me down on the bed. He joined me within moments and we made love for what seemed an age until his gentle thrusting made me explode with a passion that I had never experienced before. We lay quietly for some time before he kissed me and whispered 'I hope that now we will be together forever.'

'So do I... my darling Jeff.'

After a breakfast of toast with black coffee he drove me home and came in to meet Mother. After saying 'hello Jeff, pleased to meet you' she turned to me and said 'when I got up this morning and realised you weren't here, I thought that you were probably dead in a ditch!'

'Sorry, I should have called you' I said.

'Yes, you should have, now I'm sure you could do with a nice cup of coffee Jeff and then you can tell me all about yourself' she said and I was glad that on the drive back from Brentwood I had warned him about Mother. However, I needn't have worried because they got on splendidly and Jeff charmed Mother from the very start. She insisted that he stayed for Sunday lunch, which he did and afterwards we went for a walk in the park. We sat on the bench where I had often waited for Eric and I told Jeff all about our meetings there. He was genuinely pleased and said that without doubt Eric's guidance had brought us together. I felt the same and we kissed for awhile before walking slowly home for tea.

By the end of October I was practically living with Jeff at his flat, much to Mother's relief, and by then I had met his parents, along his brother and his family. They were all lovely and welcomed me with open arms so I felt very at home with them.

I introduced him to Dad and Nicole as well as Jane and he was an instant hit with them all. From then on it seemed to be a nonstop round of Sunday lunches and dinner parties as we prepared for Christmas.

I went with Jeff to his Spiritualist Church and, after being a little sceptical at first, soon realised what generous, open hearted people the small congregation were. I was impressed by their healing book and understood why Jeff had been able to recover from his dreadful experiences in Iraq. The Minister, Adrian, was a charming extrovert who made us all laugh and he had 'one liner's' that would have made him a hit on any comedy show. I enjoyed going to the little church and felt very uplifted every time I went with Jeff.

My divorce came through in early December and we celebrated with a romantic dinner at 'The Royal Hotel' in Chelmsford and when we arrived back at the flat, Jeff proposed to me. I said 'yes' of course, then he surprised me with a beautiful engagement ring he'd bought, it had two large diamonds set diagonally and when he slipped it on my finger it fitted perfectly. We had decided that it would be best to keep our relationship a secret at work until we were engaged, so when I told Tina that I was going to marry Jeff she was blown away!

'What old knicker sniffer?' she asked wide eyed and incredulous.

'Yes...'

'You must be mad!'

'You don't know him…'

'I'm bloody glad I don't!' she interrupted and I laughed, but she soon settled down to the idea and I was able to tell her a little about my fiancé. I think that in the end, she was quite impressed with him.

When I told Wilkes that I was engaged to Jeff he was unsure what to say other than 'I hope you'll both be very happy, Clare.' After all, he was speaking to his boss's future wife and that's a tricky situation for any manager! From then on he walked on eggshells as far as I was concerned and it was obvious that I would have to move to another job in the future to save any embarrassment.

Jeff and I had a wonderfully happy Christmas with our two families and even Mother seemed more affable and relaxed.

We were married at the Registry Office in Romford on Saint Valentine's Day! Everything went very well and at the reception we enjoyed a fabulous meal with plenty of Champagne. All the speeches were amusing and without doubt the best was from Adrian, our Minister from the Spiritualist Church, who we had invited as our special guest. We asked him to give us a Church blessing when we returned from our honeymoon and he was delighted. I danced with most of the guests and by midnight I'd had enough, so we left them to it and were given a lovely send off on our first night of married bliss!

The next day we flew to Bermuda for three weeks which was absolutely fabulous. We stayed in a five star hotel and ate, drank, made love, roasted on the beach, went sailing and played a couple of rounds of golf! Even I was surprised how good I was for a beginner, and Jeff said he was impressed.

In the months that followed we became very close and I was so very happy. My new husband was attentive and good around the house. He would often cook an evening meal or do the ironing and it touched me deeply when he said 'when a man lives on his own he soon realises that there is no one but himself to do everything… if he wants a cup of tea, he has to make it… a clean shirt, then he has to wash and iron it... an evening meal... he has to cook it - otherwise he'll starve! So it makes a man very appreciative of everything a wife does for him... because he knows from experience what's involved... it would do all men a power of good to live on their own before they get married!'

I agreed!

Jeff told me all about Evelyn and I knew from my own experience with Tony what deep sadness he had felt after being betrayed by the person he loved. You never get over the disloyalty and time never heals the wound, all that happens is the scab on top just gets thicker. We discovered years later that she never married again but went to live in Germany with a divorced school friend called Nicola, who ran a language school over there. Jeff never heard from Evelyn again.

I left Hamilton's soon after we were married and got a job as the accounts manager with Bristow's Engineering, a company that made parts for the motor industry. I made a name for myself and had a substantial raise in salary at the end of my first year... then I fell pregnant! We hadn't actually planned it but I think it was more of a happy, timely accident. The whole family were delighted and baby David Alec was born without too much bother in the following September. By then Jeff had been promoted to Southern Region Accounts Manager with an increase in salary and a bigger BMW car. We realised that we should start looking for a house as we were now becoming a bit cramped in the flat... why do little babies take up so much room?

We eventually found a three bedroom semi near Ongar that suited us and when Jeff made an offer, the owner accepted it immediately. It was all very traumatic to say the least and when we actually moved in after selling the flat we could hardly believe it!

I went happily back to work knowing that either Mother or Jeff's parents were looking after baby David every day... they took it in turns and sorted out a rota amongst themselves... sometimes parents are a blessing in disguise!

That year Jane met a lovely guy called Charles. It was obvious that they were a perfect match and after a whirlwind romance they married. We saw a lot of them and we all got on very well. Charles was such a laid back, witty person that he charmed everyone he met and was delightful company. He ran a small publishing business, which was very successful and as a result they had a very good life.

Another year passed quickly and after a lovely relaxed holiday in Portugal I was expecting again! Baby Louise May was born and we were all delighted. I remembered what Eric said when he gave me Rowena's gold ring 'take care of it and one day, give it to your daughter.' As I looked down into her beautiful little face and bright blue eyes I wondered if she was in fact Rowena returning from the spirit world for a long and happy life.

As the years passed we grew even closer as a family. Jeff progressed with his career and eventually was promoted to UK Finance Director and of course, our life changed for the better. We bought a large four bedroom house on the outskirts of Brentwood and I gave up working at Bristow's. I was sorry to leave as I had enjoyed it there and made some good friends, but there comes a time for everything to end. The children were growing up fast and needed my attention, so it was the right decision.

David eventually went on to university and studied economics at the LSE, whilst Louise studied art at the London Polytechnic. We were very proud of them both and were delighted when Louise met a young man at college and they became engaged. His name was Matthew and when she brought him home for the first time I was immediately struck by his good looks. He was tall, fair haired with blue eyes... he could have been the son of Eric and I just wondered...

Well I'm sure you want to know what happened to everyone!

I never saw Tony again but I heard a rumour, some years later that he had gone to live in America.

Simon married his accountant, so I'm sure they were made for each other in heaven and I guessed they talked about money, profit, and five year plans before they went to bed!

Rupert and Sophie moved to France but Sophie returned after six months and carried on writing poetry whilst living alone in a small cottage by the coast... with only two cats for company.

Rupert carried on writing but never enjoyed the success he had with his first novel, which was never made into a film. He wrote to Jane telling her that he'd bought a little bar in Bandol, which is on the coast near Cassis, and now divided his time between writing and serving behind the bar.

Tina married 'Dezzie' and they had four children... yes, four children, all boys, and apparently they could all dance as well as their father!

Mr Wilkes carried on at Hamilton Motors until he retired and we went to say 'goodbye' to him at his leaving party.

I have never seen Eric to speak to again but when we were on holiday in Norway, visiting the home of the Vikings, I'm sure I saw him walking passed our hotel in Oslo.

On Louise and Matthew's wedding day, I gave her Rowena's ring, just before the ceremony, she was thrilled with it... and it fitted perfectly on her little finger!

I think Eric was there outside the church... at a distance, amongst a group of people who had stopped to see my lovely daughter being photographed with her handsome husband. However, the tall man I had noticed just seemed to melt away in the crowd and so I wasn't absolutely sure it was Eric... but I like to think he was there.

When Jeff took early retirement we splashed out and bought a new sailing boat, a lovely ten metre, sparkling white beauty we called 'Rowena'. We started by sailing her along the south coast, then ventured across to the Channel Islands, then regularly to France. The years have been good to us and we are now like a comfortable pair of slippers, always cosy and warm in each other's company.

I am sure there is a guardian angel like Eric for everyone and it is truly wonderful when you find him or her. I truly believe that no one is ever alone in this world so... thank God for Eric and happy endings!

Follow Eric in his next angelic mission entitled
'ERIC AND THE TWINS'

THE FRENCH COLLECTION

AMUSING AND EROTIC TITLES
FOR ADULTS

MARSEILLE TAXI by Peter Child

This is a tantalising revelation of the twilight existence of Michel Ronay, a Marseille taxi driver. Every moment of his life is crowded with incident. Compromised by the lecherous women of Marseille, chased by the Police, harassed by the underworld and encouraged by 'gays', his life is a non-stop roller coaster. Stay with him, in his Taxi and feel the heat of the Marseille streets, smell the odours; then have a bath with someone to cleanse your body and mind of the experience.

ISBN : 0-9540910-1-9

AUGUST IN GRAMBOIS by Peter Child

Michel Ronay, a taxi driver, leaves his tiring work driving through the hot, dusty streets of Marseille and heads for the cool tranquillity of his villa in Grambois, for the whole month of August. With his second wife, Monique, her mother, two aunts and Frederik, his stepson, Michel prepares to enjoy a holiday relaxing in the peace and quiet of Provence. So what could possibly disturb him in the ample bosom of his family? His many mistresses perhaps? Or Edward Salvator? Or Jacques and Antone? Or Gerrard? Or....

ISBN : 0-9540910-2-7

CHRISTMAS IN MARSEILLE by Peter Child

Follow Michel Ronay, a taxi driver, around the cold, bright sunlit streets of Marseille in the frantic run up to Christmas. Laugh with him when he discovers that all of his wife's family are coming to stay, cry with him when the Police involve him in undercover work that goes wrong, sympathise with him when his mistresses find out about one another. His life is just a frantic kaleidoscope of drink, sex and the fear of being found out. You will never get in a taxi again without thinking of Michel Ronay.

ISBN : 0-9540910-3-5

CATASTROPHE IN LE TOUQUET by Peter Child

Michel Ronay escapes from the hustle and bustle of Marseille to Le Touquet, where he plans to start a new and prosperous life with his fiancé, Josette. After making business arrangements with his cousin, Henri, everything is set for a relaxed and wonderful future, until he meets Madame Christiane. Monique, Michel's wife, Monsieur Robardes, a solicitor and Henri, are not at all amused by what happens in Le Touquet and Josette wonders if she should ever have bothered to leave Marseille in the first place.

ISBN : 0-9540910-5-1

RETURN TO MARSEILLE by Peter Child

Michel Ronay, a taxi driver, leaves Le Touquet after a failed attempt to start a business with his cousin, Henri. With his fiancé, Josette, he sets off on the long drive back to Marseille, where all his friends and family are waiting for his return. As he drives onto the autoroute heading south he relaxes, knowing that he is going home and nothing can possibly go wrong...

ISBN : 9780-9540910-7-1

To order the above titles contact Benbow Publications at www.benbowpublications.co.uk